NAME GAMES

book five of the

James P. Dandy Elderhostel Mysteries

Bloody Bonsai
Killing Thyme
Tip A Canoe
Painted Lady

plus a novella in an anthology
Sheep in Wolf's Clothing

Peter E. Abresch

Name Games

ISBN-10 1438262868
EAN-13 9781438262864

Printed in the United States of America

The authors web site and email address

http://www.elderhostelmysteries.com
Peter@elderhostelmysteries.com

for my outlaws

John and Elizabeth Klein

Harry and Roswitha Case

Toni Lang

Kenneth and Renata Burgess

I love you all...
well, I really like you a lot

Praise for the Elderhostel Mystery Series

Action, romance and playful dialogue abound in Peter Abresch s third James P. Dandy Elderhostel mystery, Tip A Canoe... where Jim and his partner in love and crime-solving, Dodee Swisher, have come for a canoe trip. As members of their group turn up dead, our heroes realize that the killer is in their midst.   PUBLISHERS WEEKLY

Series protagonists James P. Dandy and Dodee Swisher go canoeing on the Santee lakes in South Carolina as part of a particularly lively Elderhostel program. Unfortunately, murder mixes with the usual oddball assortment of characters. For all collections. Library Journal

Jim Dandy and his girlfriend Dodee are headed down to the Carolinas... The plan is to enjoy the peaceful and inspiration surroundings while hiking and canoeing. However, Dodee has a history of leading Jim by the hand into obscure and dangerous mysteries....Fun, witty and most of the time downright humorous, Abresch spins off well thought out scenes laced with strings of laugh-out-loud lines. Reviewed by Phillip Tomasso III, The Charlotte Austin Review

This book was a "Jim Dandy" good read... I just hope that when I am old enough to retire I have the wit, stamina and energy that this group does. Sue Johnson, Myshelf.com

...fans will find plenty to enjoy. The mystery itself is challenging, with many red herrings and a surprise ending; the outdoor scenes are vivid; and the story is well paced. Abresch also offers sensitive insights on love, aging and bereavement. Recommend this series to readers who like strong, active seniors as main characters. John Rowen, Booklist

While there are a good number of mystery books out on senior-aged detectives/amateur detectives, this series has a focus on Elderhostel...a down-to-earth these-are-people-you-probably-know as well as an honest portrayal of a very popular senior group. Retirement Life

Acknowledgments

To all the folks who were on the Hiking and White Water Rafting Elderhostel at the Mountain Retreat and Learning Center in North Carolina with special thanks to:

Susan & Robert Smith
Doris Cove
Lee Knight
Vic and Martha Harrell

The author also wishes to acknowledge the generosity of ELDERHOSTEL INC. for the use of their name

On all the ELDERHOSTELS I have attended, I have found nothing but fun, camaraderie, adventurous spirits, and nary a body on any of them...

yet.

Peter E. Abresch
Peter@elderhostelmysteries.com
http://www.elderhostelmysteries.com

ONE

It killed Jim Dandy to pass by the Dairy Queen.

Well, *kill* might not be the word he wanted to use considering the lady in the seat beside him, and the surprising number of people who had died–croaked, expired on the spot, taken the big dirt nap–since he had known her.

Maybe he should get a new girlfriend.

He glanced over at Dodee Swisher, her cornflower eyes closed, head of wheaten curls propped up against the head rest, trim body from teaching aerobics slumped in the passenger seat.

Yeah, buddy, like he could ever replace her.

He was long past the L word.

He shifted in his seat, comfortable in an old pair of jeans that had been washed and faded enough for the threads to relax around the contours of his body, and resettled into the driver's seat of the Avalon.

It was a new car for him, bought nearly-new at CarMax to replace the Lincoln that had almost become their coffin the last time they had gotten together. When they had been poking about in police affairs on the Outer Banks of North Carolina.

Well, that ain't happening again.

This time he was ordering Dodee to stay out of it.

Oh yeah, like that would make an impact.

He might as well lean out the window and lip-lock a passing eighteen wheeler.

Besides, this time they would be hiking through the woods and rafting down the rivers. How many killers lurked about for a passersby in the woods? And how often did you hear of a drive-by shooting from a rubber raft?

He glanced over at Dodee again.

Her chest rose and fell in the even cadence of sleep.

But for that he'd have pulled off into the Dairy Queen.

When had he had last eaten a Blizzard?

Too long

He had stopped at a Dairy Queen that morning, a mega-gas station cum Truck Stop-Subway-Dairy Queen where route 207 ran into 95 north of Richmond, but it was still dark and the fast-food sections weren't open. All he could get was a cup of coffee and one day-old packaged Danish, which he ate while watching a two day-old TV news story about a car being blown up on Rock Creek Parkway, tying up the start of Washington's weekend traffic.

Well, actually it did more than tie up traffic as he had found out seven hours later, when he had finally rolled into the airport at Asheville and picked up Dodee.

"I almost didn't make it," she said as he put her luggage in the trunk.

He held the car door for her. "How come?"

"There was a bombing in Washington. You didn't hear about it?"

He shut the door, walked around, and got behind the wheel. "I heard about a car bomb on Friday."

"That's it." She pointed at him in that strange way of hers, with three fingers curled and the thumb and index finger pointed together. "At first they thought it might be a terrorist's bomb and they cancelled flights into Washington."

He shifted into drive and headed back out to Highway 26. "But that was on Friday. Today is Sunday. What's it got to do with you?"

"I told you, sweetheart, they were cancelling the flights into Washington. I had to change planes in Washington."

"To come from Kansas City to Asheville?"

She shrugged. "That's the way they work it nowadays."

"If I had know that, I'd have picked you up in Washington and we could have driven down together."

She shook her head. "Then I would have had to fly in yesterday and it would have been worse. Besides, I had too much stuff to do at the gallery to get away yesterday."

He turned onto Highway 26 and headed northwest, looking for Route 40 west. "How is the art gallery going?"

"Alison—my daughter Alison?"

"I remember."

"She's turning into the boss and I'm turning into the hired help. Not complaining. Leaves me time to work on my own paintings, and to come on trips with a certain dirty old gentleman I know."

"I'm not old."

She leaned across and kissed him on the cheek, then ran a hand through his hair. "You look tired, sweetheart. Want me to drive?"

And that's where he had made his mistake.

If he hadn't insisted on being James P. Dandy, Mr. Macho Man, he could be the one snoozing in the passenger seat. On the other hand, maybe she would have fallen asleep at the wheel and they would have ended up in a ditch. On the other, other hand, at least he wouldn't have known it when they passed the Dairy Queen.

He rolled his shoulders and yawned.

So now he plowed down Highway 23, looking for someplace called Dillard, Georgia.

He glanced at the map lying between the seats and back at the road.

Where the hell was Dillard?

He reached for his reading glasses, then let it go.

"Dodee, I could use some navigation help."

She popped up with a start.

"Sorry, sweetheart." She blinked a few times and ran her hands over her face. "I didn't mean to nod off. We had a late night hanging artwork for a show tomorrow—today. I guess I was sleepier than I thought." She picked up the map and the attached paper with typed directions. "Where are we?"

"That's what I want to know, lady. Somewhere along Highway 23. We're supposed to be coming into Dillard, but I ain't seen hide nor hair of it."

"We're looking for Route 246 by a Chevron Sta–stop."

He glanced in his rearview mirror and jammed on his brakes, tires screeching against the pavement.

"Sonofabitch, Dodee–"

"We take a left here."

He waited for oncoming traffic to clear and made the turn.

She leaned over in front of him.

"What are you doing?"

"Checking your odometer. It's ten miles to the entrance."

"Thank God, I'm bushed."

He drove up a curvy, two lane road with a middle passing lane on the straightaways. The land fell away on the right, giving them a view of the wooded mountainside, and up ahead white water reflected in the afternoon sun as it plummeted off a rock ledge onto more rocks fifty feet below.

Was it an omen?

They were going whitewater rafting, but he damn sure hoped it wasn't over that.

A red car popped in and out of his rearview mirror as it followed one turn behind, coming out of a curve just as Jim rounded into a new one.

The road veered into the woods with the red car tagging along. Then in one long straight stretch, passing side roads and an occasional house, it closed the gap like a meteor falling from the sky, and he recognized it as a Jaguar. It fell back again as they headed into more winding curves.

He glanced at the map in her lap. "We're out here in the middle of nowhere."

"The town of Highlands is supposed to be a short way down the road from where we turn in." She leaned over and checked the odometer again. "There's supposed to be something up here called–there it is. Lick Log Mill."

"What about it?"

"We're getting close."

"I've been getting closer since I left Southern Maryland."

He checked his rearview mirror to see the red Jaguar making another charge.

"Stop. Take a right."

He jammed on his brakes and slammed into a right hook around a wood-grained *The Mountain Retreat and Learning Center* sign as the red Jag zoomed by on his tail. He heard the screech of tires gripping the pavement and waited for the crunch of a crash.

TWO

"Damnit, Dodee," he said when the crash didn't come, "be nice if you gave me a few more inches of notice next time."

"Sorry, sweetheart."

They passed a pond and drove up a steep winding road through a mixture of deciduous and evergreen trees, eventually coming upon a long gray building with Texture 111 siding–plywood with cut groves to look like individual boards. The road continued on up the hill, but Jim spotted an Elderhostel Registration sign and pulled into the lone slot of a four-car parking lot at the building's lower end.

He climbed out, stretched, and waited while Dodee ran a brush through her short wheaten curls.

"We have arrived," he said.

"So I noticed, sweetheart."

She came around the car, placed her slender body close to his, and batted her cornflower eyes up at him.

He shook his head, smiled, and kissed her. Warm, soft lips answered his. Then he took her hand and they followed a wooden walkway tucked under the building's overhang, past two entrances to the dining hall, and into a third door with another Elderhostel Registration sign tacked to it.

Knotty-wood walls and ceiling gave the place a rustic, homey feel. A popcorn machine lived at the far end with an exit on either side to a large deck filled with rocking chairs and shaded by twenty-foot trees.

"Well, hi." A woman stood up from behind a twelve-foot aluminum table spread with folders. She looked to be in her mid-fifties, trim and tall, five foot ten, a ready smile on a broad face reminiscent of eastern Europe. "Welcome to The Mountain Retreat and Learning Center, and to the Appalachian Elderhostel." Her short cropped hair was the color of steel and her eyes as blue as deep ocean. "I'm Babs Penny."

"And I'm Duke Penny." A short, five-foot-seven, brawny man barreled in from the rocking chair deck. Hairy, muscular arms and legs stuck out of a T-shirt and shorts with a round face topped with a monk's black circle of hair. "I'm her other and greater half."

Babs's eyes rolled. "And he's also delusional." She picked up a list from the table. "You are either James P. Dandy and Dodee Swisher or–"

"That's us," Dodee said.

Babs Penny handed them each a card and Jim held his out to Dodee.

She stared at it a moment then up at him with raised eyebrows, smiled, shook her head, and took the card.

"Isn't that always the way," Babs said. "Men are just not smart enough to fill out these complicated cards."

Duke Penny grinned. "Or too smart."

"Or too lazy."

Jim turned to Duke. "Noticed a waterfall on the way up. Does it flow all the time?

The hairy man shrugged. "Far as I know. We don't live here. We're a host couple, come up from Alabama as volunteer help on the Elderhostels. But they've had a lot of rain this spring–two inches yesterday–so all the streams and rivers are full."

"Which will help when we go whitewater rafting," Babs said, picking up two folders from those spread on the table. "We won't be bumping along on the bottom."

"How white is the whitewater rafting?" Jim asked

"Enough to make it exciting," Duke said with a flick of his eyebrows.

Babs shook her head. "But not enough to worry about."

"The first river's pretty easy, but the second can really get exciting."

Babs sighed. "Not enough to worry about." She took the registration cards from Dodee and gave her the two folders. "The schedule and lowdown on The Mountain is in there along with your nametags."

The door opened and a big-boned, lardy man in his mid fifties clunked across the wooden floor in brown cowboy boots. Fleshy cheeks framed an easy smile on his big head and his T-shirted stomach jiggled over the top of a leather belt with a brass horseshoe buckle.

"Apologize, but I think I'm blocking someone in," he said in a booming voice. "There were no empty parking places."

Duke turned to his wife. "Didn't I tell you, you should move your car?"

"Well, let me register you all first, then I'll take you up the hill and show you where you're staying."

"I'm Howard Leslie." He pulled out a chair and collapsed onto it. "I signed up for a roommate."

"Oh, yes. We didn't find you one so you'll have the place to yourself."

The lardy men swung around to Jim. "I guess I'm blocking you in. Sorry about that. Name's Howard Leslie."

"James P. Dandy and this is Dodee Swisher."

"Nice to meet you both." Howard Leslie turned to the registration card and started filling it out. "Glad I didn't have to park in a slot to tell you the truth. I'm driving a red Jaguar and I don't really know what I'm doing. It's not my type of car." He looked up and gave them the easy smile. "I mean I'd like it to be my type of car, but it's a bit rich for my blood." He went back to filling out the card. "I'm afraid I'm going to scratch it or a tree will fall on it or something."

"How come you're driving it?" Dodee asked.

"My car was stolen."

Jim glanced at Dodee and could see the wheels already spinning in her head.

"Yep." The lardy man twisted around in his chair again. "In Washington, D. C. Where I live. Stole it on Friday afternoon. I was going to drive down here, but that took care of that. I had to scramble yesterday to get airline and rental car reservations. Then some flights were cancelled and I flew into

Asheville this afternoon packed like sardines. Then the rental place couldn't fill my reservation because they loaned out all their cars for some medical convention. So guess what they upgraded me to. That red Jaguar out there. It's kind of a bad luck, good luck story. Stole my car, but I was able to fly down and save that long road trip. They gave away my rental, but they upgraded me. Now I got this beautiful red Jag, but instead of showing it off somewhere, I'm going to be parking it so I can take a walk in the wild and woolly woods for a week." The easy smile again and he palmed up a fleshy hand and flopped it over. "See, bad luck, good luck."

Dodee's eyebrows arched. "And they stole it from where you work?"

"Actually," he said, "from a Metro station garage. Imagine my surprise when I walked to my reserved spot and nothing was there. I couldn't believe it. I kept turning to the other cars on each side and then back to this empty space until finally it dawned on me. Guess what. No matter how hard I studied it, my Honda was gone. Then I had to go through all this stuff with the police instead of packing my suitcase. What a mess."

She opened her mouth to speak, but Jim hooked his arm around her waist and turned her around. "Don't go there, lady. It's none of our business."

THREE

Jim followed the red Jaguar, past the dining hall and four hundred feet up the road to the top of a hill where Babs waited for them. She directed Howard to an upper parking lot on the right that led into the second floor of a two-story building, one end built into the side of a hill. Then she motioned Jim to the left, down a small road to a parking space outside the lower level.

"You're on the bottom floor, Howard's on the second," she said, leading them into an entrance at the end. "This is the lodge."

"What's the name of the building where we registered?" Dodee asked.

"The dining hall," Jim said.

"Well, it's all the same building." Babs stopped at the first door on the left, resting her hand on the knob. "But the dining hall is at the far end and the room where you registered, at the near end with the rocking chair deck, is called the Heritage Room. That's where we'll have our social hour." She pointed down the hall toward the stairs. "The room at the other end on the second floor of this building is called the Great Room. We'll be meeting there later tonight."

"And is everyone staying here in the lodge?" Jim asked.

"No. Our guest cabins and the lodge are built in a line along a ridge. Some of the cabins are further down the road where you parked and some more on the other side of the upper lot. We also have staff cabins, where Duke and I are staying, between here and the dining hall. Does that orient you?"

"I think so. And this is our room?"

"Yes, number eleven." She opened the door. "We meet in the upper parking lot at five-fifteen. Anything else I can help you with?"

Jim turned to Dodee who shook her head.

"Okay then," Babs said, big smile on her broad face. "I better go help Howard. Don't forget your nametags." She hurried down the hall and up the stairs.

Jim ushered Dodee into a smallish, but bright and cheery room. Windows faced onto a balcony that ran the full length of the lodge with trees on the other side of the railing. A few pictures hung on white painted walls and a night table with a lamp separated blue spreads and rolled up towels and blankets on twin beds.

Dodee turned to him and raised her eyebrows.

"What?"

"Twin beds."

"Ah. I guess that means I won't have to worry about you ravishing my body."

"Oh?"

He pulled her to him and wrapped his arms around her, feeling her arms encircle his neck, and kissed her in a way he couldn't at the airport. "Good to have you here again, lady."

"You haven't had me here yet?"

"Here again in my arms, dirty mind."

"Good to be here, sweetheart." She motioned with a nod of her head. "What about the twin beds?"

He looked over her shoulder. "I can move the night table and shove them together."

"As long as you don't fall through the crack." Then she slapped her hand over his lips. "Don't say it."

He smiled, gave her another quick kiss, and headed for the car. "I'll get the bags."

It took two trips. They unpacked, stacking their things on open shelves by the door and hanging clothes on a rod beside it. He went back for a third trip to get her sketchpad case and camera, and the coffee mug that he'd brought from home.

"They said we had to pack for cold and hot," Dodee said, putting a jacket on a hanger. "And bathing suits or shorts for rafting."

"I brought hot and cold stuff. Also brought a small

backpack for the hikes."

"Good, you can carry my things."

He turned to her.

She pulled her own backpack out of her bag and swung it on her finger. "I also brought a water bottle."

"So did I." He closed his suitcase, tucked it under the hanging clothes, and stretched out on one of the beds. "After the dry air we had wandering about the mountains of Colorado and New Mexico, I've learned to carry one with me."

"I bought you a present."

He raised his head and stared at two flimsy slipper-like objects with netting on top.

"Water shoes for when we go rafting. I also bought me a pair."

"Well, thank you, lady."

She looked at her watch. "We have half an hour before we meet in the parking lot. Want to look around? Or is your prone body language telling me something? Like you want to take a nap."

He stretched some more and yawned. "What a great idea."

"Maybe I will, too. Mind if I scrunch next to you on the bed?"

"You can scrunch next to me anytime you want."

She lay with her back next to him and he curled around her. Then she jiggled up and down.

"What the hell are you doing?"

"Making sure the bed doesn't squeak."

"Good thought. But after ten or eleven hours behind the wheel, I'm not sure I have a whole lot of squeak left in me."

He closed his eyes and breathed in the light touch of her perfume, letting himself drift off–

"What do you think about Howard's car being stolen?"

He popped open his eyes and stared at the back of her head. "What's to think? Someone stole it."

"And then winding up with a red Jaguar. Did you get a

look at it?"

"Just now as I followed him up from the dining hall, and before in my rearview mirror on the way up from Dillard."

"He was following us?"

"Are we napping? Is this what we do when we nap? Ask inane questions about someone else's business?"

"Sorry, sweetheart." She twisted around, gave him a kiss, and got up. "You nap. I'll find out where we're meeting and come back for you when it's time."

He watched her collect her sketchpad and camera then closed his eyes as the door clicked shut, leaving him with only the squabbling of birds outside his window to break the silence, then that too faded away.

* * *

"Sweetheart," she said, waking him a half hour later. "Time to go."

He crawled back up from the deep sleep. "Wow, I was really out of it."

He washed his face, slapped on some PS For Men cologne, put on a cap with Chincoteague embroidered on it, and they headed up the hill together.

"Um, you smell sexy."

"I am sexy." He took her hand. "Sketch anything?"

She shook her head. "I did a rough-in of the view at the other end of the lodge. There's a deck that looks down into the valley."

Twenty other Elderhostelers had already gathered by the time they reached the parking lot.

Howard Leslie, his stomach overlapping his horseshoe belt buckle, stood talking to two ladies in shorts. The shape of their faces were different, one oval, the other round, and one stood a couple of inches taller than the other, but there was a resemblance in their jaw line that indicated a relationship, although their nametags of Valerie Russin and Kelli Kee didn't reflect it. There was a similarity in their bodies as well, trim and muscular, like they could climb Mount Everest without breaking into a sweat.

A blond man with a red goatee strode up the hill and joined the gathering. He had a flat stomach and wrinkle-free face; definitely not the marks of the fifty-five year age requirement to be an Elderhosteler.

"We all here?" he asked Babs Penny.

The female half of the host couple nodded.

"Okay, everybody," he called out in a strong voice. "My name is Josiah Blue, a name my parents gave me, my father the second and my mother insisting on the first. But it's always been a bit too pretentious for me and so if you really want to get my attention, just call me Josie, like in the Clint Eastwood film, *Josie Wales*. I'll be one of your leaders on this Elderhostel." He turned to a wiry woman in khaki shirt and shorts standing next to Babs. "And this is my mentor and co-leader, Carmel Graves."

Carmel raised her hand in greeting, her face well traveled like the rest of the group, her brown hair cut short as if she had no patience with it other than a quick brush.

"Carmel is an authority on the flora and fauna in the area," Josie said.

"That's the plants and animals," Carmel said in a soft voice with a reticent smile. "And an authority is someone who knows more than Josie, which is almost everybody."

Josie smiled at that. "Carmel will be leading one of the hikes tomorrow—the long trail—and I'll be leading the other. We'll talk about that after dinner. Everybody got your nametags? We ask that you wear them when you're on campus. Helps us all to get to know one another. While we're here, see these?" He waved a hand indicating some scrub oaks with light bark on the perimeter of the parking lot. "Know what they are? Anyone want to guess?"

"Green-leaved trees," Howard Leslie said.

"Short and stubby trees," said a man with a chocolate

complexion and a head of tight gray curls, Quentin Quaries by his nametag.

"Trees that grow out of the ground," Kelli Kee said, the shorter of the two Mount Everest women.

"All right, all right." Josie Blue held up his hands in mock surrender. "I guess we won't have many shrinking violets on this trip. They are actually white oaks that normally grow to sixty or eighty feet with trunks two and three feet in diameter. Here at The Mountain they're limited to fifteen or twenty feet in height and six inches or so in diameter, and yet they are over a hundred years old. This is the way they have adapted to the wind and the weather and the altitude. The altitude actually makes our weather pattern much harsher than you would expect at our latitude. For every thousand feet of elevation the climate shifts two hundred and fifty miles north."

"The same thing has happened to bristle cone pines in the high mountains of California,"Carmel Graves said in her soft voice. "Those are the gnarled old evergreens you see with a lot of gray wood. The weather is so sharp up at twelve thousand feet, their branches grow only an inch or so a year. They are the oldest living things on the planet."

Josie smiled. "Now can you see why I call her my mentor? The other plants you see here with the white flowers"–he walked over to a bush beside the road and touched a leathery leaf–"these are mountain laurel. We're lucky to have them in bloom."

He turned around and faced the group, rubbing his hands together.

"Some quick housekeeping things. As you probably noticed, there are no televisions up here at The Mountain and no pay telephones. In an emergency our office has a phone where we can receive a call." He motioned to a gray building to the right of the parking lot. "If you need to buy stuff or a laundry mart, the town of Highlands is about ten or fifteen minutes away, depending on whether you're driving that red Jaguar over there"–he pointed to it–"or an SUV. The dining hall down the hill is open twenty-four hours. Coffee is always on and there's always water for hot tea. The Heritage Room is attached to this side of the dining hall where we'll end up, after a quick tour of The Mountain Retreat and Learning Center, for a little wine and popcorn relaxation before dinner. So, if everyone's ready, let's do it."

Jim put his arm around Dodee and followed Josie Blue past the office out onto a gently sloping rock that fell away to a valley below, foothills of humps and bumps trailing off to a far distant plain.

Josie stamped his feet on the solid outcropping. "We call this Meditation Rock. Down there somewhere," he said, pointing southeast, "the three states of North and South Carolina and Georgia come together. In fact you were in Georgia when you came through Dillard, and now we're just back across the border in North Carolina. Our whitewater rafting will be in Georgia."

"That will be on Tuesday," Babs said, a smile on her broad face.

"Right." Josie stamped his feet again. "As I said, this here is called Meditation Rock." He strode closer to the edge of the rock. "From here it's one small step to Short Meditation Rock, which is about a hundred feet below."

"Short Meditation Rock?" asked the chocolate complected Quentin Quaries. "Should be called Quick Thought Rock."

"Or Splat Rock," Howard added.

"Or Oh-shit Rock," said an older lady, somewhere in her seventies, with tight gray curls and a nametag of Debra Longstreet.

Josie Blue hung his head. "I can see I'm going to have to watch what I say every step of the way. What I'm really trying to point out is that we can see the drop-off here." He stepped away from the edge and pointed along the ridge in both directions. "But behind the cabins and lodge it is not so clear. We ask that you do not go wandering around behind the lodge or the cabins where the trees and underbrush hide similar steps into the great beyond. We don't want to have to rappel down the side to hoist your remains back up. This might be—forgive me—overkill, but here at The Mountain Center, safety is primary. We hope you will all have a fun experience and for that to happen, you have to go home under your own power."

Josie then led them back around the Center's office and to a wooden deck attached to the second floor end of the lodge, similar to the rocking chair deck outside the Heritage Room, except this one was on two levels. There were benches and more rocking chairs here, all of which were quickly occupied by Elderhostelers who needed no encouragement to sit. Josie stood at the railing and pointed to the next hill, as high or higher than them. Its green carpet, broken by rocks and cliffs, changed shades under the effect of passing clouds.

"That's Chinquapin Mountain where we'll be trekking tomorrow. We'll have three levels of hiking. The long one will start out here and head over the top of Chinquapin and down to Glen Falls where we'll eat lunch and then hike back up. Those on the short hike will take a van to a parking lot half way down, hike to the falls, then hike back up here to The Mountain. And then there's a real shortie that starts from the parking lot, goes down to the falls, and back to the parking lot. Any questions?"

"When do we eat?" Howard asked.

"Just getting around to that." Josie pointed to the peaked roofed, glassed-in end of the lodge. "First, this is the Great Room where we'll meet every evening. There is a small kitchen in the corner where there will be coffee for you early risers who don't want to make the trip down to the dining hall. All our programs are held in the Great Room, so we'll meet here after dinner at seven-thirty. Okay, if there're no more questions, let's move on down the hill to the Heritage Room and have some hospitality popcorn and beverages of your choice."

Howard fell into step with Jim and Dodee. "Don't know about you two," he said, his lardy body lumbering along like an elephant, "but I'm signing up for the long hike."

Dodee turned to Jim. "We're taking the long hike?"

"Actually, I'm thinking about sleeping all morning and meeting you when you get back." He watched her mouth fall open and smiled. "Just kidding. I'm ready to give the long hike a try if you are."

"Me too," Howard said. "I've been walking everyday at lunch for over a week. I'm ready for the wild and wooly."

"Are you worried about your stolen car?" Dodee asked.

He spread his arms in a big shrug. "Nothing I can do about it. Frankly, if it's torn up, I'd just as soon they don't find it. I didn't have anything in the glove compartment or trunk to worry about. If they'd stolen it yesterday after I packed for the trip down here, it would have been a different story. They'd have had my laptop and clothes then, and I'd be up the creek without a paddle."

"It will cost you money," Jim said. "The insurance won't cover what you'll spend to get a new one. I know, I just went through that."

Howard turned to him. "You had your car stolen?"

"Someone ran me off the road on the Outer Banks. Fortunately we weren't hurt."

"But we could have been," Dodee said. "I think he intended for us to be hurt."

"Really?" Howard's eyes widened. "Why would they try to do that?"

"Because somebody who shall remain nameless," Jim said, and glared down at Dodee, "was poking around in someone else's business. Something we are not going to do on this trip. Right?"

But for an answer, Dodee raised her nose in the air, folded her arms, and continued walking.

"Wow, that silence is deafening," Howard said. "But my car was only stolen. I can't see an ulterior motive in it. Probably someone who wanted to cut it up for parts." He looked down at Dodee and popped his easy smile. "If you're looking for something sinister, afraid you'll have to look somewhere else."

FOUR

They followed Josie four hundred feet down the road to an open set of wooden stairs, clunked down them to the rocking chair deck, and across it into the Heritage Room. Duke Penny had the popcorn machine running. Two box wines sat at one end of the aluminum table and cans of soda and beer nestled in a small plastic tub of ice on the floor.

"This is our community social time," Josie said. "We'll gather here every evening, and you're welcome to popcorn and the beverage of your choice. Take it out on the deck, rock in the chairs, and get to know one another." He reached across and picked up a small stainless steel bowl. "We take donations here to supply these goodies for the next group of Elderhostelers. As you can see, the last group did very well by you all. It's strictly voluntary. Put in whatever you like, either by day or once for the whole week."

Jim turned to Dodee. "I think I'll wait until the line dies down."

"Can I get you something, sweetheart? A glass of wine?"

He shrugged. "Okay."

He went back outside. Josie's stunted white oaks surrounded and shaded the deck, reminiscent with all the rocking chairs of the front porches on old houses in small towns of a bygone era. He sat in one by the railing and put his Chincoteague cap on the chair next to him to save it for Dodee. Then he closed his eyes and hoped no one would bother him. For a few minutes no one did, but then the empty chair on the other side of him creaked. He opened one eye to see a white-haired woman holding a cup of wine. She leaned forward and read his nametag through tired blue eyes.

"James," she said in a soft voice. "I'm Debra Longstreet. Good to meet you, James. Or do I call you Jim?"

He gave up and opened his other eye. "Nice to meet you,

Debra." He put her age somewhere in the seventies with a face that was smooth and pleasant except for some furrows on her brow and wrinkles at the corners of her eyes and lips. But what was she doing here on a hiking and whitewater rafting Elderhostel?

She sipped her wine. "Looks like we're going to be active over the next few days. I plan on going on the long hike tomorrow. That's the one my roommate signed up for, and I like to keep up with her." She took another sip of wine. "How about you, Jim?"

"I think my roommate will sign up for the long hike and I like to keep up with her." He smiled. "You don't think it might be too much for you."

"Oh no. I like to keep active."

A woman who looked to be in her early fifties sat down in the chair next to Debra—Elcee Howard on her nametag—and the old lady turned to her. "Elcee, this is my new friend, Jim Dandy."

"Jim Dandy?" Clear brown eyes stared out of a younger version of Debra Longstreet's face, this one without furrows and wrinkles, one with a freckled nose and a helmet of soft yellowish-brown curls bunched about her head. "You must take some kidding about your name."

"More than I care to mention."

"I know a little of what you mean." She sat straight-backed in her chair, as if she had come out of a southern girls's finishing school. If she was overweight she hid it well. "Before I was married I had the same name as the movie star and dancer, Leslie Carron, and everyone always wanted me to dance."

"Elcee's her nickname," Debra Longstreet said.

"Now as fate would have it, my husband gave me the name of another movie star."

"Jim's going to take the long hike with us tomorrow," Debra said.

Elcee's pink tongue licked her lower lip. "Don't you

think we should try the short one the first time out?"

"No, dear, I told you I want to go on the long hike."

Jim looked at Elcee. "Are you two roommates?"

"More. This is my Aunt Debra."

Aunt Debra swung around and looked down her nose at Jim. "Do you mean, is she my keeper?"

"No, that's not what I meant." Yeah, right. "I just noticed a resemblance." And screw it. If the feisty old lady wanted to go on the long hike, let her go and croak. "Where are you from?"

"Aunt Debra's from Greensboro; I live in Bethesda, just outside Washington. I drove down to Aunt Debra's place yesterday, spent the night, and then we made the trip this morning. Wasn't too bad that way. How about you?"

Dodee walked across the deck with two cups of wine and handed him one. "Want some popcorn?"

He shrugged. "I guess."

She handed him the second cup of wine. "Watch that." She had a way of smiling when she wanted to be smug, with the very ends of her lips turned down, not something he could do, but which her face muscles had perfected, and that's the smile she gave him now as she shook her finger at him. "Don't drink it." Then she headed back inside.

Jim turned back to Elcee. "I live in Southern Maryland, down in Calvert County. I wasn't as lucky as you. I started out before dawn this morning, drove down to Asheville, picked up Dodee at the airport, and then came on in."

"Dodee lives in Maryland?"

"Kansas City."

"Um," she said, yellowish-brown eyebrows arching, carrying a lot of meaning without actually putting the question to him.

"Dodee and I met on an Elderhostel in New Jersey a few years ago, and we've been coming on Elderhostels together ever since."

Then the wheaten-haired lady in question returned with

two cups of popcorn, exchanging one of them for her wine, and sat down next to him.

"How is it?" she asked.

"Needs salt."

"I thought I put some on. What me to go—"

"No, it's fine. Thank you."

A round-shouldered man came out of the Heritage Room carrying a cup of wine and took a rocking chair next to a chubby woman with a double chin. Paul Fetgatter, by nametag, had two-toned brown hair, one color on the sides mixed with strands of gray, and a deeper brown on top. He looked up and down the porch. "Who has the red Jaguar up at the lodge?"

"That would be me," Howard said from a rocker down at the end.

"That's some car," Paul Fetgatter said. "Do you race it?"

"I raced it here." Howard crossed his heavy legs, hiking the pants up on his cowboy boots. "I was trying to do sixty, but every time I looked down at the speedometer I had crept up to eighty-five and it felt like fifty."

"Why didn't you put it on cruise?" Duke Penny asked, sipping from his cup.

"I don't like using it. I don't feel like I have control when I do."

"No, I mean do you actually race the car?" the brown-two-toned Paul Fetgatter asked.

"I don't own it," Howard said.

"You don't own it?" asked the chubby woman with the double chin.

"I just rented it. It's really something to drive, though, I kid you not." Howard re-crossed his legs. "See, my car got stolen on Friday..."

Jim tuned the man out as he started through his long story again, and studied the chubby woman sitting across from him, Joppa Harp on her nametag. Her large, cheerful brown eyes were fixed on Howard as she stuffed popcorn in her mouth, jiggling her double chin. Joppa Harp had obviously made a few too many passes at the buffet table and seemed more fit for taking gourmet cooking than hiking and whitewater rafting.

Of course, the same thing could be said of the lardy Howard who had trained for the treks by walking at lunchtime for a week.

He glanced around at the other Elderhostelers.

None of them were as trim as Kelli Kee and Valerie Russin, the Mount Everest ladies, but none of them had reached the limits of Joppa and Howard either. Still, most of them would be packing some portly pounds up and down the hills. Maybe twenty in the chocolate-complected Quentin Quaries's case, although his large-framed body made it hard to tell. But his wife, Hallis, on the other hand, trim and petite, high cheek bones and dark eyes in a bronze complected face, could easily model clothes for senior citizen magazines.

He glanced at Dodee who kept in shape teaching aerobics a couple times a week.

No problem there.

But what about good old Jim Dandy?

He was still hefting an extra ten pounds around in spite of exercising and walking a couple of miles a day, one of the curses of living alone. Either you ate too much or too little.

Be interesting to see how the week shook out.

The other thing that struck him was the ease with which everyone sat around in the rocking chairs carrying on relaxed and animated conversations with people they almost surely hadn't known that morning. Open, was the thought that came to him. Probably not something that could be done as easily in another age group.

"Folks," Josie Blue called out, "it's time for dinner. When we head in, please put your discards in the trash. One of the things we try to do here at The Mountain, and we'll carry through when we're out in the woods, is to leave no trace behind. I think I told you the dining room is open twenty-four hours a day. Coffee is always available. And if you go into the dining room after dinner hours and you find things left out on the counter, like cookies or desserts, they are up for grabs. Another thing, when we get inside please find a place and stand behind your chair and the director of the center will say a prayer."

Jim took Dodee's hand and they made their way down a covered walkway, through the back door of the dining room, and into the rich smell of cooking food. A buffet table sat at the far end, the kitchen beyond that linked by passthroughs, and wooden tables spread out in the no-man's land in front. Strings of tiny white lights, like those seen at Christmas time, hung from the cross beams of open rafters connecting knotty wood walls with a knotty wood ceiling.

They found places at one of the wooden tables and when the room grew quiet, a dark-haired man picked up a microphone beside a second door midway down the room.

"Good evening, everyone. I want to welcome you to The Mountain Retreat and Learning Center. We are a Unitarian camp so we've decided that we should give a short, generalized prayer of thanks before our evening meals. Tonight I will do it, but in the coming days if someone else would like to step forward and say a prayer, they would be welcome."

And that's what he did, offered a prayer invoking God's blessing on their food and friendship.

Jim followed Dodee through the line, taking two slabs of meatloaf, potatoes and gravy, and green beans. He put a salad in a separate bowl, passed on milk and soda, and poured himself a glass of water. They sat with Howard and Paul Fetgatter, the man with the two-toned brown hair.

Then another man dropped into the chair opposite Howard, thin and short, a lot of skin on top of his head, and a big black mustache, like a handlebar without the handles. "You have the red Jaguar?"

"That's me. Just rented it."

"Hi, my name's Sam Moskowitz." His blue eyes bordered on indigo. "I've always dreamed about buying one. Think there'd be a chance of taking me for a spin in it while we're up here?"

"Hell, I'll let you drive it."

"Really?" Sam Moskowitz beamed. "This is like a dream come true."

Babs joined them. "Looks like everybody has enough to eat. How is it?"

"Good," Jim answered, taking another bite of meatloaf. It wasn't gourmet—he didn't think anyone should expect that on an Elderhostel—but it was wholesome and nourishing and tasty. "Will you be with us when we go on the hike tomorrow?"

"Yep." The ever ready smile spread across her broad face. "I'll be right along with the rest of you for the whole week, including the hikes and the whitewater rafting. That's one of the perks of being a host couple. We get to get to go along and do everything you folks do." Then the smile faded as she stared past Jim toward the back of the room. "That must be our latecomer." She started to rise, then sat back down. "Duke's taking care of him."

Jim turned to see her husband leading a tall, thin man back toward the Heritage Room.

"Do many people show up this late?" Dodee asked.

Babs nodded. "Sometimes. We've even had them come in the following morning, like tomorrow. But this one is a late signer-upper. He only made arrangements by phone on Thursday, and we didn't find out he was coming until yesterday. Luckily we weren't booked up."

"He's by himself?" Howard asked. "Does that mean I now have a roommate?"

She shook her head. "He specifically signed up for a single room."

"That's good because I have my laptop and clothes and stuff spread out all over."

"Is that unusual?" Dodee asked. "For someone to sign up this late?"

Babs cocked her head. "You know, I don't know. You'd have to ask someone like Josie."

Jim finished the last of his meatloaf and stood up. "I think I saw some pudding up there. Anybody interested?"

Howard raised a finger. "I'm up for it."

He crossed the room as one of the kitchen staff brought out a tray of clean dessert bowls. The young man sported a buzz haircut and a name stenciled on his apron.

"Hezekiah?" Jim asked.

The young man's face split in a grin. "My friends call me Ki," he said and headed back to the kitchen.

Jim spooned vanilla pudding into two bowls as Hallis Quaries came to stand beside him.

"Can I fill a bowl for you?" he asked.

"For my husband." An eyebrow raised over one of her dark eyes. "He asked me to bring it to him, but I bet it was so he could sneak up for a second one and nobody would know."

"Sounds like a man after my own heart."

"And if I don't watch him—you know what Josie said about leaving things out for grabs? Well, if I don't watch him he'll be sneaking up here after hours to make the grabs."

By the time he returned to the table, Duke was ushering in the new man, long and lanky, dressed in a dark suit and tie. An unruly swatch of brown hair capped a long face as white as a cave-dwelling fish. Serious brown eyes scanned the room, and something about his bearing made Jim think of a cop or a state trooper.

Or the FBI?

Except, what would an FBI man be doing here?

And even more except, why the hell should he care?

Damned if he wasn't starting to think like Dodee.

Want to know what an FBI agent would be doing here?

How about hiking and whitewater rafting.

FIVE

At seven-twenty Jim and Dodee headed upstairs for orientation and entered the Great Room, dominated by a stone fireplace on the far wall where a long table had been set up. Josie Blue rested his backside against it, his co-leader, Carmel Graves, sat behind it. A lofty wooden ceiling, held up by laminated wood beams that formed high arches, gave the place a church-like feeling. Windows on either end let in the remains of the long June evening, the ones on the right giving a golden sheen to two couches in the near corner and a piano in the far.

To Jim's left someone had set out a coffee pot and hot water with tea bags. He poured himself a cup, peeked into a small coffee kitchen tucked into the corner like an oversized closet, and continued on to two long tables by the windows where sign-up sheets had been set out.

"Which hike we going on?" he asked Dodee.

"The long one?" she asked.

He looked for the sheet so marked and handed it to her.

She smiled at him a moment then shook her head. "You want me to sign your name?"

"While you're at it."

"You know you could do it; sign both our names. That would be all right. In fact, it would be just Jim Dandy."

"Not funny, lady."

He walked back across the room and stood behind the last row of chairs arranged in a semi-circle facing the fireplace. Most of the dinner crowd was already there, seated and engaged in conversation.

One thing about Elderhostelers, tell them to be somewhere at a certain time and they'll all be there. Don't have to send someone out to round them up. But then the late signer-upper, Tristin Fontaine by nametag, came in, still dressed like an undertaker in his dark suit and tie. He gazed around the room for a moment, then took a seat behind Debra Longstreet and her niece Elcee.

Dodee slipped her arm around his waist. "We could sit up front."

"You could sit up front," he said and turned to the two couches that lurked in the corner.

"No, sweetheart." She sat down in the last row of chairs and looked up at him. "We ought to at least join the crowd."

He gave a last glance at the comfortable couches, then sat down beside her. She rewarded him by placing her hand on his as Duke and Penny came in and sat a few seats over.

Josie Blue glanced at his watch, said something to Carmel, then cleared his throat.

"Okay, everybody, like to take a few minutes to go over what we're going to be doing over the next few days. Tomorrow's hikes will be easy, about seven miles for the long one, four miles for the short, over uneven terrain. Over the hills and through the woods—"

"To grandmother's house we go?" Valerie Russin asked with a wink, she the taller of the two Everest climbers.

"No." Josie shook his head. "No grandmother."

"How about mountain mamma?" Howard asked. "Like in mountain momma take me home.".

"Wait a minute." Josie held out his hands. "No mountain mamma. No grandmother. The long hike will start from the bottom of the lodge, wind along a trail over to Chinquapin Mountain and down to Glen Falls, have lunch, then back up again to the lodge. For the short hike we'll drive to a parking lot halfway down, trek to the falls and then back up here to the lodge. And the really short one is just from the van to the falls and back to the van. We also want to remember, folks, that this should be a fun, relaxed walk. Don't hesitate to ask the leader to make a rest stop. And if you start out on the long hike and decide on the way back up that you'd rather take the van back, you can do that."

Howard raised his hand. "You mentioned lunch—"

"Yes, at breakfast the cooks will put out sandwich stuff, snackies and drinks, and brown bags to carry it in. How much or how little is up to you. You'll be responsible for packing your own lunch in and out, as well as your own water bottle. There'll be an opportunity to refill it from the van when you get to the parking lot."

Carmel Graves stood up, her wiry body dressed in khaki shirt and shorts and hiking boots.

"Perhaps this is a good time to mention that whatever we take into the woods we want to take out." Her flat voice was soft and unhurried and contained a touch of country twang in it. "There are no facilities on the hike. In keeping with the Appalachian Trail motto to leave no trace behind, this will include any waste material we might need to dispose of. I suggest taking a Baggie or two along for any paper products. And if you have to go off in the woods to answer a nature call, you either bury and cover it over, or cart it out in a Baggie. Babs and Duke Penny are our sweeps. Where are they?"

The Pennys raised their hands.

"If you do go off to answer a nature call, make sure the sweep knows about it. I'll be leading one hike and Josie the other, but the sweeps are the last ones in line to make sure we not only don't leave any trace behind, but we don't leave any bodies behind as well."

Josie Blue grinned. "Right. We don't want to leave any bodies behind. It makes for too much paperwork." The smile faded. "Seriously, safety is one of the main things we stress here at The Mountain. This includes the hikes and walking around the campus. When we go whitewater rafting we use the Nantahala Outdoor Center for the same reason, because it is the oldest with the best safety record." Josie motioned toward the tables by the window. "Has everybody signed up for tomorrow? If not, please do so. Oh, and if you are not going on the hike, or if you change you mind, please, please let us know so we don't hold everyone up waiting for you. Any questions?"

"What if it rains?" Hallis asked.

Carmel Graves nodded.   "We go regardless of the
weather. I believe your instructions said to bring hiking boots,
water bottles, *and* rain gear.   If it starts to lightning and
thunder, we get to shelter as fast as we can. But, as Josie said,
these will be easy hikes and we'll have plenty of rest stops along
the way."

She opened a folding aluminum tube and placed the tip
on the floor. "If you have a hiking stick, bring it along if you
like. They're especially helpful to some for crossing streams
and climbing steep grades. I bought this one three years ago
and its served me well, but you can also find a stick in the
woods. Just be careful you don't get it tangled in someone's
legs, including your own."

"Okay, some housekeeping matters," Josie said. "I told
you the dining hall is always open if you want coffee, but we
also have a kitchen here." He pointed to the door in the corner.
"We have a coffeemaker for those of you who get up early and
would like to make a pot. We just ask that if you empty it, you
clean it for those who follow." He paused a moment, bit his lip,
then shrugged. "I know a lot of you have had a long drive in
today, so we'll let you go now to get a good night's sleep."

Duke stood up and turned to Dodee. "Well, tomorrow
we'll be off on a new adventure," he said, running a hand over
his monk's circle of black hair

The plump Joppa Harp sauntered over. "How tricky is
that whitewater rafting on Tuesday?"

Duke flicked his bushy eyebrows. "Enough to make it
exciting."

Babs rolled her eyes. "Not enough to worry about."

Jim took Dodee's hand and they headed downstairs.
"Think some people are concerned over the whitewater
rafting?"

She glanced up at him. "Maybe, but they signed up for
it."

He shrugged. "I suppose it's a little like waiting in line
for a roller coaster. You're there and you're buying your ticket,

and you're looking forward to the thrill, but way back in your brain a voice is screaming, 'are you out of your freaking mind?'"

They entered the room and she stopped dead, turned, and stared up at him.

"What?"

"I didn't come all this way, sweetheart, not to sleep in your arms."

He glanced over her shoulder to the twin beds separated by the night table.

"You're saying you want me to put the beds together."

"I'm saying I want you to put the beds together."

He unplugged the lamp and set it on the desk. Then he manhandled the night table out from between the beds and banged it against the door as he set it down.

"Shh."

He stared into her big blues.

She glanced at the ceiling and back. "We don't want the whole building to know."

"Dodee, we're sharing a room. Don't you think the whole building knows?"

"But they don't need to know we're rearranging furniture."

"That makes it more wanton?"

Her breasts rose and fell. "Are we moving these beds or—"

"Okay, okay."

He shoved the near bed over to the one by the windows then moved the night table back against the wall where the bed had been. "How's that?"

"Not perfect, but better."

"If you fall between them in the middle of the night, I ain't coming to your rescue."

But she was already pulling out sheets and blankets and rearranging them to cover the span.

He pulled off his shoes and socks and peeled off his shirt.

"While you're putting our nest together," he said, grabbing his shaving case and pajamas, "mind if I brush my teeth?"

She turned and put her arms around his neck. "I'm sorry." She ran her a hand through his hair and stared into his face. "You look tired."

"It was a long trip down."

She gave him a feather kiss. "Why don't we just snuggle in tonight and save the fireworks."

"After you had me play furniture man?"

"I wanted to be near you, sweetheart, not pressure you to run a footrace after you've already completed a marathon day."

He kissed her. "Yeah, maybe we'll save the footrace. Is that what we're calling it this time?"

She slapped him on the rear. "Go brush your teeth before you fall asleep standing up."

He did as he was told and when he was finished, she took over the bathroom. He cracked the windows, crawled into bed, and realized how right she had been. He was half asleep when she slipped in beside him. He put his arms around her as she rested her head on his shoulder.

The split between the two beds might come apart in the night and dump them on the floor or leave a crease on their bodies, but for now it was okay.

She gave him an innocent kiss, her lips tasting of toothpaste. "Good night, sweetheart."

"Good night, lady."

And he let the long day melt away.

SIX

He awoke to the chirping of some dumb bird acting like a rooster as the first signs of light seeped into the night.

Screw 'em.

He breathed in the lady curled next to him, smelling of soap and sleep, and the warmth of her body made him think about the footrace he'd been too tired to run the night before.

He was ready to race now.

Unfortunately it took Dodee a long time to shift from sleep to wakefulness, and while she wasn't exactly grumpy–well, she was, in spite of how nicely she tried to cover it up.

He kissed her softly on the neck, carefully untangled himself, and made his way into the bathroom. He thought about shaving, passed on it, and washed up. When he came out, enough morning had crept through the windows for him to find his jeans, a sweatshirt, and his Chincoteague cap. He grabbed the coffee mug he had brought from home, slipped out the door, and barefooted it up the stairs.

He skirted a table in the gloom of the Great Room and found the light switch in the small coffee kitchen tucked into one corner like an oversized closet. A few cabinets, an under-counter fridge, and a coffee machine to which someone had thoughtfully added water and a prepackaged pack of coffee. All he had to do was flip the switch. He flipped the switch.

Then he turned off the light and stepped out onto the balcony, cold against his bare feet. He placed his hands on the railing damp with dew, breathed in the musty odor of the woods, and gazed down at the humps and bumps of mountains and foothills rising like castle keeps out of the mist that clung to the lowlands. All the kingdoms of the world were stretched out before him to end where the first golden haze topped the clouds on the horizon.

The birds bid it welcome.

And so did he.

God had done it again, spinning the world silently through the night until the sun could reclaim his majesty.

Thank you, God, for the day.

The door opened behind him, and he turned to see Elcee's clear brown eyes, her helmet of soft, yellowish brown curls in slight disarray.

"Good morning, Jim. Did you put the coffee on?"

He nodded. "Should be done soon."

"Already is."

"Your Aunt Debra awake?"

"Oh, what a beautiful sight." She stood at the railing in a light jacket, shorts and sneaks, her posture finishing-school straight. "I think I'll run and get my camera."

She swung around and rushed off. He caught the door before it closed and stepped into the inviting aroma of the kitchen. He filled his mug, added some half-and-half from the fridge, and barefooted back out onto the cold deck.

Now this was living.

Muscles rejuvenated during the night, sleep drained from his eyes, the first rays of sun peeking through the clouds, and a rich cup of coffee to snap in that little zing.

Maybe the rest of the day would be hell in a bucket, but he'd take it as payment for the morning.

Elcee returned and took a few shots with her camera "It's so pretty up here. Now for coffee." She popped into the kitchen and popped out a few moments later with a foam cup. "All set for the big hike?"

"I'm ready for breakfast."

She smiled and it lit up her face, highlighting a few freckles around her nose he hadn't noticed before.

"How about your aunt? Is she–"

"She's on her way up."

"You don't think the long hike might be too much–"

"For Aunt Debra?" She licked her lower lip. "Yes, I do.

That's why I signed us up for the shorter hike. But she's tough. And you can bet she'll be insulted. Even so, I think she should take it easy the first time out." Elcee turned to him. "She's the one who wanted to come on this Elderhostel. I just wanted to get out of Dodge for awhile."

"Greensboro?"

"Washington area. More glad than I thought I'd be when I signed up."

"How come?"

"My job is intense right now. A lot of pressure. And Friday's explosion didn't help."

"Yeah, I heard about that." He turned to her. "A car blew up on Rock Creek Parkway?"

"Nobody was hurt, except the driver, but everyone in D. C. is paranoid about a terrorist attack."

"No idea what caused it?"

She lifted her shoulders and arched her eyebrows. "I was on my way out of town when I heard about it. Haven't see anything since."

He turned back to watch the last vestiges of the night fading before the onrushing day.

"How about Dodee?" Elcee asked. "She awake?"

"No way." He smiled. "She might paint some nice sunsets, but I don't think she'll do many dawns."

"She paints?"

"Dodee's an artist. She has her own gallery in Kansas that her daughter mostly runs now, leaving her free to concentrate on her own painting and go on trips with me. But as far as the morning goes, she'll hang under the covers as long as she can, and even then I'll have to bring her a cup of coffee to pry her eyelids apart."

"Must be nice to have someone to bring you coffee."

He nodded. "And nice to have someone to bring it to."

The door opened and Aunt Debra came out dressed in shorts, anklet socks, and hiking shoes.

"Hi, Jim." Her hair might be gray, and she might have

wrinkles on her brow and around her lips, but her tired blue eyes held a glint of determination. "Great morning."

"Yes, it is."

"Dodee awake?"

"We just went all through that, Aunt Debra."

"Speaking of Dodee, I better get inside and see about her cup of coffee."

He bumped into the late-signer-upper, Tristin Fontaine, in the kitchen. What had been a merely unruly swatch of brown hair the night before was now a wild bird's nest, and sleep still rested in the eyes of his cave-dweller face. He had traded in his suit and tie for a cream-colored dress shirt, chino slacks, and soft walking shoes, not something you'd want to wear for a seven mile hike.

But then, maybe he wasn't going on the hike.

"Good morning," Jim said.

Tristin Fontaine gave him a brief nod.

"Did you sign up for a hike?"

The man nodded again and carried a foam cup with the tab of a tea bag hanging over its side out onto the balcony.

Jim turned to the coffee pot.

Gleaned a whole of information there.

He refilled his mug and poured a cup for Dodee.

On the other hand, wasn't that something he was always getting on Dodee for, not minding her own business?

Physician heal thyself.

He added Equal and half-and-half to her cup and strode out into the Great Room now filled with sunlight slanting in through the windows, splashing the laminated beams and exposed wood ceiling with golden light and soft shadows.

He ran into Howard. The lardy man was dressed in a short-sleeved, red plaid shirt and shorts that stretched tight around fat legs. A laptop hung from his hand.

"Doing some homework?"

"Uh huh." Howard lifted the laptop as if Jim couldn't see it. "Couldn't leave everything behind. Got an environmental group breathing down my neck." He sniffed. "Do I smell coffee?"

"Around the corner."

He continued down to his room, setting his mug on the floor to open the door.

Dodee was no longer in bed.

Either someone had carted her off or, from the sound of running water, she was up and about in the bathroom. He knocked on the door.

Nothing.

"I have coffee."

The door opened a crack, a hand reached out. He deposited the cup and the hand withdrew.

He stared out the window at the woods on the other side of the balcony railing. From here it was hard to see how the underbrush might hide a step off into the great beyond, as Josie Blue had called it, but if you weren't warned, and you were careless, maybe so.

The bathroom door opened and Dodee came out dressed in a tan shirt with small lapels, cargo shorts which set off her legs, and white socks stuffed into hiking boots.

The same sun that had streamed into the Great Room now turned her wheaten hair yellow and decorated her big blues with flecks of gold, but the smile on her lips was all her own.

"Thank you for the coffee, sweetheart," she said, putting her arms around his neck and kissing him.

He smelled her mixture of soap and herbal perfume, tasted her peppermint toothpaste, and felt her trim body pressed up against his, like it was footrace time.

She broke off the kiss as if reading his mind, or his body signs, and stared him in the eye. "It's almost time for breakfast."

"We could skip breakfast."

"Skip breakfast and we skip lunch if we're not there to make it."

"I've been thinking of going on a diet."

She smiled, gave him a quick kiss, and broke away. "Later, sweetheart. But keep the fire burning."

She started making the bed. "You don't look like you're ready for the woods."

"I'll get there." He exchanged his jeans and sweatshirt for his own cargo shorts, socks, and walking shoes. "All ready."

She opened the door barely enough to get out, waved him through, followed, and quickly shut it behind her.

"What are you doing?" he asked.

"People don't need to know we've rearranged the furniture."

He shook his head and patted her on the rear end as they headed out into the cool morning for breakfast. They strolled past mountain laurel lining the road, their glossy green leaves contrasted by delicate white flowers, some sprinkled onto the blacktop. They entered the chow hall and marched to the buffet table, engulfed in the warmth of frying bacon.

Jim scooped scrambled eggs onto his plate along with a sausage patty and five strips of bacon, then added a toasted English muffin, two patties of butter, and a small container of grape jelly to his tray. He picked up another cup of coffee and followed Dodee to an empty table, passing other Elderhostelers streaming in the door like bloodhounds picking up the scent of food.

He picked up a piece of bacon and saw Dodee smiling at him.

"Yes?"

"Tell me again, sweetheart, about this diet you are going on."

"I believe in eating a good breakfast--"

"I know, it sets you right up for a good lunch."

He cocked his head. "You've been hanging out with me too long."

"May we join you?" Kelli Kee asked as pony-tailed Valerie Russin came up behind her.

"Please do," Dodee said.

Then Howard came clunking over and plopped down across from Jim. "Good morning, Dodee." He nodded to the two Mount Everest women. "Kelli, Valerie. Already said good morning to Jim." His plate was piled high with a separate plate containing four pieces of toast. "Well, we all ready for the wild and wooly?"

Sam Moskowitz, the short man with the big black mustache, joined the table. "Hi, everybody." He turned to Howard. "Haven't forgotten about letting me drive the Jaguar?"

"Nope. How about after the hike?"

Sam beamed, dark blue eyes taking in the table. "This is like a dream come true."

"No problem," Howard said, and dug into his eggs.

"I see you believe in a good breakfast like Jim," Dodee said.

"Gotta stoke up for the long haul. Don't want to lose energy halfway down the trail."

"Or halfway back up?" Valerie asked with a wink.

Howard shoveled in a sausage patty. "On the way back up I'll have my lunch stocked up to keep me going." He gave them all his easy smile. "Got it all figured out."

SEVEN

Hezekiah, the buzz-cut kid from the kitchen staff, stopped by the table to let them know the lunch fixings had been set out.

Jim watched him move from table to table and head back toward the kitchen.

There were some unusual names this trip. Aside from Hezekiah, there was Joppa and Hallis. And Tristin and Quentin, for that matter. Also Babs and Duke, a little more common, but still unusual.

Dodee stood up. "Want me to make lunch for you, sweetheart?"

"No, I'll come with you." They started across the room. "After a breakfast like that, I want to go light for lunch."

"You make your own meals at home?"

"Mostly." He opened a brown bag and stuck in a small package of Health Chips. "I eat out about once a week, and maybe I'll order take-in once a week." He made a ham and cheese sandwich and added it to the brown bag along with a banana. "But yeah, if I can't con one of the kids into inviting me for dinner, I make my own."

"Alison and I often eat at the gallery. If we run late hanging paintings for a showing, like Saturday night, we'll treat ourselves to a dinner out after we close. When I'm working in my studio on a painting of my own, I can lose all track of time. Then it's all I can do to grab a sandwich before dropping into bed. But sometimes, if Alison has a date or something, I get to eat alone. Not so bad once or twice a week, but eating alone every night must be... lonely?"

He shrugged. "At least no one interrupts me when I'm reading the paper." He turned to her. "And sometimes I eat while I'm talking long distance to a lovely lady out in Kansas."

She smiled. "We'll have to do that more often."

They dropped off their trays at the kitchen window and returned to their room. Jim took his water bottle into the bathroom, but the faucet was too low and the shower head too wide.

"Going up to fill my water bottle. Want me to take yours?"

She tossed it to him. "Thank you, sweetheart."

He hurried up the stairs and started filling the bottles from the tall, curved faucet in the small kitchen's sink.

"Ah." Kelli Kee came in with two water bottles of her own. "Thought I saw a high faucet here when I came up earlier for juice and coffee.

"Juice?"

"Val and I keep some in the fridge. Juice first and coffee after. Hydrate then caffeinate. You're welcome to some if you like."

He finished with Dodee's bottle and reached for Kelli's. "Here, I'll fill those for you."

"Well, thank you. You're here with Dodee, right? You two come on a lot of Elderhostels together?'

"We haven't been on as many as some people, but we always go together."

"That's like Valerie and me. I think we've done fourteen of them so far."

Jim handed her one of the bottles and started filling the other. "Have you known each other long."

She smiled. "Only all my life. Val's my sister."

He turned to her. "I thought I saw a resemblance–"

"Around the jaw line?"

"Well, yes, I guess, but the names didn't give me a clue."

"Our maiden name was Hargrove. Val's taller and, of course, our hair is different, but we're sisters."

"How about your husbands?" He handed her the second bottle and collected his own. "Don't they ever come with you?"

"We keep trying, but they claim they can't take the time off."

"Where's this?" he asked as they started across Great Room together.

"We live in D. C. My husband works on Capitol Hill and Val's is a lobbyist. You going on Carmel's hike?"

"The one meeting at the bottom of the lodge?"

Kelli nodded. "Us too. See you there."

He skipped down the stairs and entered the room. "You know those two ladies that sat with us at breakfast? They're sisters."

"I figured that." She stuffed her water bottle into her pack and turned to him. "Ready?"

He swung his backpack over his shoulder and followed her out.

They gathered almost outside the back door to the lodge.

Carmel Graves, khaki shirt and shorts covering her wiry body, hiking boots with short socks folded over the tops, stood leaning on her aluminum walking stick. Babs Penny, similarly dressed with a polished wood walking stick, stood next to her, the alpha and omega for the hike.

Quentin Quaries gazed down the hill with his hands on his hips.

"Good morning," Dodee said to him. "Hallis going with us?"

The lips turned down on his chocolate face. "If she ever gets here. She's always late. That is the story of my life."

But instead of Hallis popping out of a cabin down the hill, Paul Fegatter's two-toned brown head rounded a curve up the hill. Following right behind was the chubby, double-chinned Joppa Harp dressed in a tan blouse and shorts with a cellphone strapped to her waist.

"Top of the morning," she said.

"Hi, Joppa," Dodee said.

"Everyone ready for the big hike?" Paul asked.

Now that he was up close, Jim realized the two-toned hair was the result of his wearing a toupee.

"Ah." Quentin raised his arms and let them flop as his

wife came out of one of the cabins and strolled up the hill toward them. "Here she is. Finally."

Hallis smiled. "Hi. Am I the last one?"

"Yes, as usual."

But then Howard rushed out of the lodge still dressed in his red plaid shirt and tight fitting shorts, and Jim saw that he, too, had a cellphone on his waist.

What was this?

Have we become such talk junkies that we can't take a walk in the woods without being in touch with the rest of the world?

Valerie and Kelli followed a moment later.

Then came the white-faced Tristin Fontaine, changed now from his chino pants and cream-colored dress shirt into what looked like brand new trail clothes—cargo pants, canvas shirt, hiking boots—as if he had just been outfitted by REI. He wasn't wearing his tie, but he had a red bandana wrapped loosely around his neck.

Babs counted the people as Dodee snapped off a few pictures with her camera. "I think we're all here."

"Wait." Tristin raised his hand. "I thought Debra Longstreet was on this list—"

"She was, but she changed to the shorter hike."

"Okay," Carmel said. "We've had a lot of rain so crossing some of the streams is going to be tricky." Her words rolled out in a soft, unmodulated voice. "We'll help each other and hopefully keep our shoes dry. If you need a rest stop or a nature call, there are some places that will facilitate this. Pass the word and I'll hold up. We don't want anyone to feel overburdened. Babs will be our sweep."

"That's me," Babs said, raising her hand.

"We'll head down into a saddle area and back up onto Chinquapin Mountain and on down to Glen Falls. Any questions before we head out?"

"Yeah," Howard said, big grin on his face, "when do we eat lunch?"

"At the falls. Remember, if I'm going too fast, yell at me. When we come to an intersection of two trails, I'll stop and wait until I see Babs before going on. Okay, as they used to say when wagoning across country in the olden days"—she raised a hand, gave it a little twirl, then stretched it straight out—"westward ho."

Howard took off right behind her, then Quentin and Hallis, and Dodee after them.

Jim fell in step behind her, traveling along a well-defined trail through the woods, wide enough for two people to walk abreast, if they were very thin and very cozy, and easy going despite it being rocky in places. Birds joined the cacophony of human conversation, and he breathed the woodsy smell of trees and moss and earth, all combining to push yesterday's long road trip far down in his mind.

Carmel stopped part way down the mountain, climbed a two-foot boulder on the side of the path, and turned to face them.

"I like to stand here because the rock amplifies my voice so you all can hear." And it did help, but only marginally. She looked down at her feet as she shifted them to one side. "I always try to be careful of the lichen on this rock. Everybody see it?" She pointed with her walking stick. "I try not to damage it because it's slow growing and it takes so long to recover." She looked out at the group. "You notice the white flowers on the mountain laurel?" She pointed to the leathery-leaved bushes. "If you pull off a section of the blossom, the inside is sticky and you can press them against your earlobe." She did so and it stayed in place. "They make nice earrings, something Indian maidens would have used. Also notice that flowering bush next to Joppa Harp?"

The chubby woman spun around to gaze at it.

"That's honeysuckle azalea, a wild native to these hills and one of the few azaleas that has an aroma."

So everyone started smelling it.

Dodee turned to Jim. "You going to sniff it?"

"If they call it honeysuckle azalea, it's got to smell like"—he held out his hand--"guess what? And if I've smelled one honeysuckle, I've smelled a million. However." He bent down and picked up a couple of fallen mountain laurel blossoms and stuck them to her earlobes. "Now you look like an Indian maiden."

She gave him a quick kiss, and they hurried to reclaim their place in line.

The path leveled off in the saddle between the two mountains, and Carmel held up at a cross trail with wooden signs pointing in various directions.

"This is the end of The Mountain property and the start of the U. S. Forest Service's," she said when everyone had caught up. "Everybody see this tree?" She touched a bush with long, saw-toothed leaves. "Can anyone tell me what this is?"

"A green-leaved plant," Howard Leslie said.

"A short and bushy tree," Quentin Quaries said, a grin splitting his chocolate face.

"A tree that grows out of the ground," Valerie Russin said, winking at her sister.

Carmel shook her head. "You would think I'd have learned not to ask questions like that after Josie made the same mistake." She looked back to the plant. "This is an American chestnut. At one time it was the dominant tree in the eastern United States in number and size and economic value. It grew eighty and a hundred feet tall. Around nineteen hundred a blight was introduced into the country, and it attacked the American chestnuts and wiped them out. The blight doesn't affect the roots so they keep sending up new shoots. The trees may reach ten or fifteen feet, sometimes even flowering and bearing fruit, before they die back again."

"Aren't there some places in the midwest that escaped the blight?" Jim asked. "I think I read that there're some full grown trees out there."

"That's right. There's a lot of research going on to bring the trees back."

Howard raised his hand. "There're hundreds of people, maybe thousands, of volunteers working on trying to develop a blight-free American chestnut. They're also looking at a gene in the Italian Chestnut that's resistant to the blight to see if they can alter the DNA to take care of the problem."

"You work for the Forest Service?"

"Department of Agriculture, but the altering of DNA is one of the things I monitor."

Carmel nodded. "Everyone ready to move on? It's uphill here."

"Lead on, MacDuff," Howard said. "Off into the wild and woolies."

Shafts of sun poked through the canopy of oaks, maples, white pines, and hemlocks, dappling the trail in light and shade like bright spots on a drama stage. Every so often Dodee stopped to snap a few pictures of something that appealed to her artist's eye, but it looked the same as the last bend in the road to him. The going became steep and he concentrated more on where to put his feet than the forest around him, so he was startled when they broke out into clear light on top of a large boulder, a small breeze bidding him welcome. Sunshine glowed on green treetops down in the small valley they had just crossed.

Carmel stood about five feet from the rock's edge. "We don't want to go any farther than this. The first step might be exhilarating, but the second is a cruncher."

"How far down is it?" Paul asked, patting his head as if to make sure his hairpiece was in place.

"What's that over there?" Quentin asked, pointing to a building on the mountain across the saddle.

"That's the lodge where we started out this morning. And the fall from here is about the same as from the lodge down to the bottom."

Hallis rested an arm on her husband's shoulder. "We've come a long way."

"Not so far," Kelli said.

The lanky Tristin Fontaine, red bandana still tied around his neck, came out onto the rock, carefully placing each foot as if walking on uneven ground was a new experience.

Joppa Harp straggled out of the woods next, puffing to catch her breath. "When I get back home, I'm going to get in an exercise program. How much farther up is up? Are we at the top yet?"

"This is it. From here on it's downhill to Glen Falls. Just remember when you're enjoying all that down, you have all that up on the return trip.

Dodee snapped off a few pictures and came over to huddle next to Jim. "How are you doing, sweetheart?"

"I'se doin' jus' fine. How you'se doing?"

"Jus' fine also."

They started off again and three hundred feet farther along, Carmel stopped beside a large boulder at the side of the path, eight feet long and protruding five feet out of the shady ground, like someone had plopped down the covered body of a pickup truck. She rested her arm on top and leaned her wiry body against it. When they all caught up, she pointed her walking stick at a fungus growing on the rock, looking like two or three inch gray leaves.

"The Cherokee name for this large lichen is blood leather. If you got a serious wound, like from an arrow in battle, you put this on it, wrapped it up, and it would stop the bleeding. It's also called rock trout. The Indians used to boil it in a stew if they were starving and eat it. If you break off a small piece and chew it for fifteen minutes you'll get a flavor."

"Good flavor?" Joppa asked.

"Nope."

"Forget it." She gave a sweep of her pudgy hand. "I'm not working my jaws fifteen minutes for a lousy flavor."

"Howard!" Carmel jerked around. "Stop!"

The lardy man had blazed a path off to the right, between the rock and a large oak, tramping the underbrush and sparse grass like a one-man herd of elephants. He stopped five feet from where the woods cleared and prickly stalks of a bush grew in the sun.

"Aren't these blackberries?"

"Yes, but those blackberries are right at the edge of a hidden cliff. If you pick them, assuming there are any this early in the season, you'd better eat them fast because you could end up going splat. Turn around. Come back."

Howard turned around. And came back.

EIGHT

Jim heard the first stream before they came to it, a gurgle as it squeezed by a rock, a splash as it rolled over a fallen-tree dam, a crash as it tumbled over a mini waterfall.

Traversing it was a simple matter of jumping across, he ahead of Dodee, then reaching back to take her hand.

But after climbing over the next rise and coming down to the second stream, it became a little more tricky. And the same for the third and the fourth. Fortunately a heavy boulder lodged in the middle facilitated one crossing, a log that spanned from bank to bank took them across the next, and Tristin found a place where some bouncy branches got them over the last with only the soles of their shoes getting wet.

But then they came to the mother of all stream crossings which required going from a wobbly rock, to a pointed one in the middle, then to a slanted one barely awash before finally reaching the bank.

They stood watching the clear mountain runoff, six or eight inches deep.

Then Carmel struck out, using her walking stick for support and extending her free arm for balance, she stepped nimbly from bank to wobbly rock to pointed rock to slanted rock awash, and landed on the edge of the opposite bank. She flailed her arms as she fought to keep from falling back, then regained her balance, and turned to face them with a triumphant smile.

And everyone cheered.

She braced herself and stretched out a hand to help the next one across.

Jim scooted to the front of the line to stand on the bank opposite her and extended his hand to help from his side. "Come on, Hallis, you can do it."

The dark eyes flashed at him. "Yeah, thanks a lot." She

took his hand in a death grip, reached one foot out, then looked back to him. "If I fall, you're dead."

She clambered from bank to wobbly rock to pointed rock, still clutching Jim's hand in a death grip, forcing him to lean   way out over the rushing water. Then she screamed and in a moment of truth let go, stepped onto the slanted rock awash, and grabbed Carmel's hand as she jumped safely to the other side. She spun around and threw up her arms

And everyone cheered again.

Quentin followed his wife and when he made it, he turned and offered a second hand to those making the crossing.

Valerie and Kelli crossed with ease, then Joppa screaming all the way, and Dodee laughing.   Tristin next, moving like an aloof member of royalty with his red bandana carefully knotted around his neck and his new trail clothes hardly wrinkled. Paul with the speed of a gazelle. Howard with a lot of squeals, arm waving, and tottering before making it to the opposite shore.

"Yes," he shouted, raising two fists in the air, "one small step for man, one giant step for Howard Leslie."

"Let's go, Babs," Jim said, reaching for her hand.

"Nope, I'm the sweep. You go first."

"But you might need help."

"It's my job to help." She snapped her fingers. "You take my hand."

He took her hand and started across, felt the world shake under him as he put his weight on the wobbly rock, rested his other foot on the pointed rock, and stared at the slanted rock, barely awash. The slanting part had moss growing on it, unseen from the bank. If he didn't hit it just right he'd be in the drink. But then, everyone else had made it.

He shifted his weight to the pointed rock as he let go of Babs, concentrated on putting his foot on the edge of the slanted rock awash, hit it just right, felt a hand grab his and jumped for the other side.

"All right," he said, landing both feet on dry soil.

"Thanks, Quentin."

"No problem."

They all turned to face Babs who grabbed her walking stick and started across without preamble. She made it to the wobbly rock, then the pointed rock, but as she stepped for the slanted rock awash, she reached out to grab a hand, and in that moment of inattention hit the slippery moss slope and went down with a scream. She plopped rear end into the drink, sending water flying as the stream gurgled and splashed around the new obstacle in its path.

"Oh Lord, that's cold."

"Are you all right?" Quentin asked.

But she popped up as quickly as she had gone down, hands on hips, feet flat in the stream, water running over her boot tops. She turned to them and grinned. "I'm glad it was me."

"Are you all right?" Quentin asked again. "You could have twisted something."

Jim took her hand as she sloshed to shore. "If you're hurt," he said, starting to tell her was a physical therapist, but Hallis cut him off.

"Quentin's a physician."

Jim nodded.

A doctor probably trumped a physical therapist.

"I'm fine, I'm fine." She patted her short-cropped, steel-gray hair. "A little embarrassed that's all. My backpack didn't get wet, and I have some dry clothes in there."

"You want to change?" Carmel asked.

"No, I'm ready. It's a warm day. I'll dry out along the trail."

So they started off again, Carmel once more taking point and Babs sweeping the rear with a wet rear.

Half an hour later they met Josie Blue leading his short-hike crew from the parking lot and starting up the trail. Tristin exchanged a few words with Aunt Debra and Elcee as they passed, and Duke Penny waved to his wife. "How was the hike, dear?"

"Don't ask," Babs said, and turned around to show him her wet seat. "I took a tumble in the crick."

He smiled. "In the crick is better 'n the creek."

"She zigged when she should have zagged," Carmel said.

"Hi," Dodee said, coming abreast of the seventy-something Aunt Debra. "How are you doing?"

"Just fine, Dodee. We got a nice climb ahead of us?"

"Not too bad. I thought you were going on the long hike with us."

"I was," she said with a steely glance at Elcee, "but my niece talked me out of it."

Elcee rolled her eyes. "I thought it might be too much for her, but I haven't stopped hearing about it since."

"Not too much for me, dear. I was primed for the long hike, but maybe too much for you."

"Yes, Aunt Debra. We won't make that mistake on Wednesday's hike."

"I didn't make the mistake. You did."

Elcee rolled her eyes again and followed her older version up the trail after Josie Blue.

Duke gave Babs a kiss. "See you at the cabin, honey." He flicked his brushy eyebrows. "I'll help you dry off your bottom." Then he took off after the others, taking up his position as sweep at the end of the line.

Next to the parking lot they found a wooded clearing with railroad ties laid out to form a square circle, a burned out campfire in its center. At the far end log seats overlooked the valley and flatlands, and on the far right, opposite the parking lot, the trail continued on down to Glen Falls.

Carmel dropped her backpack on one of the railroad ties. "Okay, we'll rest here for a few minutes. The van is open in the parking lot if you'd like to refill your water bottles." She pointed to the small path off the trail they had just come down. "Women can go that way." Then pointed to the overlook. "Men go that way."

Howard grinned. "Suppose you're a boy?"

"You say you're that small?" Valerie asked.

"You say you need someone to help you find it?" Kelli asked.

"Okay, okay." Howard held up his hands. "I'm off with the men." He took a few steps, then turned. "Although helping me find it might be fun."

Jim collected Dodee's water bottle along with his own and took them out to the white passenger van. He filled both bottles and glanced around the parking lot at two Camrys, a blue Ford Taurus, a white Chrysler, a Chevrolet pickup, and a green Lincoln SUV, all deserted

So where were the people? Down at the falls?

He moseyed back to the clearing to find a small group gathered around Carmel, who was pointing out some flora or fauna, Tristin standing off by himself, wiping his flushed face with the red bandana, and Dodee walking back from the au naturel ladies room.

"I filled your water bottle."

"Thank you, sweetheart."

Carmel called them all together again and they started off through the woods. The path got steeper the further they traveled, turning into winding switchbacks. Then came the sound of splashing water, growing louder until it reached a crescendo as they broke out of the trees at the top of Glen Falls. All the streams they had crossed, plus all their brethren, must have come together to charge out of the forest into the bright sunlight and race over a rock cliff into an abyss below.

Dodee snapped a few pictures from behind the protection of a board fence designed to keep the unwary from being accidentally swept away.

"What do you think, sweetheart?"

"Hope that's not part of our rafting trip."

"Yeah," Howard said, and turned to Carmel. "This part of tomorrow's rafting trip?"

"Nope. Thursday's trip."

"I ain't going," Hallis said.

Carmel gave her a reticent smile. "Just kidding. On Thursday we'll face only one class four falls. All the rest are class three or less."

"What class is this?" Jim asked.

"Five million."

They followed the switch-back trail down the hillside as the water fell in stages: a sheer drop of forty feet crashing onto rocks with a roar that drowned the sounds of the forest; falling again off a ten foot ledge, adding to the noise; then splashing on more rocks to spread out in a series of cascades, the white water flashing in the brilliant sunshine that glowed green on the leaves of the trees lining the shore where ferns and bushes lurked in the shadows.

When they reached the bottom, Carmel spread the word that it was lunch time.

Jim found a slanted rock to lean his butt against and shared it with Dodee. "Seems like Carmel could have picked a better place for a lunch," he said, pulling out his sandwich and taking a bite. "No place to sit here."

"You're right there," Howard said. "Mind if I rest my bag on your rock?"

"Sure," Dodee said and moved to one side. She pointed to the falling water smashing against the rocks. "Maybe she thought it would be nice to eat by the falls."

"Maybe so." Howard chomped on a sandwich, taking half of it in one bite, and pulled out his cellphone. "But it also makes it damn hard to hear."

"Can I put my bag on your rock?" Joppa Harp asked.

Dodee moved further to the side. "Be my guest."

"Doesn't seem to be anyplace to sit except on the wet ground."

Howard inhaled the rest of his sandwich as he shook his big head and put his phone away. "No signal," he said, pulling out another sandwich. "I probably wouldn't have heard them anyway."

"Calling home?" Joppa asked.

The lardy man shook his head again. "Don't have anyone at home to call. Trying to get my office."

"Would they even miss you if you didn't call?" Jim asked.

"Not normally, but I have an environmental case I'm tracking. It could turn political if I don't handle it just right." He finished off his second sandwich and grabbed a third. "Need to stoke up on energy for the trip back."

"Stoke up too much and it will sit in your stomach like a lump of lead."

"No problem. I'm a fast digester."

Jim turned to Joppa. "See you brought a cellphone, too."

Joppa nodded, jiggling her double chin. "My office requires me to carry it."

"What do you do?"

"I'm a partner in a lobbyist firm," she said and turned to Howard. "What kind of case are you tracking?"

"Confidential." He bit into his sandwich and a blob of mayonnaise squirted out onto his red plaid shirt. "Kind of tricky, and political, and I'd like to tell you about it." He wiped the mayonnaise blob off with his finger and licked it, leaving a smear behind. "But, as I say, it's confidential."

Carmel walked past them and made one switchback where she had a commanding view of the hikers. "While you're eating let me relay some things to you. First of all, I don't think I've ever seen this much water going over the falls. We've had a lot of rain this spring–two inches on Saturday alone–but this will help when we go rafting. When we finish our lunch, we'll head back up to the parking lot where you can refill your water bottles from the van if you haven't already done so. Those of you who've had enough hiking can take the van back to The Mountain. For those who are going on, we'll have plenty of rest stops along the way, and when we get up near the top of Chinquapin Mountain, we'll do something a little different. I'll give you each a chance to experience the trail as it was before the white man came."

NINE

He breathed in the faint sounds of the forest.

The long, steep switchback trail from the falls to the parking lot, deserted now except for the van and the green SUV, had convinced Hallis Quaries that she was riding back up to The Mountain. Had convinced good old Jim Dandy, too, for that matter. Go back to the room and take a nap. Except when they reached the parking lot, Dodee had informed him she was for going all the way. Which meant—sonofabitch—if he wanted to maintain his machismo, he had to tag along as well. Sometimes she really pissed him off. But after they had filled their water bottles, rested, and been assured by Carmel that the worst of the climb was over, everyone had bucked up for the long haul.

Including Hallis.

And including good old Jim Dandy.

He was glad now that he had.

Of course, he knew he wasn't alone.

"Okay, while you're resting," Carmel had said near the top of Chinquapin Mountain, "I'd like everyone to be as quiet as you can. Let the silence settle in. I'm going to start out along the trail and when I'm out of sight, I want the next person to start after me, and when that person is out of sight, the next person. Stay on the trail." She'd glanced up as a bird called out from the tree tops. "That's a Bireo," she had said, her soft voice barely above a whisper. "If you listen, it sounds like it's saying, 'Look up, see me, here I am.' I always look up and never see him. It will be interesting to see what else we hear. Remain silent, not only for yourself, but out of respect for the rest of the group, so that we'll all get some small sense of what it's like to hike alone." She had started to go, then turned back. "Remember, stay on the trail."

So while he couldn't see anyone, he knew Dodee was somewhere not too far up ahead, with Valerie, Kelli, and Carmel out in front of her.

Somewhere behind, the rest of the group.

But for now, good old Jim Dandy marched alone to the tune of the forest: a woodpecker whacking at a dead tree, a bird singing to its mate, the rustle of leaves and the whisper of pines, with only the occasional soft crunch of his footfall striking a discordant note. He breathed deeply of the woodsy odors and the smell triggered an instant memory.

He is a kid again at Boy Scout camp, walking back through the woods after swimming in a stream-fed lake, cold enough to tingle his toes, with only the warmth of the summer day to towel him dry. His step is light and without effort, young bones and supple muscles taking up the slack like steel springs and ball bearings. Only the sounds of the surrounding woods–a scolding blue jay, the bark of a squirrel, a lone odd crow calling from the top of a dead chestnut tree–keep him company. The pungent smell of a wood fire reaches out through the clean air to welcome him, and as he closes the camp it mingles with that of bubbling stew–food to be transferred from cast iron pots into cast iron stomachs, grander than any feast set before a king.

He shortcutted a switchback bend in the trail, and in the exuberance of his memory, hopped over a log, landing with a jar that rippled through his body and reminded him that Boy Scout camp had been more than half a century ago.

He sipped from his water bottle and continued on.

Never carried bottles in those days.

Instead they had depended on the streams to supply them with water, confident that their young bodies would be able to fight off whatever trace contaminant or bacteria they contained.

Now, with acid rain and pollution, he wasn't ready to put that to the test.

He slowed as he caught a whiff of alien air by the pickup-sized boulder where Carmel had pointed out the rock trout lichen. He sniffed again, but now all he could detect was the smell of pines and moss and mold.

He continued on and in a few hundred feet, after hiking perhaps a total of fifteen minutes alone, came upon the others waiting on the rock outcropping that overlooked the saddle between the mountains and the lodge on the other side.

Carmel put her finger to her lips as he joined them, feeling the sun on his face and an unobstructed breeze riffling his hair.

Dodee smiled and held up her arms to him.

He wrapped her in close and she kissed him, warm and tender and not quite so innocent.

Now that was one thing he hadn't gotten at Boy Scout camp.

And the words of one of his cronies, spoken with alcoholic authority on their annual Chincoteague fishing trip, slid in to tickle him.

"When I was seventeen I kept wondering when I was going to get laid next. Now that I'm seventy-one I keep wondering when I got laid last."

He hoped to take care of both of those problems when he and Dodee got back to their room.

"Did you enjoy the silence?" she whispered in his ear. "I really felt like I was alone out there."

"No unseen eyes staring at you from behind the trees?" he whispered back.

She blinked, then put her lips against his ear again. "You know, I did at one point. Thought I heard someone cough, but I ignored it knowing you were within shouting distance."

"Maybe a wood-goblin was watching you from the shadows."

She frowned. "The only goblin around here is standing next to me."

"If we get some nap time in, I hope to show you a real goblin."

She cocked back her head, looked down her nose at him, and gave him that little smug smile of hers where the ends of her lips turned down.

The plump Joppa Harp came puffing in, raising her arms to catch the breeze. Then came two-toned Paul followed by Tristin minus his red bandana. Then Hallis and Quentin. Finally, when Babs Penny brought up the rear, everyone started talking at once, as if they could no longer contain the silence.

"That was great," Quentin said. "Reminded me of playing in the woods behind my house when I was a boy."

"The farther I walked, the more things I could hear," Kelli said.

Hallis nodded. "Me, too. Including another Bireo, saying, 'Look up, see me, here I am'."

Carmel smiled. "Aren't they loudmouths?"

Babs turned to Carmel. "We haven't done this on our hikes before, have we?"

"Nope. The last time I was working on the Appalachian Trail, I got to thinking we might give this a try. Did you like it?"

"Yeah, we ought to do it from now on."

"Know what it brought home to me?" Joppa rested her hands on her wide hips. "I wouldn't do this if I was really alone. Even if I was sure I was really alone, I wouldn't feel comfortable doing it in today's age."

Carmel shrugged. "I've spent days hiking alone along the Appalachian Trail. I love the idea of just nature and me."

"Maybe so, but I wouldn't be able to do it. Not because of the isolation and the silence—I think I'd like that—but because of the fear that someone could be stalking me, ready to do me harm if they got the chance. But that's just me. Maybe it's my Hackensack, New Jersey upbringing."

"That's one of the reasons Val and I always go together," Kelli said.

Carmel pointed her walking stick toward the trail. "Everyone ready to go on?"

Jim glanced around at the crowd, then searched them again. "Where's Howard?"

A stunned silence fell like a shroud as everyone looked around, as if he was hiding somewhere.

"Was he with us from the parking lot?" Carmel asked, turning to Babs.

"Yes. I watched him walk off just like everyone else."

"Maybe he wandered off the trail," Hallis said.

"Wasn't he interested in those blackberry bushes?" Paul asked.

Jim moved back onto the trail and looked down the way they had come, Carmel coming to stand at his side.

"We need to retrace our steps," he said. "He could have fallen and hit his head."

She looked at him, then turned to the others. "Babs, why don't you all stay here while Jim and I make a quick reconnaissance."

Quentin raised his hand "I'll go with you. I'm a doctor."

Paul stepped forward as well. "I'll go."

"Me, too," Dodee said stepping besides Jim.

Carmel showed them the palm of her hand. "Hold up. We don't want everybody."

"No," Jim said, "but if you stay on the trail, we could spread out, two people on each side, just in case Howard decided to make a quick pit stop somewhere."

"I guess that makes sense."

Carmel nodded and they started out, Jim and Dodee tracking twenty feet off to the left, Paul and Quentin somewhere off on the right, everyone calling out as they went. But if Howard was out there, he wasn't answering.

Jim skirted a large mountain laurel and looked back. "You okay?"

"Right behind you," Dodee said. "What do you think happened?"

"We'll ask when we find him."

"If we find him. Could a bear have hauled him off?"

"Someone would have heard it. We weren't that far apart. I'm more concerned that he went off the trail to go to the bathroom and had a heart attack."

He pushed a tree branch out of the way and stopped at

the sight of a white cigarette stub contrasting with the green pine needles covering the forest floor.

"I found the blackberry bush," Paul called out. "Looks like someone could have crashed through it."

Jim and Dodee rushed back to the trail where Paul stood with Quentin and Carmel beside the pickup-sized boulder. Paul pointed toward a path an elephant could have made, crunching underlying plants and sparse grass all the way out to where the woods thinned and the blackberry bush grew in the sun, and then kept on charging.

"It doesn't look good."

He was right about that.

Carmel crossed over to the bush and tentatively leaned out.

"See anything?" Paul asked.

"I need to get further out," she said, lowering herself to the ground.

"Let me do that," Jim said, "I'm longer."

"Be careful, sweetheart. I don't want to lose you."

"Nobody's losing me."

He hurried over and dropped down on all fours beside Carmel. He tried to see over the edge of the cliff, but there was a rock lip three feet down that blocked his way, and some bushes growing past that as well. He lay flat out on the ground.

"Somebody hold onto my ankles, just in case."

He pulled his Chincoteague cap down to shade his eyes and inched forward on a layer of loamy soil as he felt Quentin and Paul grab his ankles, just in case. He gingerly picked his way through the blackberry stickers growing out of cracks in the outcropping, but he still couldn't see over the rock lip.

"Hang onto me. I need to go a little further."

"Forget it, sweetheart. Come back."

He stretched all the way out and inched forward.

"Right," Carmel said, "it's too dangerous—"

"Just a little bit more."

"We got you," Quentin said. "See anything?"

He craned his neck, rib cage hanging past the edge now, and gazed down over the rock lip. "Broken branches growing out of the–"

He moved his head to peer through a clear spot, and down on the rocky floor, forty or fifty feet below, he saw a red plaid shirt.

TEN

"Howard," he called out, but even before he shouted he knew that only his echo would answer.

"He's down there?" Quentin asked.

"He's down there." He turned his head. "Pull me back."

"I told everyone to stay on the trail," Carmel said. "You all heard that. Why would he wander off?"

"For the blackberries?" Paul asked, as if it were a real question.

Jim rolled back from the edge and stood up.

Quentin stared at him. "Any sign of life?"

He shook his head.

"We have to get down there," he said in unison with Quentin, both apparently thinking the same thought.

"Anyone have a cellphone?" Carmel asked.

"Yeah," Paul said, "I saw someone with one earlier–oh, yeah." He motioned toward the cliff. "Howard, but he couldn't get a signal anyway."

Quentin turned to Carmel. "What's the fastest way down?"

"Howard took the fastest way," Paul said, his crooked smile chinking his cheeks out of line.

Dodee shook her head. "That's not funny."

Carmel led the way back to the trail. "C'mon. We'll send the others back to call for a search and rescue helicopter while we work our way around the mountain."

Quentin and Paul followed behind her. Jim waved Dodee ahead, leaving him to bring up the rear.

"You know," she whispered, "we might have just screwed up a crime scene."

"What crime scene? You think some bear dragged him to the cliff so he could have Howard and blackberries for lunch? There's nobody out here."

"Nobody, but us."

Carmel called out when the others came into view. "Anyone have a cellphone?"

"I do," Kelli said, "but I can't get a signal up here. Did you find Howard?"

"He took a Humpty Dumpty," Paul said, his crooked smile chinking his face out of line again.

"What?" Babs said, blue eyes wide.

"We think he's injured," Jim said before Paul could open his mouth again. "I saw his shirt at the bottom of a ravine."

"Babs," Carmel said, "I need to you take everyone back to the compound."

"I have a cellphone," Joppa said.

"Can you get a sig—"

"It's a satellite phone. I can get a signal." She pulled it out of the case on her hip and showed it to them. "Who do you want me to call?"

"Can you get The Mountain? Tell them we need a rescue helicopter."

Carmel called out the number and Joppa punched it in and held the phone to her ear. "Hello, we've had some trouble out here on the hike and need a rescue helicopter. Hold a minute and I'll put Carmel on." She handed her the phone. "Just remember there's a slight time delay."

"This is Carmel. We need a rescue helicopter."

Joppa turned to Jim. "What happened?"

He shrugged. "Remember when Carmel stopped Howard from going out to that blackberry bush? Well, a trail had been trampled out to it and when I looked over the cliff edge, I saw him on the rocks below." He motioned to Carmel talking on the phone. "How does that work?"

"Like any cellphone, just that it has a little delay as the signal reaches up to the satellite and back to the ground. I need it for work. I have to be in contact no matter where I am. I also have a cell for when I'm in a good area."

"Right, hold on," Carmel said and turned to Joppa. "Can

someone call in on this?"

She nodded. "I wrote it on the side with black magic marker."

Carmel read it to those on the other end and clicked off. "Okay, Babs, you lead everyone back to the lodge," she said, her voice carrying an excited inflection in it for the first time. "Kelli and Val, can you two act as sweeps? We don't want to lose anyone else." She turned to Joppa and held up the phone. "Can I hang onto this?"

"No, I can't do that, but I'll come along and bring it with me."

"We'll be moving out?"

Joppa nodded, jiggling her double chin. "I'll try to keep up."

Dodee stepped beside her. "I'll hang out with Joppa, in case we fall behind."

"Okay. Quentin and Jim come with me."

They hurried down to the bottom of the trail where they left the others and cut off through the woods, Carmel leading, followed by Quentin and Jim with Dodee and Joppa.

"This reminds me of the hiker's prayer," Paul said, the round-shouldered man tagging along uninvited. "Lord, if you pick 'em up, I'll put 'em down."

"Try to keep up and in visual contact," Carmel said. "If you lose sight of the person ahead, sing out and we'll hold up."

"Do we need to break some branches to mark our way back out?" Paul asked.

"I'll take care of that."

They worked their way around the mountain, rough going now, pushing branches out of the way and tracking through underbrush.

Jim divided his time between looking where he was going, back to make sure Dodee was still in sight, and up toward the mountain for Howard

"Up there," he said finally, spotting the red shirt forty feet up a slope.

"Think I'll stay down here," Joppa said. "Call down if you need me to relay anything."

Carmel charged off and Jim puffed along behind her, hearing Quentin puffing along behind him. They climbed up the steep slope between trees and around boulders until they reached a clearing carved out by large slabs of rock slanting down from the base of the cliff. Howard lay on the middle of one, arms extended, face turned up to the afternoon sun. Blood had splattered the craggy surface, running down and seeping into small crevices before it had congealed.

"Be careful of the blood," Quentin said, puffing up beside them. "As a precaution."

Carmel stood aside and Quentin squatted down beside Howard. He put a hand on the fat throat, touching the carotid artery with a gentleness one would show a sleeping baby, opened the man's eyelids to peek into his eyes, then stood up and shook his head.

Howard had taken his last ride in the red Jaguar.

Jim felt a hand in his and turned to see that Dodee had followed along.

Forty feet down the slope Joppa's phone rang. "Helicopter's on the way," she called.

Carmel scanned the area and looked up to the treetops. "We'll have to winch him out and let them report it to the sheriff."

"What do you think happened?" Dodee asked.

"I think he ignored my advice to stay on the trail, decided instead to pick some blackberries, and fell." Her brow wrinkled and she palmed up her hands as her eyes shifted between them. "What else?"

Jim stared back down at the body.

In a way that sounded like Howard. Always worrying about stoking up on energy for the long haul back. But would he have gone out there after being warned to stay away?

He heard the first faint sounds of a far off helicopter and grabbed Dodee's camera.

"If they're going to take the body out of here, we'd better get some pictures for the sheriff."

He snapped off six shots from various angles as the beating of the helicopter drew near. Carmel waved it down and the chopper came in to hover above their heads. A crew member dropped out of the side door and came down on a cable, landing deftly on the rock. He un-clipped his harness as Quentin talked to him for a few minutes, then the man nodded and spoke into a phone hanging from his neck. A stretcher cage dropped from the helicopter, Jim helped place the body in it, and someone above winched it up.

"I wonder if Howard's ever ridden in a helicopter before," Paul said.

The crew member was winched back aboard and the helicopter lowered its nose and sped away, the beating of its blades echoing off the side of the mountain.

Carmel pulled a roll of toilet paper out of her pack.

Paul smiled at her. "Goin' for a lone walk in the woods?"

But she started wrapping bushes with it. "Need to mark the site in case the sheriff wants to check it out. It's biodegradable so if we don't get back, it should melt away in the first few rains."

Jim led the way down to where Joppa sat on a boulder waiting for them.

"Could hear your phone ring from up there."

"Need it that way in case I'm in a noisy place."

Then they started back for the trail, Carmel taking the lead, Jim bringing up the rear as the newly appointed temporary sweep, and everyone trying to maintain visual contact in the dense woods.

"Are you sure you're following your broken-off branches?" Paul asked, patting his hairpiece as he ducked under a tree branch.

"I didn't break any off."

"Then how are we gonna find the trail?"

"I'm standing on it," Carmel said as they gathered

around her. "We're almost home. Need a rest or are we ready to go on?"

They all turned to the chubby Joppa.

"Why is everyone looking at me? I can see I'm going to have to think about an exercise program when I get home. I'm ready to go on if everyone else is."

So they soldiered on, but Carmel's idea of being almost there didn't account for it being all uphill. Finally, three quarters of an hour later, they trudged up the road that led by the cabins, and Hallis came out to meet them looking fresh and clean.

"What about Howard?"

Quentin shook his head. "I need a shower and a nap."

"I strongly recommend the shower, honey, but if you want to make it to the community time and dinner, you'll have to skip the nap."

He raised his hands and let them flop. "No rest for the weary. See you all later."

They continued up the hill to the lodge where a car with a roof rack of dome lights waited. Two men in uniform got out as they approached. The man on the driver's side was tall and slim, the other short, mid forties, with a round face and a rounding stomach.

"Carmel Graves?"

"That would be me."

"Yes, ma'am, my name's Sheriff Graham." The short man shut the door and walked around the front of the car and motioned to the tall and slim man. "This is my deputy, Bob Jones. What was the man's name, Jonesy?"

"Howard Leslie."

"Right." He turned back to Carmel. "Fell off a cliff I understand." His eyes roamed among the group. "You all were there?"

"No one saw him go over," Jim said. "We helped recover the body, if that's what you're asking."

"We think he went out to pick blackberries," Joppa said.

"They're right at the edge of a cliff," Carmel said.

Paul shrugged. "He took a Humpty Dumpty."

Sheriff Graham squinted an eye at Paul for a moment, then turned back to Carmel. "How is it no one saw him?"

Carmel explained about walking alone in the woods and Howard failing to show up.

The Sheriff rubbed the chin of his round face. "How far is it out there?"

"Forty-five minutes or so."

"You up to showing us were it happened?"

"I can do that. I marked it with some white paper. Won't be hard to find. Sure you're dressed for a hike?"

"No problem." He turned to his deputy. "Jonesy, dig out a camera and bring it along."

Dodee held up her camera. "Jim took some pictures before they moved the body."

"Good thinking. Hang onto it. We'll probably want to talk to all of you when we get back."

They started down the hill, but Carmel turned back. "Ask Babs to save the three of us some dinner."

Jim nodded and led Dodee into the lodge as Joppa and Paul headed up the hill.

"You know," he said, opening the door to their room for her, "we don't have to go to the social hour."

She turned to him. "Yes, we do. I want to hear if anyone's found out anything."

"What's to find out?"

"That's what I want to find out. Besides, dinner is right after that. Do you want to skip dinner?"

He took a deep breath and let it out.

Sonofabitch.

"Now I know how Quentin feels." He raised his hands and let them flop. "No rest for the weary."

"It's no rest for the wicked, sweetheart. And there's no time for that either."

ELEVEN

They both took quick showers, Jim squeezing in a shave after his, slapping on some PS for Men aftershave. They dressed in fresh togs and headed out of the room.

"Let's take the stairs," Dodee said. "We can come out on top of the hill."

He followed along, but she hesitated when she reached the second floor. "If we knew Howard's room number we could take a quick look."

"What for?"

"To see if there's anything strange in there."

"Right, like your fingerprints all over the place." He took her hand and led her out into the afternoon sun, still high in the June sky.

"Doesn't all this seem odd to you?" she asked.

"What seems odd? No. Don't tell me. It's none of my business."

"Okay."

The walked on a few moments then he stopped, swinging her around to face him.

"All right. Tell me. What's odd?"

"Someone steals Howard's car in Washington. So he rents a red Jaguar in Asheville. Then when he gets up here, he falls to his death."

He stared into her big blues for a long moment, then shook his head and started walking again. "That doesn't make sense."

"But you have to admit it's odd."

"You act like it's a logical progression of events. Someone steals his car so he has to take a plane down here and rent a car. Well, that is a logical progression. But not a red Jaguar."

"Exactly."

"Exactly?"

"Exactly."

"And then he comes up here, goes on a hike, and falls off a cliff. Where's the logic—"

"Or was pushed."

He stopped and stared into her big blues again.

"You mean like somebody was hanging around in case Howard came traipsing by?"

She shrugged.

"That still isn't logical. It's like saying a man gets up in the morning, rings a bell, and his balls fall off."

She smiled. "Don't ring any bells before tonight, sweetheart."

He shook his head and started walking. They passed the observation tower and clunked down wooden steps shaded by the stunted white oaks to the rocking chair deck where Elderhostelers were already taking their ease.

"Hey, there's Jim and Dodee." Paul raised his cup of wine and gave them his crooked smile. "I was just telling them about Howard's Humpty Dumpty."

"That's an insensitive way to put it," Dodee said.

Paul palmed up a flat hand. "Maybe, but all the king's horses and all the king's men..."

Jim continued into the Heritage Room, poured two plastic cups of wine while Dodee fixed two cups of popcorn. They traded cup for cup and sat outside under the shade trees where a zephyr slipped across the deck and trifled with a dried leaf.

He popped some popcorn into his mouth and scanned the gathering.

It felt strange listening to the animated conversation, not unusual for Elderhostelers, but in the midst of all this life, Howard was gone.

Took a Humpty Dumpty as Paul insisted on calling it.

Joppa came clumping down the wooden steps. "Howard's red Jaguar is missing."

"I have it," Sam Moskowitz said, the thin man sitting in a rocker at the far end. "Howard gave me the keys this morning so I could try it out when I got back from the short hike." He smiled, spreading his heavy mustache. "Hell of a car. A hell of a rush. I have a slight heart problem and I kept my nitroglycerine tablets handy"—he shook his finger—"just in case. But it's one hell of a car. When I got back all the spaces in the top parking lot were filled, so I parked it in front of my cabin."

Babs Penny came out of the Heritage Room and clapped her hands. "Everybody. Hello." She kept clapping her hands until everyone quieted. "Dinner is ready. Remember to stand behind your chair for a generalized prayer."

Jim caught up with her. "Carmel asked if you could save some dinner for her and the sheriff and his deputy. They went out to the accident site."

She nodded as they entered the dining hall. "I'll take care of it."

Jim and Dodee joined her and Duke and they ended up at a table with Hallis and Quentin, Valerie and Kelli, pretty much the same crew that had been out on the hike. Except, of course, for Howard. And Joppa and Paul who had joined a full table with Elcee and Aunt Debra.

And Tristin Fontaine?

He scanned the room, but the man wasn't there.

Josie Blue tapped on the mike beside the side door of the dining hall. "I want to remind everyone that we'll be meeting in the Great Room after dinner, at seven-thirty." He stroked his red goatee as he looked around the room, then shrugged. "I guess I'll give the generalized prayer this evening." He bowed his head. "Oh, God, one of our number is no longer with us tonight. We commend him into your hands. Watch over the rest of us this week and keep us safe. We thank you for this meal, our camaraderie, and our day. Amen. Let's eat."

Jim took two pork chops, scalloped potatoes, peas, a side of salad splashed with ranch dressing, and a bottle of juice.

"You ought to take a dish of vanilla pudding," he said to

Dodee as he added one to his tray.

A small smile played on her lips. "Suppose I don't want one?"

"You might have a friend."

"You mean Paul Fetgatter?"

"Fat chance." He placed a dish on her tray and followed her back to the table.

He forked in some potatoes and stared over Babs's shoulder as two men in suits came in the side door. One had a pasty complection and a shock of brown hair on a balding head. The other was overweight with black hair and eyes and a swarthy complection.

"Know those guys?" he asked.

Babs looked over her shoulder as Josie Blue got up to meet them. "Uh uh."

Duke turned and shook his head. "Hope they're not more latecomers to the program."

"Whoever they are," Hallis said, "they're coming this way."

Josie led them up to the table. "Babs, Duke, this is Agent Smith and Agent Brown from the FBI. They're investigating Howard Leslie's death. Babs and Duke Penny are our host couple for this week."

The one with the pasty complection, Agent Smith, nodded at Babs. "I understand you were along when Mr. Howard met his death."

"That's right." She glanced around the table. "We all were."

"None of us actually saw it," Quentin said.

Jim stared up at the men. "Why is the FBI investigating this?"

"He was a government employee," the pasty Agent Smith said.

"Do you go around investigating every accidental death of a government employee?"

"It also happened in a National Forest," the dark-haired

Agent Brown said in a deep voice.

"Are you saying it wasn't an accident?" Dodee asked.

Agent Brown sighed and looked at his partner.

"We're not saying anything. We're just checking it out." He turned to Babs. "I understand you have the key to Mr. Leslie's room?"

"Yes, the sheriff told me to lock it."

Agent Brown's dark eyebrows rose. "The sheriff's here?"

Duke nodded. "Around somewhere."

"On the trail," Babs said. "Carmel Graves took him down to the site of the accident."

"Or was it something besides an accident?" Dodee asked.

Agent Brown sighed again and turned to Agent Smith who turned back to Babs.

"I hate to interrupt your dinner, but we need to look at Mr. Leslie's room."

She started to stand, but Duke turned to her. "Wait a minute." He ran a fork across his plate, stuffed it in his mouth, and stood up. "Give me the key, dear. I have to go to the bathroom anyway."

Jim watched them leave by the side door and a few minutes later a green SUV drove past the windows and up the hill.

"Don't they need a search warrant for something like that?" Dodee asked.

Quentin shrugged. "Maybe not if Howard's dead.

Kelli leaned forward from the other end of the table. "For FBI they didn't seem to be very competent."

"Acted like they didn't know why they were here," Valerie said, sitting across from her sister.

"Except to get into Howard's room," Babs said.

Kelli leaned forward again. "They didn't act like they believed Howard's death was an accident."

"That's what I was thinking," Dodee said.

Jim turned to Babs. "Where did Howard fit into the line up? I mean, who was in front and behind him?"

Her deep blue eyes blinked. "Let me see." She lowered her fork and knitted her brows. "Carmel was first, of course–"

"Kelli was next," Valerie said, winking from down at the end of the table, "then me."

Dodee raised her hand. "Then me and Jim."

Babs thought for a moment. "Then Howard followed by...Paul Fetgatter."

Jim turned and stared across to where Paul sat at the full table with Elcee and her aunt Debra. "Howard followed me?"

Hallis shook her head. "No, I don't think so." She turned to her husband. "Who was it?"

"Don't ask me, woman," Quentin said. "You're the memory of the family."

Babs pinched her lip. "If it wasn't Jim, who was ahead–oh,"–she snapped her fingers–"I know who it was. Tristin Fontaine."

Jim scanned the room again.

And Trinstin Fontaine, the latecomer to the Elderhostel, had missed the social hour and now was missing dinner–but no. He had slipped in like a cave-dwelling shadow and sat eating dinner at a table by himself.

TWELVE

After dinner they strolled back up the hill in the deepening evening. Long shadows stretched out on the road. A small breeze brought a whiff of pine needles.

Jim jumped as a car tooted and a red Hyundai Tiburon sped past to pull into the upper parking lot. A young man hopped out and turned to face them. Five foot six, flaming red hair, and a freckled face, freckles on freckles.

"Hi," he said in a high pitched, squeaky voice that sounded like it could crack with adolescence. He was dressed in a blue striped shirt, red tie, chino pants, and scuffed Reeboks. He looked like he could use a couple of passes to the buffet table, maybe a few of the ones Joppa had overused. "I'm Billy Riley with station WHLC. I'm investigating the accidental death up here today."

He looked like he was fourteen, but was more likely in his early twenties.

"What was the man's name again?"

"Howard Leslie," Dodee said, face to face with the short man.

"Oooo-kay." He had a pen in his left hand and a pad in his right and wrote it down. "And how did it happen?"

"He fell off a cliff," Dodee said, turning to Jim.

"We think he strayed off the trail to pick some blackberries. It was right at the edge of a drop-off, and he must have slipped and fallen."

"You say must have?" His red eyebrows shot up. "Hey, like no one witnessed it?"

He told Billy Riley about the hike.

"And that's it? How high was the drop-off?"

"Enough to kill him."

"He landed on a rock," Dodee said.

"Cool. And you were there when the helicopter came?"

She nodded.

"Cool. Thanks for your help. Could I have your names?"

"Dodee Swisher and James P. Dandy," she said.

"Wait a minute," Jim said. "If you're going to quote us—"

"No, I just want to have names to back up what we talked about." He gave them a thumbs up. "I'll check with the sheriff—he's investigating it, isn't he? I'll check with him before I work it up." He pulled a business card out of his pocket and handed it to Dodee. "Thanks for your help. Later."

They watched the sporty Hyundai Tiburon speed back down the hill, like a kid rushing out on a date.

"That was short and quick," Dodee said.

"You seemed eager to help him."

"Well, he looked young and... eager. Like it's his first job out of college. I didn't tell him about the FBI, did I?"

"That was only because he scooted out of here."

They headed for the entrance of the lodge and saw Carmel Graves and the short, round-faced Sheriff coming up the road from the trail with the tall, thin deputy a few steps behind.

"See you made it back," Jim said.

"Oh yeah," the sheriff said, breathing hard.

Carmel gave them a reticent smile. "Hope someone left some supper for us."

"Babs did," Dodee said. "Did you find anything suspicious?"

"No," the sheriff said. "We yellow-taped it to take another look tomorrow, just to cover the bases."

"The FBI might want to go out there with you."

Sheriff Graham looked up at that. "The FBI? What's this to do with the FBI?"

"They were here investigating Howard's death," Dodee said.

"Why would they get involved?"

Jim shrugged. "Said because Howard was a government employee and it happened on National Forest land."

"That's baloney. Never heard of it. Where are these guys?"

Jim looked for the green SUV, but he didn't see it. "I don't know. Maybe they left."

"If you run into them, tell 'em I want to see them." The sheriff turned to Carmel. "I'd like to talk to everyone who was on the hike. Think we can do that?"

"Probably." She looked at her watch. "We have a meeting starting here shortly."

"Good." He smiled. "In the meantime, maybe we can investigate that dinner that was supposed to be saved for us."

"We can do that."

They started toward the chow hall when the sheriff turned back.

"What about Howard's room? I asked someone to lock it up."

Jim nodded. "Babs did, but Duke opened it for the FBI."

"The FBI? Where's this room?" He turned to Carmel and his deputy. "Why don't you two go on ahead and I'll catch up."

Jim turned to Dodee.

"I know where it is," she said and led the way.

Sheriff Graham tried the door. "It's locked now. Who was it you said locked it?"

"Babs Penny."

"Good. If you see her, tell her not to open it for anyone, including the FBI. I'll be back after dinner."

They watched him start down the hill.

"For a minute there," Dodee said, "I thought we'd get a peek inside. He seems upset with the FBI."

"It's not our business."

"I wonder what they wanted."

"Hello. It is not our business. Am I talking to myself here?"

"Don't you think it's strange that the FBI would be here investigating an accidental death?"

He spread out his hands. "I am talking to myself."

Babs and Duke Penny came out of one of the employee cabins and started towards them.

"You just missed the sheriff," Jim said. "He wants to make sure Howard's room remains locked until he gets back."

Dodee turned to Duke. "Did the FBI find anything?"

"I don't know." He ran a hand over his monk's rim of hair. "I opened the door and left to go to the bathroom. They seemed to be concerned about talking to the sheriff, but when I got back, they were already gone."

"Did they take anything?" Dodee asked as they walked into the Great Room, chairs set up to face the fireplace.

Duke shrugged. "I wasn't there. I locked the door again and left it at that."

While Babs and Duke went about setting up for the evening, making coffee and hot water for tea, Jim plopped down in one of the couches on the right side of the room and stretched out his legs.

"This is the most comfortable I've been all day."

"You don't want to sit up front?"

"I don't want to sit up front."

"You don't want to sit in the chairs?"

"I don't want to sit in the chairs."

She stared at him a moment, then crossed over and sat on the other side of him, shoulder touching shoulder. He bent down and kissed her lips. Soft lips. Warm kiss.

"I hope you're not so comfortable that you get sleepy."

He kissed her again. "You mean like before we get back to our room?"

"Something like that."

Others started drifting in and finally Josie Blue entered and strode to the front of the room.

"Okay," he said with a big smile, "everyone make it back from the hike okay?" Then the smile faded and he shook his head. "That was meant to be a joke. I guess you all heard about Howard?" He shook his head again. "To tell you the truth, we've never had anyone not make it back from a hike before. Never had anyone not make it back from anything." He paused, folded his arms, and glanced around the room. "Is everybody here?"

Aunt Debra raised her hand. "Tristin Fontaine isn't here."

"I saw him at dinner," Babs said. "He usually shows up late."

Josie nodded. "Well, speaking of whitewater rafting, tomorrow we'll be doing it on the Nantahala River. We'll mainly have class one and class two falls, at least for the part we'll be on. It's a good river for the inexperienced rafter. We'll be using the services of the Nantahala Outdoor Center who have been in the business longest and have the best safety record. They'll give us instructions and provide us with PFDs, personal floatation devices. We're all required to wear them."

Jim leaned over to Dodee. "You're not anxious about tomorrow, because we can stay–"

"No, I'm looking forward to it. You anxious about it?"

He shook his head.

Him anxious?

No, terrified was more like it.

"The Nantahala is dam fed so the water depth is always about the same. The temperature as well. We'll be on the river for a couple of hours, rain or shine."

Babs stood up in the last row. "They're calling for a clear day tomorrow so it should be a lot of fun. We've done it in the rain and it was still fun, but the sun is better. Bring sun block."

"How many times have you made the trip, Babs?" Josie asked.

"Oh"–she looked at Duke–"how many, dear? Five or six. Enjoyed it every time."

"The Nantahala has just enough white water to make it exciting," Duke said.

"Not enough to worry about," Babs said.

Duke wiggled his eyebrows. "Now on Thursday, the

Chattooga can really get exciting."

Babs stuck her hands on her hips. "But not enough to worry about."

Jim sighed.

Just what he needed. Enough to make it exciting, not enough to worry about. Not to worry because if he could figure any way out of it, he wasn't going.

"We'll leave here after breakfast," Josie said, "and pack our brown bag lunches again. They have picnic tables down at the river and we'll have lunch after we pull the rafts out."

Babs raised her hand. "There's also an outfitter's store there, and we'll probably have time to look around."

Josie nodded. "They'll also be taking photographs of us going over at least one of the falls that they'll put up for sale."

"What about the temperature?" Elcee asked, sitting next to her Aunt Debra. "Should we bring long sleeves?"

Babs stood up again. "The outfitters will supply us with long-sleeved oar jackets if you think you'll be chilly. But with all the splashing, you will get wet so bring a towel and dry clothes. There's a place to change after we get off the water. It's going to be fun."

"Any more questions about tomorrow?" Josie asked.

The wiry Carmel Graves slipped into the room, knelt down behind Babs, and whispered in her ear.

"How far is it?" Paul asked.

"The van trip down should be an hour and half or so, depending on traffic."

Babs handed a key to Carmel and Jim watched her leave. Obviously the search of Howard's room was about to begin.

"Any more questions?" Josie looked around the room. "Okay. Babs and Duke have something they want to do with you so I'll see you in the morning. Get a good night's sleep."

"The first thing we have to do," Babs said, standing, "is make a circle."

Duke started manhandling the chairs. "Let's go, everybody help."

Dodee jumped up. "Come on. We need chairs in the circle."

He looked up at her. "I don't have a chair. I have a couch."

"Come on, sweetheart. It will be fun."

He stood up and helped form the circle of chairs.

"We need a chair for Babs," Hallis said.

"No, not one for me." Babs ran her hand through her steel-gray hair. "Here's what we're going to do. I'll call out something, like I spy with my little eye people who are over sixty. Then everyone over sixty has to change chairs. And while you're changing chairs I'm going to try to grab one for myself. That's going to leave one of us without a chair. That will be the next person who will say I spy with my little eye, and we'll change chairs again."

"Does it have to be someone's age?" Hallis asked. "I don't like that idea."

"No, no, it can be anything, like"–she softly snapped her fingers–"like people wearing sandals or people with gray hair or whatever. Everyone see? Okay? Ready?" She looked around the room. "I spy with my little eye"–a smile lit up her broad face–"people whose first or last name begins with an H."

Six Elderhostelers jumped up and raced for an empty chair, the women screaming as they ran. When the dust had settled, Elcee stood erect in her finishing-school posture with no place to go.

"I guess that means I'm it." She turned, scanning the circle. "I see–no, what is it? I spy with my little eye, people wearing shorts."

Jim waited until Dodee jumped up then shifted into her chair as she raced across the room and Elcee grabbed his vacated chair. More screaming and laughter and when the shifting was over, Dodee was left standing.

"Traitor," she said, fixing her eye on Jim. "You took my seat fast enough."

He shrugged. "That's because you have a very pretty

seat."

That brought groans and laughter.

Dodee turned to Babs. "Suppose I say I spy with my little eye people named Jim Dandy?"

"No way," he said. "Has to be at least two persons if you're going to say people."

"Okay, I spy with my little eye, people... with gray hair."

He raced past two occupied chairs to one just vacated by Aunt Debra while Dodee grabbed Quentin's leaving the good doctor standing in the middle.

An ivory grin split his dark face. "I gotta learn to move faster."

Jim looked over Quentin's shoulder and saw the round sheriff beckoning him from the doorway.

He stood up. "I spy with my little eye, Sheriff Graham, who wants to see Dodee and me."

THIRTEEN

They sat in an unassigned room; Dodee and Jim on the bed, the sheriff in a chair by the desk. Deputy Jones stood in the doorway, propping his lanky frame against the jamb.

"Well, sir, ma'am, we just want to go over some things to verify what Carmel Graves has told us. If you could tell us what you know about Howard Leslie and the hike, I'm sure it will be a help."

Dodee leaned forward. "Do you think somebody murdered Howard?"

"Whoa, wait a minute, ma'am." The sheriff held up both hands. "Don't know where you came up with that idea. As far as we know, this was an accident, pure and simple."

Jim put his arm around Dodee's waist. "My friend is always seeing conspiracies where none exist." And always nosing into police business, not that he was going to mention that. "But aren't you spending a lot time investigating something that's a simple accident?"

The deputy straightened in the doorway. "We're mainly trying to get a complete picture of what happened. Right, Sheriff?"

"Right, Jonesy. I believe in being thorough, the reason we went the extra mile in hiking out to the scene this evening. Going the extra mile, or three or four as it turned out. We probably wouldn't be having this conversation if the FBI hadn't shown up. But since they have, I want to make sure I know what's going on."

Jim took a deep breath and let it out. "To tell you the truth," he said, glancing at Dodee, "we don't know a whole lot."

"We know his car was stolen before he came out here," Dodee said. "In Washington, D. C."

And between the two of them, each filling in what the other missed, they told the sheriff about the hike, about

Howard turning up missing, about the blackberry bush at the edge of the cliff, and about finding Howard's body on a rock slab below.

"No one actually saw him fall," Jim said. He raised his eyebrows at Dodee. "Or heard him either."

She shook her head and turned to the sheriff. "Did you search his room?"

"Well, ma'am, we did." The sheriff bit his lip. "We have it taped off, and we'll be back for a closer look tomorrow. But since you asked, do you know if Mr. Leslie had a CD player or a computer?"

Dodee looked at Jim.

He shrugged, but then nodded. "Yes, come to think of it. He came up for coffee this morning carrying a laptop. Said he had some work to do. Why do you ask?"

The sheriff rubbed the back of his neck and yawned before looking up. "We found two CDs in a jacket he had hung on a hanger, but no laptop. No CD player either."

"Did you check the Jaguar?"

The sheriff's eyebrows rose.

"He drove up here in a rented red Jaguar. I'm sure it's the only one here. I think Sam Moskowitz has the keys."

"Why would that be?"

"He asked Howard if he could drive it sometime, and since he was going on the short hike, meaning he would be back before we were, Howard gave him the keys."

The sheriff looked up at the deputy. "Got that, Jonesy?"

"Sam Moskowitz. Got it."

"Did the FBI take the laptop?" Dodee asked.

The sheriff shrugged. "They were gone by the time we got back here." Graham fished in his pocket for a card and handed it to Jim. "I want to thank you for your help. If you think of anything else, please call me."

When they got back to the Great Room, the group had broken up, everyone leaving or left, so they went downstairs to their room.

"What do you think?" she asked, turning to him as he shut the door.

"I think we should mind our own business. That and I'm bushed."

She put her arms around his neck. "How bushed are you?"

"Not that bushed." He kissed her. "But I'll probably conk out on my feet if we get into a lengthy discussion about the sheriff and Howard Leslie."

"Howard who?" She kissed him back. "You want the bathroom first?"

"I'll wait. Don't be long."

She wasn't.

By the time he had opened the windows, stripped down to his shorts, and grabbed pjs and shaving kit, she was out, wearing a shorty nightgown with a big rabbit in the front and the word "Thumper" underneath.

He hurried through brushing his teeth and washing his face and slapped on some PS for Men cologne. He took off his shorts and started to put on the pjs, but then gave it up as a waste of effort. He turned off the light and opened the door.

A gibbous moon sneaked through the upper window and bathed the room in a soft glow. A breeze trifled in after it, cooling his skin enough so that the covers felt good. Even better when he found Dodee had lost her nightgown somewhere along the way.

She wrapped her arms around his neck, engulfing him in a light herbal perfume, and gave him a long kiss.

"I love you, lady."

"And I love you, sweetheart. Most times."

"Most times? Ha, I like that. And when–"

She shut off his words with her lips and stroked his tongue with hers, tasting of toothpaste. They caressed each other with their bodies as crickets serenaded outside the open windows.

"It's been a while, sweetheart."

"Too long."

And they slipped into a moonlit garden where the light is drained of color, turning flowers passionate and the familiar mysterious. They raced along with abandon, calling out into the night, gasping as air was sucked out of their lungs, and burst into a white hot light as blinding as a strobe of lightening. Then they crashed back to earth in a crumpled heap, fighting for breath, pounding hearts shoving blood to oxygen-starved muscles, and slowly, slowly settled into a languid embrace.

A long sigh floated on the air, echoed by another.

"Thank you, sweetheart."

He kissed the top of her head. "Thank you, lady."

He eased his weight off the crack between the beds and she snuggled in close, shifting arms and legs and resting her head on his shoulder.

"Are you quite comfortable?"

"I'm getting there."

"Love me sometimes? What does that mean?"

"You can be stodgy sometimes."

"Stodgy? Me?"

"Like when I mentioned it was strange that someone stole Howard's car back in Washington, then he has to rent a red Jaguar, and then when he gets up here, he's murdered–"

"Wait a minute. Who said he was murdered? No, wait a minute again. It's none of our business."

"See. Stodgy."

"Not stodgy. Practical. Logical."

She rested a hand on his stomach and shifted her head.

"It was an accident," he said finally. "How could you think it was murder?"

"Suppose the men who stole his car came down to bump him off?"

"Bump him off?"

"So they hide in the woods and wait for him."

"Like they knew he'd take that path? It's not logical."

"Suppose they knew because they followed us and saw

where we were going? Or suppose it was Tristin Fontaine or Paul?" She rose up and looked down at him. "One could have slowed down or the other run up, and then pushed him off."

"You're forgetting it was silence time," he said as she lay back down. "We'd have heard them if there was a scuffle."

"Suppose they knocked him over the head?"

"You can build supposes for anything, but it doesn't make it logical."

"People are not always logical, sweetheart."

He smiled as the words rolled out to the tip of his tongue, but the opening was too easy and he pulled them back.

"The most log–the most likely thing is that Howard went out to check on the blackberries and fell."

She raised up again. "You're forgetting it was silence time. How come we didn't hear him scream?"

"Because he knocked his head on a rock."

She grunted and lay back against his shoulder.

But she did have a point.

He stared up at the ceiling, just a dark outline in the somber room.

No one had heard a scream.

And what about the FBI guys?

What did they want?

And why take the laptop and leave the CDs behind for the sheriff to find?

Still, someone lying in wait along the trail in case Howard showed up was a stretch.

He closed his eyes and let it all go. Then popped them open again.

Except for the cigarette butt he found in the woods.

"I wonder how long it would take for a cigarette to disintegrate," he said. "Say with all the rain they've had here."

But Dodee's deep breathing told him he wasn't going to get an answer tonight.

He closed his eyes and let it go again, this time not coming back.

FOURTEEN

He awoke to an avian alarm clock squabbling outside the window, unfortunately one he couldn't switch off. He eased out of bed, washed, dressed, grabbed the mug he brought from home, and stole upstairs to the small coffee kitchen off the Great Room. He switched on the coffee pot and stepped out on the balcony to watch God create a new day.

Down below white mists hung in the valleys between the humps of foot hills, while up above a few grazing clouds turned golden in sunlight not yet peeking over the horizon. Then the golden orb itself popped up to disperse the shadows of night and claim sovereignty over the morning.

Not a bad job.

Yeah, buddy.

He heard the coffee pot sputtering and went inside, filled his mug, and took a sip.

Not a bad job himself.

Elcee came around the corner wrapped in a pink bathrobe, her brown eyes not yet awake, her curly yellow-brown hair slightly disheveled. "Morning, Jim. Please tell me there's still some of that coffee I smell."

"There's a whole pot."

"Had a rough night," she said, pouring herself a cup.

"You don't feel well?"

"Aunt Debra snored without let up." She took a sip of coffee. "Um, that's good. What kind of day we got out there?"

He held the balcony door for her and then followed her out.

She smiled. "What a glorious morning."

"Yep, God did a pretty good job."

They stared at it a bit before she turned to him. "Are you retired?"

"Semi retired. I'm a physical therapist down in Southern

Maryland, but I only work a couple of days a week now, just to keep my skills up."

"You're not far from me. I live in Bethesda."

"Work for the government?"

"Doesn't everybody? Well, that's glib to say out here on an Elderhostel. I think only Howard and I work for the government." Elcee set her cup on the railing. "Well, Howard did. What about him? Have you heard anything?"

He shrugged. "If the sheriff or the FBI hadn't shown up, I'd say he went to pick some blackberries and fell off the cliff, as unlikely as that sounds even as I'm saying it. But any other explanation is even more unlikely."

She shook her head. "He was a nice man. A little boisterous, but nice."

"Do you know what he did? For a living, I mean."

"He worked in computers, same as I, only he was with Agriculture while I'm with Commerce."

"Did you know him?"

She shook her head. "He worked across the mall. Our agencies are so large he could have worked in the same wing and I probably wouldn't have known him."

"You're a programmer?"

"Uh huh. I set up and test programs, mostly for Internet access. Like, you know the rules the federal government is always promulgating? I set it up so interested people can make comments on line in support of or in opposition to a regulation. Gives everyone a chance to get their say in, whether they're lobbyists or private citizens, in Washington or not. I developed the program and still monitor it."

"You sound proud of it."

"I am." She licked her lower lip with a pink tongue. "We're having some troubles right now, but I'll get it squared away."

The door opened and they turned to see Aunt Debra, an older version of her niece with her hair in a gray permanent. She was dressed in khaki shorts and a white open-collared shirt and looked ready for the day.

"There you are, Elcee. I had a marvelous sleep last night."

Elcee glanced at Jim and raised her eyebrows.

The old lady sipped from her cup. "What a great day for our raft trip. I am pumped."

He smiled and turned toward the windows of the Great Room to see that the sisters, Kelli and Valerie, had also come in. Valerie took a container of orange juice from the fridge and poured a large glass for each of them. They had also dressed for the day in shorts, shirts, and light jackets.

"I better get some coffee for Dodee." He went back into the small kitchen. "Morning, ladies." He hefted the coffee pot, looking at its contents. "You having coffee?"

Kelli held up her juice glass. "Hydrate first, then caffeinate."

"I want to take a cup down to Dodee. You want–"

"Go ahead," Valerie said. "We can make some more."

He filled his mug and a Styrofoam cup, hoofed it downstairs, and, both hands full, tapped the door with his knuckle to see if she was up. The door opened a crack and she peeked out.

"You better have coffee."

He held up the cup. She smiled and opened the door, giving him a warm kiss as he entered. They finished dressing, a blouse and lipstick coating for Dodee, shoes and socks for him, then started down the road for breakfast, running into Carmel Graves by the stairs to the rocking chair deck.

"You going with us on the raft trip or do you just lead the hikes?" Dodee asked.

"I was planning on it, but I promised to take the sheriff back out to the accident site."

Dodee nodded. "It's getting to sound less and less like an accident, don't you think?"

Carmel cocked her head as if to hear better.

Dodee shrugged. "If it was just an accident, why go

through so much investigation?"

Jim turned to Carmel when they reached the rocking chair deck. "Know how long it takes a cigarette to disintegrate in the woods?" Both women faced him. "When we were tracking along off the trail looking for Howard, I came upon a cigarette butt."

"You didn't tell me about that," Dodee said.

"That's because just as I saw it, Paul called out about the blackberry bush and we rushed back to the trail. I didn't think about it anymore until I was falling asleep last night."

"Did it look fresh?" Dodee asked.

"I don't know. It was easy to pick out, white against the green needle carpet." He motioned for them to go ahead on the wooden walk toward the dining room. "How long before it would disintegrate?"

Carmel shrugged. "With all the rain we've been having, I would think the tobacco would wash out fairly quickly, although the paper might remain." She turned to him at the chow hall door. "If it had been left by someone who knows about hiking in the woods, they would have field stripped it, making sure it was out and the tobacco scattered. If it was intact, it could have been left by anybody, even one of our own hikers."

"Any of our group smoke?" Dodee asked as they crossed to the buffet table.

"Tristin Fontaine?" Carmel asked. "Does he smoke?"

Now Dodee shrugged.

Jim picked up a tray. "You might want to mention it to the sheriff. It was by a big hemlock, almost directly across from where Howard went over the edge."

He loaded up with pancakes, butter, and syrup, got a glass of orange juice, another coffee, and a sweet roll. They sat at a table with Elcee and Aunt Debra.

"Good morning," Dodee said. "What a beautiful day. I'm looking forward to our whitewater trip."

"Me too, Dodee," Aunt Debra said, and smacked her fist

against the table. "I'm pumped."

He shoveled in a mouthful of pancakes.

What the hell was this?

He would just as soon skip the whole rafting thing and here these women were raring to go.

The combination of pancakes, sweet syrup, and butter soothed his taste buds, but did nothing for his psyche.

There had to be something wrong with them.

Or was it a woman thing?

Like maybe a death wish?

Yeah, buddy.

FIFTEEN

He and Dodee joined the other Elderhostelers outside the dining hall for the trip down to the Nantahala River. They wore a wide assortment of shorts, ankle-length Spandex, and boxer-type bathing suits. Most had light jackets for the cool morning. And he saw they all carried backpacks containing brown bag lunches and the change of clothes they had been warned to bring.

See, that didn't sound good right there.

Everyone was engaged in animated babble, acting like they were going for a leisurely cruise down the river on a sunny afternoon.

Was good old Jim Dandy the only one to realize they were about to embark on a one-way raft ride to doom?

Good old Jim Dandy turned to mention this to good old Dodee Swisher, but she, Elcee, and Debra were laughing at something.

Laughing.

Great.

One last light-hearted moment in the face of death.

Just great.

Then they started loading the three vans, and his window of opportunity for turning back was slowly closing.

He climbed in, Dodee following, and sat directly behind the brawny Duke Penny in the driver's seat.

"The rafting this morning is easy," Duke called over his shoulder as he started the engine. "The Nantahala is fed by a dam so the water level is fairly constant, and we have a bright sunny day so we'll have a lot of fun."

"You been on this river before?" Paul asked from the back of the van.

"Four or five times. As host couple we do all the things you do."

Jim leaned forward and spoke over Duke's shoulder. "Ever fall out of the raft?"

Duke turned to give him a quick grin and a flick of his eyebrows. "Not yet."

Jim nodded.

What did that mean?

That little grin?

Malicious little grin.

We did Howard in yesterday, buddy boy, and today it's good old Jim Dandy's turn.

Just absolutely great.

They traveled down the mountain and wound through some back roads, picking up and following a river for a few miles. Finally they crossed a bridge and pulled down into a large parking lot circled by the rustic buildings of the Nantahala Outdoor Center.

Duke dropped them off at the restroom and changing station. "I'll park the van and leave it open in case you forget something, but I'll lock it up while we're on the water."

Jim and Dodee changed into their dorky-looking water shoes, and Dodee pulled out a throwaway waterproof camera, leaving everything else in the van—packs, spare clothes for changing, and lunches.

"I bought one for each rafting day," she said, strapping the camera to her wrist as they climbed out. "Might catch something I can use for a painting."

"Like me going over a waterfall and sinking below the surface with one fist clutching for air?"

Her eyebrows rose and she smiled. "Knowing you, sweetheart, the clutched fist will have an extended finger."

They gathered to one side of a building marked *Guide Assisted Trips*, under a shaded hut with benches facing a small television. A man stood beside it in a yellow PFD with *Nantahala Outfitters* stenciled on it.

"We're going to show a little safety film, folks," the man said. "We don't want anyone to get alarmed, but we're dealing with Mother Nature here, and whenever you do that it's always better to be prepared. Safety first. Think of it as a lifeboat drill on the cruise liner. After that we'll get everyone suited up and head out."

The man punched a button on the VCR and after some flickering an instructional film showed them how to don a PFD, personal flotation device, the importance of getting the correct size, and of making sure it was cinched up tight.

Jim nodded.

No need to worry about that sucker.

He'd have the damned thing cinched up tight enough to turn blue in the face.

It also instructed him on the importance of keeping the top strap snapped so the floatation in back would keep his head above water in case he was knocked out.

In case he'd was knocked out?

Great, just great.

The screen changed to a graphic of a man in the water, head above the surface, body below, and rocks along the bottom.

"If you should happen to end up in the water, float on your back with your feet up and pointing down stream until someone pulls you back on board or until you can slowly work your way to the side of the river. Do not try to stand."

A new graphic popped up with the figure's feet on the rocky bottom and its face down in the river.

"If you try to stand, your feet could get lodged beneath a rock and the force of the current could drag your head under."

Just absolutely great.

Afterwards the outfitters helped them find oar jackets which were like light windbreakers, and PFDs to wear over them. When they were all suited up, they moved to another set of benches where the lead guide waited for them, spinning a paddle in his hands so that the spade end twirled on the ground.

"Each raft will have six people and a guide." He motioned to five young people in yellow PFDs. "He will issue instructions—he or she." He bowed to the lone woman guide. "If the guide says all forward, everyone does what?"

"Paddle forward," the group of Elderhostels sang out.

"Good. If the guide says, give me three strokes, of course you paddle only three times. Now he might say, right forward, left back. Then, depending on which side of the raft you are on, you act accordingly. This will align the raft with the river or rocks that might be coming up."

He wrapped his hand around the end of the paddle.

"The other thing is to keep your hands on the top of this animal. The raft is crowded and it's easy to clunk someone on the head. We don't want that, so if you keep one hand on the end no one will end up with a headache."

He twisted the paddle in his hands again.

"Okay. The raft has two rubber cross beams called thwarts. You want to sit on the side of the raft, not the thwarts, so that when you paddle you get power behind your stroke. You can tuck your feet under the thwarts and the side for support to keep from being knocked overboard. But if you do find yourself falling out, try to grab the raft line, that's a line running around the outside of the raft."

The man put the paddle aside and rubbed his hands.

"Finally, if you do have an out-of-raft experience-—"

The Elderhostelers broke out in laughter at that, some genuine, some nervous.

"If you should have an out-of-raft experience, remember to float on your back with your feet up and pointing down stream. Your PFD is designed to keep your head above water. Don't try to stand. You could catch your feet under a rock and the current could force your face beneath the water. Also, hang onto your paddle and use it to try to work your way back to the raft or towards the shore. In the meantime, everyone in the raft listen to the guide who will immediately bring the raft alongside the one in the water."

The lead guide motioned for Babs, sitting in front, to come up.

"When we reach for someone in the water, we want to grab the shoulder straps of the PFD."

He turned Babs around and grabbed the PFD straps going over her shoulders.

"This will give us the strongest and most secure hold on the person in the water. When you got a good hold, don't try to lift up, just hang on and fall backwards onto the raft floor. The momentum will pull the person back on board with the least strain and the most success. This is the reason we want to make sure our PFDs are good and snug. Don't want them yanked off and us left behind in the water."

Jim grabbed his PFD and tried to yank it up and down.

He might not be able to breath, but there was no way that sucker was coming off.

"Any questions?" the lead guide asked. "Remember, these are safety instructions to ensure that we have a fun time out there this morning, not to frighten you. If we are prepared for these possibilities, there's no reason to panic and we will have a good time."

He patted Babs on the back.

"Thanks for your help." He turned back to face the Elderhostelers. "One more thing I should mention. Right out here we have the Nantahala Falls." He pointed to the river behind them. "It's a class three falls, the most you will encounter today. It also has a bit of hydraulic component to it, the water whirling in a circular motion as it comes off the falls. In the unlikely event you should find yourself caught up in the hydraulic action, roll up into a ball and when you pop out go back into the feet-downstream posture. And, in the even more unlikely event you lose your guide, work your way to the riverbank as quickly as you can. Certainly before you pass under the bridge you came over because there's a class five falls down there and you didn't pay enough money to try something like that. Any questions."

Jim stared at the man.

Any questions?

Hell yeah, was it too late for him to turn back?

"Okay," the guide said, "let's get started on our adventure."

SIXTEEN

They rode school buses upriver, roof racks built on top to hold the seven-person rafts. The lead guide stood up at the front of the bus and talked above the noise of the engine.

"If you could arrange yourselves in groups of six when we get off, that would be a big help. This is a national river and to protect the environment we can't drive right up to the water's edge. The bus will drop us off on the side of the road, and we'll have to carry the rafts to the put-in spot. Any questions?"

Jim glanced around.

No one raised a hand. No one voiced anything. No one jumped up and screamed to get off the bus.

Elcee turned from the seat in front of him. "May Aunt Debra and I join your group?"

"We don't have a group," Jim said.

Dodee nodded. "We have four now. We need two more."

"Hey," Paul said from across the aisle, "count me in."

"Me, too," said the plump Joppa Harp.

Dodee smiled Jim. "I guess we have a group now."

He nodded.

Just great.

The bus crossed a bridge and pulled off in a small clearing.

They had arrived.

The window of opportunity for turning back had closed to a crack.

He got off the bus and gathered with Dodee, Aunt Debra, Elcee, Paul and Joppa, into their group of six. He looked around at the others, also forming into groups, everyone smiling and joking.

Eat, drink, and be merry for tomorrow–tomorrow, hell–in a few minutes you'll be dead, croaked, taking the long dirt nap.

The driver and one of the guides stood on top of the bus and tossed rafts down to those on the ground. Two of them carried one over and dumped it at Jim's feet.

The instrument of death.

A yellow inner-tube shaped into oblong sides and ends with two inner-tube thwarts spaced out in the middle for braces, and a rubber floor. A line threaded around the outside of the oblong inner-tube, the raft line you were suppose to grab if you found yourself going over the side.

A young man in his early twenties joined them. "Hi, I'm Hank." He had black curly hair and eyebrows, broad shoulders, and a white-toothed grin. "I'll be your pilot this morning, and we'll be cruising at minus six inches."

The women laughed, Paul grinned, and Jim nodded.

If they remained at six inches he could handle it.

"I won't be turning the seatbelt sign on, but you won't be free to move around the plane."

Only grins this time.

"We'll need everyone to help carry this to the river," Hank said. "If you'll grab the raft line, we'll get on with it, but if you get tired, sing out and we'll stop and rest.

They carried the raft down a tree-shaded dirt path that turned rocky as the sound of running water got closer.

"Thank you for buying these water shoes," he whispered to Dodee as he walked on the pebbly surface. "They may look dorky, but they work."

They made it to the put-in spot in one straight shot, a wooden pier built alongside a shady inlet, and dropped the raft into the drink.

"Okay," Hank said, "let's have the men in the front. We need the most powerful paddlers up there. Make it quick while I hold the raft against the pier."

"Go, Jim," Paul said.

He stepped on board, the rubber bottom wobbling under his feet as he moved to the right front section just ahead of the first thwart. Paul flopped on the other side with Debra and

Elcee behind him while Dodee and Joppa lined up behind Jim. Hank pushed off and sat in the center at the back, using his paddle as a rudder.

"Okay, all forward ten strokes."

Jim held his paddle as he had been instructed, one hand on the end to keep from shlocking someone on the noggin, and joined the others in giving Hank his ten strokes.

"Good job," Hank called. "Let's wait for the others."

He rested the paddle across his legs as they drifted at the edge of the inlet. The bordering trees, filled with the cry of songbirds, freckled the still water with shadows, but out in the full sun of the river, the bubbling and gurgling Nantahala beckoned.

Sonofabitch.

His window of opportunity for turning back had just slammed shut.

"Okay," Hank said, "let's practice a little bit while we're waiting. Left forward, right back."

It took Jim a second to remember that he was right and had to stroke backwards, but when he put the action into practice, the raft circled in place.

"Okay, right forward, left back two strokes."

The raft stopped spinning and steadied in the water.

"All back two strokes."

He gave Hank the two backs and they drifted away from the bumpy river.

"Good job. We just went through all the commands. Most of the time I'll be steering and you can relax and enjoy the scenery. Break out your cameras if you like. Sometimes we'll see deer along the banks. I'll give you plenty of warning when things start to get tricky. This is an easy river, nothing to worry about."

"How long have you been doing this?" Elcee asked.

"This is my first."

Jim swung around to face him. "This is your first trip?"

Hank smiled. "No, my first year. I've been doing this

almost every day for three months. Okay, we're ready to go. Everyone forward."

They moved out into the river, leaving the shade behind, the sun warm and welcoming. Three of the Elderhostel rafts strung out like yellow inner-tubes in front of them with two more following behind. The water turned bumpy as they headed over some small rapids, the inner-tube raft twisting and undulating as it tried to accommodate the surface.

Jim gripped the paddle with both hands, ready for the call to action as they rumbled over a small waterfall. The raft dipped and he looked down into a hole in the river into which water poured and bubbled and splashed before rising up in a hump on the other side. And they raced into it, crashed into the bottom, popped up over the hump, and hardly as it started, drifted in flat water again.

He blinked.

That was it?

He could take that.

He turned and grinned at Dodee.

"You okay, lady?"

"Isn't this fun?"

Paul turned toward the guide. "See that rock ahead of us?"

Jim swung around as the current smashed them into a boulder.

The raft jerked backwards.

Good old Jim Dandy kept right on going.

Sonofabitch.

He grabbed a fast breath before the water closed over him and all the instructions raced through his head.

Hang-onto-the-paddle. Lie-on-your-back. Point-your-feet-downstream. Look-for-the–

The world burst into view again as his shoulder straps yanked him out of the river and back onboard the raft, staring up at the clear blue sky.

"You okay, sweetheart?" Dodee yelled.

He lay on the floor of the raft with someone fumbling underneath him. He clambered back onto his inner-tube seat and turned to see Paul climbing onto the other side.

"You moved fast."

Paul grinned. "How was your out-of-raft experience?"

"Wet."

"Did you see a mysterious light?"

"I saw the water."

"Did you get your feet up?" Joppa asked.

"I kept trying to remember all the things I was supposed to do, but I didn't have time to do shit before I was jerked aboard."

"How do you feel?" Dodee asked.

"Damp." He turned to Paul. "Thanks."

The man's crooked smile cocked his face out of line as he checked his hairpiece. "I was like you. I was thinking of all the things I was supposed to do, but before I had a plan of action, I had already grabbed you by the straps and fallen back. My one concern was that I might end up with only your life preserver."

"No need to worry about that. I have it on so tight I'll probably end up with gangrene."

"Right side back," Hank shouted, "left side forward."

Jim started stroking in reverse as another large rock poked up out of the river and water dipped into a trough beside it.

"All forward."

And he dug in, putting his arms, shoulders, back and stomach into it, his physical therapist's brain ticking off the muscles coming into play—triceps, deltoids, upper trapezius, middle trapezius, latisimus dorsi, rhomboids and holy shit—they fell off into the trough, like driving a Humvee into a deep ditch, and bounced up on the other side. They slid around two more rocks, rumbled over hidden stones while the raft twisted and turned, and then everything flattened out in smooth water.

"Good job."

He took a deep breath and let it out.

Awright. He could handle this. And even if he fell overboard again—

Screw that shit.

He stuck his right foot under the front of the raft and braced his left against the thwart.

No more overboard again.

Yeah, buddy.

"All forward"

He dug in as they rumbled down another series of cascades, rocks banging on the bottom of the raft like a car on a washboard road, then into a flat calm again.

"Good job. You can relax for awhile."

Okay, he wasn't ready for another swim, but he could handle the white water. Except there was still that class three falls at the end with the hydraulic effect.

He'd worry about it when they came to it.

He turned to Dodee. "What did you think when I went over?"

"I held on until Paul grabbed your PFD. You were out and in so fast that there wasn't time to worry."

"Well I wasn't out and in so fast that I didn't get wet." He looked down at his legs and wet water shoes and turned to Paul. "Thanks again."

"No problem. I just reacted."

They drifted along on smooth water, enjoying the full sun out in the middle of the river while along the banks overhanging trees speckled the surface with shadows. The call of songbirds gave way to the rumbling of a train running somewhere off to the left. Then a line of container cars came partially into view, playing hide and seek behind tree trunks like the flickering of an old time peep show, and the smell of a diesel engine contaminated the fresh mountain air.

They rounded a small bend and—oh shit—rushed back into white water. They lunged over waterfalls and rapids and cataracts, the sound of splashing and roaring magnified by the proximity of the violence around them. The raft's angle of attack shifted and they charged catty-corner down a fluid hill, bounced on the bottom, and squirted out of a trough like being shot from a cannon.

"Right forward, left back, three strokes."

He dug his paddle into it and they swung around, pointed downstream again, threaded a gauntlet of protruding rocks, and finally shot into calm water.

He blew out a breath, puffing his cheeks.

"You know what?" He turned to the others. "This reminds me of what a woman said about sailing. Men love it because it's like war; hours of boredom interspersed with moments of sheer terror."

They bounced along over more falls, rumbled over more cataracts, and lolled in the smooth spots between–boredom interspersed with terror–until the lead guide waved them over to bunch up on one bank.

"We're coming up on Nantahala Falls now," he called. "Nothing to panic about. Listen to your guides, brace yourselves in your rafts, and you shouldn't have any trouble. Just remember, if you happen to fall out and get momentarily caught in the hydraulic effect, roll yourself in a ball until you are out of it."

Screw that.

He braced his right foot against the front of the raft and left against the thwart.

No way he was going over the side again.

They started downriver with three rafts stretched out before them in a yellow line.

"Okay," Hank said, "we want to get lined up so we can take the falls head on and then power through it. When I give the command for all ahead, I want everyone to really dig in."

Jim watched the lead raft suddenly drop out of sight as it went over the falls. After a million years it popped up like a roller coaster cresting a rise before diving again as one of its passengers flew into the air and vanished over the side.

Sonofabitch.

Then a second raft disappeared.

Son-of-a-bitch.

He wanted to go back—now—reopen that damn window of opportunity.

"Left forward, right back."

He dug his paddle into the drink.

And, oh shit, he could see it now.

A two-foot drop onto a shelf, then a four-foot hell-ride to oblivion.

"All ahead, dig in, dig in."

He dug in, paddling with all his strength, stroke after stroke, and sonofabitch—

They plunged onto the shelf, smashing into it as the water twisted them around forty-five degrees, then washed off the edge of the world. Jim's side of the raft dropped into the trough first, tipping it on its side and he leaned inboard as a wall of water swirled around him. Something slammed him in the back and he caught sight of Paul falling to the rubber floor. Then his side of the raft popped up, yanking his stomach into his mouth as the other side dropped into the trough, throwing Paul back against the thwart. They dipped into another hole then catapulted into the air like a plane on takeoff, but crashed down again like a lead Zeppelin, sending spray flying everywhere. They bobbled on the surface a couple of times before the hydraulic action spit them out onto level water full of boil and bubble. They were soaking wet, and the raft swamped, but they were past the falls and were still alive.

Hoo rah.

Yeah, buddy.

Paul grinned at him. "Hey, we all made it."

"Think again," Dodee yelled. "We lost our guide."

"Everybody back," Joppa called.

Jim dug in, backing the raft up.

Only, shit, did he really want to get back into that hydraulic?

Hank, you is gonna die.

But then he heard the man's voice. "All forward."

He didn't have to say it twice.

"Right forward, left back."

Jim caught sight of the curly-haired man climbing into the raft.

"Okay, all hard forward. Everybody dig in. The raft is flooded and it's going to be hard to get across the river before the current carries us downstream."

Downstream, oh yeah, like to the class five falls.

Bullshit on that.

He put his back into it, digging into the water, but the raft moved only sluggishly forward while the banks rushed rapidly by. He dug in again and again as they inched toward the sandy pullout beach. Only–sonofabitch–they weren't going to make it. Hank yelled for help and guides on shore rushed down the beach, waded out waist deep, caught hold as they drifted by, and pulled them onto the bank.

Jim climbed out and stood there, staring back at the falls.

The others laughed and high-fived each other, but he was just glad to have made it.

In one piece.

Still holding onto his privates.

Dodee turned to him. "Now wasn't that fun?"

He nodded.

"Oh, yeah. Like a roller coaster."

Only, he never did like roller coasters.

SEVENTEEN

He retrieved his spare clothes from the van and dragged himself to the changing house, the last one to get there, and had to wait until the others finished before he got a spot on a bench to sit. He dried off, put on the fresh clothes, feeling warm and relaxed, and had to admit, it had been a good trip. The minutes of boredom interspersed with seconds of sheer terror had left him alive and invigorated.

And ready for a nap.

When he went outside he found Dodee waiting for him, clutching her brown bag.

"You okay, sweetheart?"

"Yeah, why?"

"Just worried because you took so long. They took pictures of us coming over Nantahala Falls, and I want to buy some before the bus leaves."

He glanced at the empty parking lot and down to the deserted vans parked in a shady spot beside some picnic tables.

"Where's everybody?"

"Either in the store buying pictures or they've crossed the bridge to the outfitters shop. You want to get your lunch and come with me?"

"No, you go ahead. You need some money?"

"I'll put them on my credit card."

He watched her rush off and walked to their van. He stowed his wet clothes, grabbed his brown bag, and sat down at one of the picnic tables.

Decision time.

Should he gobble down his sandwich now and take a nap afterwards, or nap now and eat the sandwich on the trip back?

He looked into the bag, then neatly folded the top, and placed it on the table before him. He stretched out on the bleached-wood bench-seat, and closed his eyes, listening to the faint sounds of rushing water from the nearby river, and the call of birds from the overhead trees.

All right, let the world go away—

"Excuse me, are you with the group from The Mountain?"

He popped open one eye to stare up at a sandy-haired man with piercing blue eyes and a trim shape, probably in his late thirties.

"This group—what is it?" he asked, turning to another trim man at his side.

The second guy, also in his late thirties with dark eyes and two balding spots that gave him an extended black widow's peak, looked at a notepad. "An Elderhostel group with The Mountain Learning Center."

"Right. You with the Elderhostel group?"

Jim opened the other eye and sat up.

So much for his nap.

"We're looking for Howard Leslie," Sandy Hair said.

Jim studied the two men, their stone faces telling him nothing. "Mind telling me who you are?"

Sandy Hair pulled out a leather fold that showed a badge and FBI identification. "I'm Agent Gordon Grigory of the FBI, and this is Agent John Blackstone."

"Mind telling me what you want him for?"

"Yes, I would. Mind telling me who you are?"

"I'm James P. Dandy. Howard Leslie was killed yesterday."

That put a crack in their stone faces. Their eyes widened as they looked at one another.

"The other agents already know about it," Jim said.

"Other agents?" Grigory asked

"FBI. Like you two. They were here last night. Not here, but up at The Mountain."

"What were they doing?"

"Same as you, investigating Howard's death."

Blackstone's dark eyes focused on him. "There wasn't an

explosion, was there?"

Grigory gave Blackstone a small backhand tap on the arm and the man fell silent.

"How did he die?" Grigory asked.

"Howard? He fell off a cliff when a group of us were out hiking."

"And you say two FBI agents investigated it?"

"Yes. I thought it was strange the FBI would be there and asked them about it. The sheriff thought so, too. But now here you two are so maybe—"

"What did they tell you?"

"What did they tell me?"

Grigory took a breath and let it out. "You said you asked why—"

"Because Howard was a federal employee. When I asked if they investigated the death of every government employee, they said it was also because it happened on National Forest land. Which brings up the third question. Why are you two here?"

"You said there's a local sheriff involved?"

"Sheriff Graham. Didn't anyone tell you this up at The Mountain?"

Blackstone put his foot up on the bleached-wood bench-seat of the picnic table and glanced at his notebook. "I talked to a Hezekiah. Know him? Works in the kitchen? He said everyone was down here."

"The sheriff went out to the accident site last evening. While he was gone, the FBI guys showed up. You don't know about them?"

The stone faces had returned.

"Did they show you ID?" Grigory asked.

"No, but I didn't meet them when they came in the door. Josie Blue, one of the coordinators, is around here somewhere. He did. Maybe they were from a local FBI office."

Blackstone shook his head. "I'm assigned to what you would call the local office."

"Then maybe they're out of Washington."

He motioned to his partner. "Grigory flew in this morning from Washington."

"You know if the sheriff checked their IDs?" Grigory asked.

"The sheriff never met them. These guys came into the dining hall while the sheriff was out at the accident site and said they wanted to look at Howard's room. Duke Penny–he's also around here somewhere–he took them. When the sheriff got back, the two men had already split." He looked from one agent to the other. "How about answering one question for me? You obviously couldn't be investigating Howard's death because you didn't know he was dead. So, why are you here?"

Grigory's steel blue eyes riveted him. "You seem to be overly inquisitive about this?"

Jim smiled.

"Something funny?"

"You're lucky my nosey girlfriend isn't here."

And that got another little chink in the armor as the tips of his lips turned up. "These two people you mentioned. Josie Blue and Duke..."

"Duke Penny." He scanned the area and saw them coming across the parking lot. "There they are. Both of them."

Grigory nodded and started towards them, but Blackstone pulled out a card. "You say the sheriff is up at The Mountain Learning Center?"

Jim shrugged. "He said he was coming back this morning, but I didn't actually see him. What about the two men from yesterday?"

"They could be dangerous." He gave Jim his card. "If you see them, stay away and give me a call."

He watched Blackstone hurry out to where Grigory had intercepted Josie and Duke.

Why the hell was everybody after Howard?

He unfolded his brown bag.

First the two guys last night and now these two guys.

He pulled out his ham and cheese sandwich.

He didn't know about the guys last night, but there was no question the guys today were the real things.

He took a bite and watched as Duke spread his arms in a big shrug.

Blackstone said the other two guys could be dangerous, but how could he know that if he didn't know who they were? And what was that business about an explosion before Grigory shut him up?

He caught sight of Dodee, Debra, and Elcee leaving the store, laughing at something as they came across the parking lot.

Dodee rounded the picnic table and sat next to him, revealing two photos of them going over Nantahala Falls. He put on his reading glasses and studied them. The first had been taken just as they had started to slip off the shelf, the yellow raft bright in the sunlight with a backdrop of dark rocks that he hadn't been aware were there. Everyone was paddling except Paul who was leaning inboard. No wonder the man crashed into him. Anxious looks adorned everyone's face with his own jaw hanging slack.

"Look at your legs," Dodee said.

His leg muscles bulged from the strain of wedging himself in.

He smiled at her. "Damned if I was going to have another out-of-raft experience. Not there."

She flipped to the second picture which showed them at the bottom of the falls; steeper, deeper, and with more white water than he had realized. The raft was tipped way over, water bubbling under the high side bright in the sunlight, but the low side of the raft was hidden from the camera, except tucked in among a swirling wall of water, white face strained in concentration or fear, good old Jim Dandy hung on for dear life.

He smiled again and shook his head. "If I had seen these first, you can bet all the sweet parts of your body I'd have never made that trip."

Aunt Debra nodded. "That's what I said. I'm glad I didn't see the pictures first. But they make it look more dramatic than it was. Makes us look like we're in one of those ECO races." She studied the picture a moment, then looked up and smiled. "There's supposed to be an even bigger falls on Thursday's trip. I can't wait." She raised a fist in the air and brought it down. "I am pumped."

Jim stared into her tired blue eyes.

The woman had obviously taken leave of her senses.

They piled into the van soon after that, and soon after that he was asleep, wedged in between Dodee and the window. But it was a fitful sleep that left him groggy when he climbed out back at The Mountain. He squinted in the late afternoon sun and turned toward the lodge to see the round-faced Sheriff Graham resting his butt against his police car.

The sheriff stood up straight as they approached. "Jim Dandy, right? Dodee Swisher?"

Jim nodded.

"Like to ask you a few questions. Only take a couple of minutes."

Jim palmed up his hands. "Okay." He turned to Dodee. "You want to go on to the room?"

"She can stay," Graham said. He motioned to the other Elderhostelers and waited until they cleared the area. "Last night you told me you saw Mr. Leslie with a laptop. Isn't that correct?"

"Yesterday morning. He came into the Great Room to get some coffee and he was carrying it. Said he had some work to do before starting on the hike. Some others there must have seen him with it, Elcee, Aunt Debra, Tristin Fontaine."

"Yes, Tristin Fontaine. Did he go on the rafting trip?"

Jim shrugged and turned to Dodee who shrugged in turn.

"You didn't find the laptop?" she asked.

"Not so far. Would you mind if we looked in your room and checked out your car?"

Jim shrugged again. "No problem. How about Howard's car?"

"The FBI impounded it this afternoon. Oh, you mean did we search it for the computer?" He nodded, then rubbed his jaw and cocked his head. "You meet the FBI guys last night?"

"They stopped at our table during dinner."

"You didn't happen to see their ID?"

"No, Josie Blue said they were the FBI. I assumed they had showed him identification. But I thought it was strange the FBI would be investigating an accident."

"Seems like no one saw their ID."

"How about the FBI guys from today?" he asked, and regretted it when he saw Dodee's jaw drop.

"No, they're the real item." Sheriff Graham turned down his lips and nodded. "Not only had IDs, but I checked them out with the office before turning over the Jaguar."

"What FBI guys from today?" Dodee asked.

"The ones who showed up this afternoon." He turned to Jim. "You talked to them I understand."

He nodded, feeling Dodee's eyes on him. "They were surprised when I told them Howard was dead. So why were they looking for him?"

The sheriff gave a little shrug.

Apparently the information highway was a one way street.

Except for the slip Agent Blackstone had made.

"Because of the explosion?" he asked, giving it a try.

Sheriff Graham's eyebrows rose at that. Then he nodded. "That's why they wanted the Jaguar."

Jim nodded back.

Because of the explosion?

What explosion?

He nodded again, trying to urge the sheriff on, but the man stood up, apparently having said all he was going to say. Then he looked back to them

"Did Mr. Leslie appear out of the ordinary to you? I

mean, did he say anything that might sound subversive?"

Jim shrugged yet again. "Like what?"

"Like why he would be carrying explosives around in his car?"

EIGHTEEN

"What was that about?" Dodee asked as soon as the door to their room closed. "And what about the other men from the FBI? You didn't tell me anything about them."

"Well," he put his arms around her, "I didn't have a chance."

"Bullshit," she said and gave him a light punch in the stomach.

"Ugh."

"You had no intention, sweetheart, Jim Dandy, James P. Dandy, no intention of telling me."

"You want to use the shower first?"

That got him another poke in the stomach.

"Ugh. You're a dangerous woman, you know that?"

Then she brought her arms up around his neck and gave him a long, lingering kiss. "Are you going to tell me about the FBI agents?"

"Well, lady—"

She raised her chin and looked down her nose at him. "Then we can use the shower together."

"It's a really small shower."

"Exactly."

So he told her about meeting Grigory and Blackstone as he pulled off his shoes and socks.

"They didn't know about Howard's death?" she asked.

"That's what I just told you."

"Then why were they here?"

"When I told them Howard was dead, Blackstone asked me if there had been an explosion. Apparently that was a slip because Grigory cut him off and changed the subject."

"What explosion?"

"I don't know." He pulled off his pants and hung them up. "That's why I tried it out on the sheriff."

"And that's why he asked us about Howard carrying explosives. He thought you knew more than you did." She smiled. "That's very devious of you, sweetheart."

"I can be sneaky when I want to. Right now I'm going to sneak into the shower. You can stay and talk to the wall or come with me."

The tips of her lips turned down. "Get the water warm and I'll tag along." And she slapped him on his naked rear as he walked by.

He had been right about the shower. It was small. Both of them scrunched together under the hot water as he washed her shoulders and back. Then she squeezed around to face him and he bent to kiss her.

"How did they know Howard had the explosives?"

He stared down into her big blues and some of the erotic moment slipped away. "They found them in the Jaguar?"

"How did they know he had a Jaguar?"

He shrugged and put his arms around her. "Who cares. Maybe someone told them."

"But you said they only talked to Hezekiah, and he sent them down to the whitewater outfitters. How did a cook know he had a Jaguar?"

"I don't know. I don't care." He pulled her to him. "Enough with the Jag and the FBI. You're ruining a moment here." And he kissed her.

What the hell difference did it make how they had found out about the Jag?

Except.

He broke off the kiss. "Howard flew down. Picked up the Jag in Asheville. If Grigory flew in from Washington to investigate the explosives Howard had in his car, he couldn't be talking about the Jag."

"That's right."

"So he had to be talking about Howard's own car."

"That's right," she said again. "And Howard said someone stole his car. But then how did the FBI know the explosives belonged to Howard and not to the thief?"

"Good question."

"Any answers?"

"Let me think on it." He kissed her again and ran his hands down her back to her rear end.

She broke the kiss. "I think you're thinking about something else, sweetheart."

"What makes you think I'm thinking about something else?"

"Because your brain has gone stiff."

"Very funny."

She reached up, wrapped her arms around his neck and gave him a wanton kiss, their bodies pressed together in the cramped shower, his body caressing hers until he broke off the kiss.

"This is not going to work. If we were in our teens or twenties, maybe, but now?"

"Are you saying we need to dry off and beat a hasty retreat to the bed?"

"I'm saying we need to dry off and beat a hasty retreat to the bed."

They dried off and beat a hasty retreat to the bed.

And they made love like innocents on a sunny afternoon.

Not with the agility of teenagers racing along to the strains of the *William Tell Overture* banging in their ears.

But with the sedate and stately grace of *Pomp and Circumstance*, reaching the top all the same, and falling off on the other side, their cries and whimperings joining the cacophony of birds bickering on the balcony outside.

Afterwards he lay on his back, Dodee's head on his shoulder, her hand gently caressing his stomach. Mountain air, just cool enough to be refreshing, drifted through the open window. And he felt himself drifting down to a fuzzy place on the edge of slumber.

"We have to get going soon," she whispered.

"Where we going?"

"Down to the social hour."

"Screw the social hour."

"No, I want to hear what the latest rumors are. Besides, if we don't show up, everyone will know who it was who was making all those licentious noises in their room." She raised herself up on one elbow and stared down at him. "You know what bothers me about all this?"

That popped his eyes open. "Bothers you? I thought you enjoyed it?"

"No, not us, sweetheart," she said and kissed him. "You were magnificent."

"Yes, I was, wasn't I?"

"And so humble about it. No, I was thinking about the FBI."

"Ah, back to the questions without answers."

"Why did they take so long to investigate?"

Her breast was within easy reach so he nibbled on it.

"You're not going to get any answers there."

"What do you mean, it took them so long?"

"If they knew Howard had explosives in his car, why didn't they come on Sunday or yesterday? Why wait until today?"

"It was reported stolen, right? Maybe they just found the car yesterday and hopped on a plane today."

She raised her eyebrows and turned down her lips. "But that brings us back to the other problem. Howard was a government employee. So why would they think he had the explosives rather than the thief?"

"Maybe they didn't. Maybe they were just checking to make sure."

"Then why not pick up the phone and call? Why make the trip all the way down here?"

"Because of the heightened security in Washington. Everyone's jumpy about a terrorist attack..." He bit the side of his lip.

"What?"

He sat up. "The car that blew up in Rock Creek Park on Friday."

"Where's Rock Creek—"

"In Washington. That cancelled the airline flights." He stared into her big blues. "Suppose that was Howard's car?"

"Someone stole the car and the explosives went off? Howard would have to be pretty cool to come down here afterwards and act as if nothing happened."

"Unless he didn't know it was his car. The explosives demolished it and killed the driver. It could have taken them a few days to track down who owned it, which would explain why the FBI waited to hop a plane down here."

Her lips turned down again. "Howard would still have to be pretty cool to come down here while a thief was running around Washington with his explosives."

"There's one other possibility. He might not have known the explosives were in the car."

"You mean they belonged to the thief—"

"That doesn't quite work either. If they belonged to the thief, why did they blow up and kill him? But suppose somebody rigged Howard's car with a bomb, set it on a timer so it wouldn't go off downtown where every government agent would be scrambling over it, but somewhere on his trip home?"

"You mean they were trying to kill him?"

"Right, only somebody steals the car, not knowing about the bomb, and kaplooie. Must have been a rude awakening for the thief."

"That means Howard's death wasn't an accident."

He raised his shoulders, held them there for a moment, then dropped them. "If someone did rig his car, a big if, then probably not. When they realized that he hadn't been driving, they tracked him down here and finished the job."

"But why would they want to kill Howard?"

"Why would they want steal his laptop?"

"Right." Dodee pointed at him with her thumb and forefinger extended. "That means the FBI guys from yesterday are involved."

"Phony FBI guys."

"And it also means it has something to do with the CDs the sheriff found. Which means it probably had something to do with his work. Where did he work?"

"Department of Agriculture."

"What did he do for them?"

Jim shrugged. "Something with computers."

Her big blues turned toward the windows and glazed over. "How can we find out what he was working on?"

He waved his hand in front of her face until she turned to him.

"We don't," he said. "It's not our job. The real FBI guys said the phony FBI guys are dangerous. So stay out of it. I'm sure the FBI can handle this without our help."

"Um." She pressed her lips together, staring off into the distance again. "You know what that means?"

"I'm sure you're going to tell me."

"If the phony guys threw Howard off the cliff, they had to know he'd be out there." Her big blues locked onto him. "Which means somebody here on the Elderhostel had to be tracking him."

Jim took a deep breath and let it out.

Not a pleasant thought.

NINETEEN

They strolled down the road toward Heritage Hall and the social hour. The sun skimmed the treetops, still high, but definitely on the downward track that stretched June days into long evenings. A short-sleeve breeze carried the sound of birds and the scent of pines spiced with the smell of cooking food.

He felt alive and emotionally sated, one with the world. He stopped and pulled Dodee around to face him, big blues opening wide in question. He kissed her.

"I love you, lady."

A smile spread on her face, the smug one with ends turned down. "You're supposed to say that before you have your way with me." She put her arms around his neck and kissed him back. "I love you, too, sweetheart."

They continued on, hand in hand, down the steps to the rocking chair porch.

"Hey," Paul called out, raising his cup, "here's to the first one to have an out-of-raft experience. We weren't on the water ten minutes before Jim was over the side."

He smiled. "I wasn't only one. Who else went in?"

Quentin frowned and raised his hand, followed by two others he hardly knew, a tall dark man named Rabin Hetch and a plump woman named Sally O'Sullivan, then Kelli smiled and gave a half hearted wave.

"But I didn't lose it until we went over the last falls," she said. "Our guide went in at the same time so I don't feel so bad."

"Did you get caught in the hydraulic?"

"I don't know. It all happened so fast. I was in the water, my feet were up, and then Duke yanked me back into the raft."

"That was a class three today," Valerie said, giving them a wink. "Supposed to be a class four on Thursday."

"Nothing to be anxious about," Babs said from the doorway of the Heritage Room. "We'll stop and climb up on the rocks so you can take a look at it first. If you decide you don't want to try, there's a path that leads downstream and you can pick up the raft on the other side."

"I'm going to have to look at it real close," Quentin said with raised eyebrows, showing a lot of the white of his eyes. "Being the only physician along, I should pass in case someone gets hurt and needs attention."

"Oh, groan," Hallis said holding one hand over her heart. "The old I-have-to-pass-because-I might-be-needed ploy."

"Well, I might. Beside, I have to be careful of my hands."

"Oh, groan. The old I-have-to-be-careful-of-my-hands ploy.

He stuck those hands on his hips. "How about the old I'm-gonna-get-a-divorce-when-I-get-back ploy?"

She clapped her hands over her mouth, but they didn't hide the broad smile on her bronze face.

"I'll be your witness, Quentin," Paul said. "That's cruel and unusual punishment."

"Oh, there's nothing unusual about this punishment."

"I think you went too far, Hallis," Elcee said, a smile rearranging the freckles on her face.

"Oh, he needs me too much to divorce me. A maid would cost a fortune and Lord knows he can't cook a lick."

Quentin raised his eyes to the heavens and shook his head.

"Besides," Hallis said, caressing the doctor's forearm, "he loves me too much for that."

He knitted his brows and stared at her, but then a smile escaped and spread across his face. "What I'm really worried about is the old I'll-take-you-for-every-cent-you-got ploy."

Hallis grinned. "That too."

Dodee came out of the Heritage Room with a cup of popcorn held between two cups of wine. "Want to share the popcorn, or shall I—"

"No." He took the popcorn and one wine, then handed back the popcorn. "You can have it."

She took a sip of her wine. "Seen Tristin Fontaine?"

He scanned the group and shook his head. "Why?"

She turned to the others. "Anybody seen Tristin? Did he go on the raft trip?"

"He wasn't feeling well, couldn't make it," Babs said. "Which reminds me"—she softly snapped her fingers—"I better go check on him."

Duke came around the corner from the chow hall. "Okay, everybody, it's dinner time. You can stay out here and eat popcorn of you want, but I'm going to dig into some serious vittles, as the mountain boys say."

And he didn't have to say it twice, the mass exodus a testament to healthy appetites, no doubt built up by the exertion and excitement of the day.

After the thanksgiving prayer, Jim followed Dodee through the line—spaghetti and meat sauce with meatballs on the side, garlic bread, and squares of chocolate cake. They sat down at a table with the Quarieses.

"Tomorrow's the long hike," Quentin said, taking a bite of garlic bread. "Longer than Monday."

"There's also a short one," Hallis said. "Think I'll go on that."

Valerie took the chair next to Jim. "You all talking about hiking the Appalachian Trail tomorrow?" she asked as Killi sat across from her.

"I was just telling them I think I'll go on the short hike."

"I think they're both the same, just starting from different ends."

Kelli nodded. "One has a long easy climb uphill and then a short steep path back down the other side. The second starts with the short, steep climb and ends with the long path to the bottom."

Jim twirled spaghetti on his fork. "I want to go on the steep hike up and the long trail down. Get the climb out of the way when I'm fresh."

Dodee nudged him. "There's Tristin."

He watched the man load up his plate from the buffet table, stop to talk to Aunt Debra who was getting a glass of juice, then join her at a table with Elcee.

Jim took bite of garlic bread and turned back to see Tristin shoveling food into his mouth.

If Dodee was right about someone having fingered Howard out on the trail, Tristin was a prime candidate. He had registered at the last minute, had immediately preceded Howard on the silent hike, and if he was really sick, it wasn't affecting his appetite.

But if he was involved, why hang around? Why not skip out while everyone was rafting?

He finished his spaghetti and started on the square of chocolate cake.

Unless that would have been too obvious.

And maybe Tristin was too obvious.

If you were going to bump someone off–oh yeah, bump him off. He was beginning to sound like Dodee. But if you were going to bump him off, why draw attention to yourself? Why not slip in, shoot the sucker, and slip out?

That made more sense.

After dinner they headed up the hill to the Great Room for the evening program. The chairs had been arranged in a semicircle around a large, bearded man who sat on a stool up front. He held a small black-walnut banjo with a white stretched-paper drum, and even if you couldn't lick a sound out of it, it would still be worth having for its beauty.

Jim flopped on one of the couches off to the right and Dodee stared at him. "You don't want to sit in one of the chairs up front?"

"Nope. You go sit there if you like."

She sighed and sat down next to him.

"No, go ahead," he said. "Sit up there. I don't mind."

"I mind. I like sitting next to you."

He stared into her big blues a moment, then gave her a feather kiss. "That doesn't mean I'm moving."

The bearded man played the banjo, which sounded every bit as great as it looked, and broke into a mountain song.

"Hi, everybody," he said when he finished. "I'm Lee Knight. I've lived here in the Allegheny Mountain area since the sixties. Came down from upstate New York to help out during the civil rights movement and stayed. I fell in love with the land and the people, immersed myself in the culture, and collected stories and folk songs over the years. Many of them were in danger of being lost, others still are. And some are gone forever."

He shifted on his stool.

"I want to sing an Indian song for you now. It's a chant really. The Indian's belief in spirits was such that they did things to gain their favor and stay on their good side."

He placed the banjo into a floor stand and picked up a rattle made from a polished tortoise shell.

"This is a typical Cherokee chant that comes from the green corn ceremony. It's about a long drought. When this happens plants become stressed and produce more flowers and fruit and seeds than normal. In the past few years we've been in a drought and you never saw such spectacular flowering of rhododendrons and mountain laurel. Never saw so many holly berries, either. So instead of birds starving in these drought conditions, they are able to survive by eating berries that you and I can't. The Cherokee call this chant the pheasant dance, using the word pheasant to mean all game birds. The bird they're actually referring to is the ruffed grouse. If you are out in the woods and hear a sound like an engine trying to start, that's a ruffed grouse."

He shook the tortoise shell rattle.

"The chant has no real English translation. It's meant to be the sound of the birds surrounding the holly tree and giving thanks to it for providing the food that saved their lives."

He used the rattle as accompaniment and sang the chant,

starting off low and finishing off in a crescendo. He shook the rattle and repeated the cry, or another that sounded just like it, then came to a close.

And everyone clapped.

Lee shook the rattle a few more times and gave a little laugh.

"The Indian concept of marriage was different from ours. Men and women were easily attached and detached. Frequently the most important male in a child's life was not his father, but one of his maternal uncles. They had an interesting way of getting divorced. The brave would go out hunting one day and come home to find all his stuff on the back porch. The marriage was over. Time to go home to mother."

Dodee turned to Jim. "Just like out west on the Santa Fe Trail Elderhostel, remember? The woman puts her husband's stuff outside the teepee. The marriage is over."

"You like that idea, don't you. Are you planning to put my stuff outside our door tonight."

She raised her eyebrows and gave him one of her turned down smiles.

He felt a tap on his shoulder as someone knelt down beside the arm of the couch. He turned to see the freckled face and flaming red hair of Billy Riley, the newsman from WHLC. He looked like a transplanted cub reporter from the nineteen thirties. All he needed was a porkpie hat with the brim turned up in the front and back. "Could I talk to one of you for a minute?"

"I'll go," Dodee said.

He watched them leave and turned back to Lee Knight as the man began singing another mountain folk song, this time playing a dulcimer.

Dodee and Billy Riley were a good match for one another, a conspirer and a conspiree with enough supposition to fill a book.

Except, if things got out of hand, where would that leave him?

Knee deep in swamp muck.
He jumped up and rushed out after them.

TWENTY

"Where can we talk?" Billy asked. He had traded his tie and jacket for a University of North Carolina T-shirt which made him look like a student.

Jim motioned to the door. "Let's go down to the dining hall. Coffee's supposed to be on twenty-four hours a day."

Billy gave him a thumbs up. "I have my car. It's sitting in the middle of the lot and I'll have to re-park it anyway."

So they rode down and went inside. Jim led the way to the coffee urn and he filled his cup.

"How about your wife?" Billy asked, filling his.

Jim glanced over to Dodee, sitting at one of the tables. "She doesn't drink coffee in the evening."

They started to join her, but Billy paused at the dessert tray of chocolate cake squares left over from dinner. "Oh, man, look at these."

"I have it on good authority that anything left out here is up for grabs."

"Really?" he said, and put two squares on a paper plate. "This is living."

They sat down at the table, Jim next to Dodee and the news reporter, stuffing one of the squares in his mouth, on the opposite side.

"This is a trick, isn't it?" Jim asked. "Get us down to the dining hall so you can eat chocolate cake?"

Billy shook his head, pointing to his full mouth, then took a sip of coffee. "I heard the FBI was here last night." He pulled out his notebook and flipped it open. "You know anything about that?"

Dodee nodded. "Not only that, but—"

"Wait a minute," Jim said, staring at Billy Riley. "Why did you pick us out of the crowd?"

"Because you helped me yesterday." He held out his

hands, one containing a square of cake, the other a cup of coffee. "I'll keep you out of it." He heaved a big sigh and shook his head. "Like I've been at this job since I got out of college. Like it's a dead-ender. Like if I stay here too long, I'll never get out. This is the first thing to come along that could light up the airways and get me exposure. It's, like maybe, my only ticket out of here to a bigger station and audience"

"The FBI was here yesterday," Dodee said, obviously taken by the idea of helping the young man and giving Jim a look that dared him to stop her. "And today."

"Cool," Billy said, grasping a pen in his left hand. "Why were they here?"

Jim shook his head.

No way he was going to stop her so together they told Billy of the phony FBI guys who claimed they were investigating Howard's death because he was a government employee and because it happened on national forest land. Then they told him about the real FBI guys who showed up because they suspected Howard was carrying explosives around in his car.

"Oh, wow. So you think the guy was murdered? Hey, what's his name?" Billy flipped back through his notes. "Howard Leslie. So he was murdered?"

Dodee looked at Jim.

"We don't know that, but it sure seems strange that those phony FBI guys showed up the same afternoon Howard passed on to that big Elderhostel in the sky."

"And they took Howard's laptop," Dodee said, "but left some CDs behind."

Billy looked down at his plate, then stood up. "Excuse me a minute." He hurried back to the dessert tray and returned with three more chocolate cake squares. "I haven't had any dinner," he said, taking a big bite out of one. "So what about the explosives? Any theory on that?"

Dodee leaned her elbows on the table. "This is what we think—"

"Wait a minute," Jim said. "We don't know anything.

You're just surmising–"

"He asked if we had any *theories*, sweetheart."

Billy nodded. "Yeah, it's cool. Any ideas, I'll look into 'em."

She grimaced at Jim and turned back to Billy. "We found out that a car exploded in Washington last Friday evening. Howard had his car stolen the same day."

"Oh, wow. You think Howard set off the explosion in his car, reported it stolen to the police, and then came down here to cover his tracks?"

Jim blinked at the freckled-faced man, and then at Dodee. "That's a possibility I hadn't thought of."

Billy held out his hands again. "Then what else?

"We were thinking that maybe the explosives weren't Howard's."

"You mean they belonged to the guy who stole the car?"

"How about they belonged to the phony FBI guys who showed up here yesterday?"

The eager eyes flicked from him to Dodee and back. "And these guys used Howard's car to transport the explosives, but they blew up on the way?"

Jim frowned. "That's another possibility I hadn't thought of."

Dodee placed her hands flat on the table. "But then why would they come chasing after Howard?"

Billy shrugged. "Because they were afraid he'd talk and they wanted to cover their tracks? Or, or–oh wow–they figured Howard skipped out with their explosives and came looking for him. When they found out he didn't have them, they decided to shut him up to keep him from talking."

Jim frowned again. "I'm getting theory overload here."

"What we thought," Dodee said, folding her hands, "was that they planted the explosives in Howard's car to kill him, but then someone stole it and it blew up the thief instead."

"Oooo-kay." Billy's lips turned down as he stared at the last piece of cake on his plate. "But it seems inept of the FBI to let someone steal the car when they had loaded it with explosives."

"What makes you think they were the real FBI?" Jim asked.

Billy's eyes met his for a moment, then he slapped his hand against his head. "Right, they were just the phonies. Now it makes sense. But they're still inept if they stole the computer and left the disks behind." He stuffed the last piece of cake in his mouth. "And it still doesn't explain why they wanted to kill him." He stood up. "What I'll do is track down the sheriff and the real FBI and see what they have to say about it. When I find out something I'll get back to you. Keep you informed. Is that cool? In the meantime, Ms. Swisher–"

"Dodee."

"Dodee," he said and gave her his card again, as if he knew a co-conspirator when he saw one, "if you hear anything, you let me know. Man, you guys have helped me a lot."

They declined Billy's offer of a ride back, and watched him hop in his car and charge off down the hill in pursuit of his career, if he didn't rack up the Hyundai Tiburon on the curves first. They strolled back to the lodge listening to the whoo whoo of a nearby owl, and an answering whoo whoo whoo from one further off in the valley.

"What do you think of Riley?" she asked, rubbing her neck.

"Are you all right?"

"Just a little stiff. Of course, if my friend who's handsome and humble and who just happens to be a physical therapist, was to massage it–"

"Sonofabitch, I fell right into that. Might as well stick a fishhook in my lip and reel me in."

She wrapped both her arms around one of his. "You don't have to, sweetheart."

"Ah. Now the guilt trip. How can I refuse?"

When they got back to their room, he hung up his clothes and dug out his pjs while Dodee used the bathroom. When she came out in a pink nightgown, smelling of soap and a hint of vanilla perfume, he sat her between his legs and started massaging the base of her neck.

"You didn't answer my question about Billy. I think he's a sweet young man full of ambition."

"That works for me."

"No, tell me what you think–oh, God that feels good, sweetheart. I could–"

"I know, you could kill for this."

She twisted around, big blues staring at him.

He gave her a phony grin. "You always say that."

"Well, I could." She turned back around. "What about Billy?"

"Like you say, a personable young man." He moved down the base of her neck and started on her shoulders. "Looks like a teenager though. Except he came up with a lot more theories than I had."

"He was right about one thing. Those phony FBI guys were inept if they took the laptop and left the disks."

He shrugged. "Maybe, but they were un-inept enough–"

"Un-inept?"

"All right, they were epted–you like that–epted enough to drop Howard off a cliff, if he was dropped off the cliff." He kissed her on the back of her neck, patted her on the rear as a signal to get up, and grabbed his pj's. "And they are epted enough so that I don't want to run into them during a walk in the woods."

He brushed his teeth, washed his face, changed into the pjs, and came out to a darkened bedroom. He slipped under the sheet and Dodee snuggled up next to him, resting her head on his chest.

"You quite comfortable?"

"Um." She draped one leg over him. "Now I am."

"I wouldn't want to put you out."

"The thing is, do any of Riley's theories hold water?" she asked as if the conversation hadn't been interrupted.

He replayed the chow hall conversation in his mind.

His first theory had been that Howard set off the explosion, reported the car stolen, then came down here to cover his tracks.

How did that work?

Not very well. Why would he set off the explosives when the only one killed was the driver?

Unless the driver was the only one he wanted to kill.

"Think Howard could have used the explosives to kill the guy driving the car?" he whispered.

But Dodee's even breathing told him he wasn't going to get an answer from that source before morning.

There was another problem if that was the case. Why would the phony FBI guys then trace Howard down and whack him?

Unless the driver Howard whacked was one of their guys. Then they might want to come down and whack him back.

Billy's second theory had been that Howard let someone use his car to transport explosives and when they went off, he reported it stolen.

Except Howard had been signed up for the Elderhostel for some time. How could he predict when the car was going to blow up? It might work for Tristin Fontaine who showed up at the last minute, but not Howard.

Unless they had made a mistake and killed the wrong person, Howard instead of Tristin?

He took a breath and let it out.

Before he had been on theory overload; now he was on possibility overload.

Billy said he would keep them updated.

Until then the equation had too many unknown Xs and Ys for him to sort out.

He closed his eyes as the whoo whoo whoo of the distant owl drifted in on a soft breeze and he let the day slip away.

TWENTY-ONE

Sometime during the night the who's whoo of the owl world had passed the torch to a group of nestlings whose sharp cheep-cheep sounded like a demand for a piece of the early worm. Dawn had already broken. Sunrise couldn't be far away.

He slipped out of bed, went through the morning ritual in the bathroom, slipped on jeans and a shirt, grabbed his mug and barefooted up to the Great Room to make coffee. But when he got there he found it had already been made.

Or was it left over from the night before?

He filled his mug and took a sip.

Whenever and whoever, it tasted fine to him.

He carried it out on the balcony, the wood decking cold on the soles of his bare feet, to watch his Father bring up the sun.

Down below the mist still lurked between the humps and bumps of the foothills, looking like white water swirling around rocks in a stream. Golden sheep grazed in a deep blue ocean overhead, dotted with a few lingering stars.

He took a deep breath, the air rich with the smells of the forest tinged with that of his coffee, and he took a sip, letting the hot liquid roll around in his mouth before swallowing it.

Then the sun burst forth out of the dark green of Chinquapin Mountain, filling the earth with light and warmth.

Good show, Father.

Certainly better than anything Dreamworks could do.

He heard the door open and turned to see the long face and nest of brown hair belonging to Tristin Fontaine.

"Good morning," Jim said.

The pale lips spread slightly and the man nodded. He nestled a cup with a tea bag in bony hands and leaned on the railing, bending his lanky body into a curve as he stared out on the lowlands.

Jim followed his gaze, wondering what the non-communicatory man was taking in. A wealth of information he was not.

But maybe if he asked him some general questions the man might open up a bit.

So, sucker, why did you kill Howard?

"Are you retired?"

The long face turned to him and blinked. "No, I'm a prosthetist."

"Really. You like it?"

The serious brown eyes blinked again. "You know what I'm talking about?"

"I'm a physical therapist."

"Ah." His pale lips thinned again in what might be interpreted as a smile. "Yes, to answer your question, I like it. We are doing some marvelous things today that we could only dream about a few years ago, using digital technology and microcomputers."

"Really?"

"Yes. We can make a knee and leg so closely approximate a man's gait that you would never be able to tell he was wearing a prosthesis. At one time we needed a patient to return to the office for adjustments, but now, if there is a microprocessor in the prosthesis, we can sometimes do it online."

"And arms and elbows–"

"We can do it all. Some things better than others. And unusual things. For instance in FTM cases–I don't do them myself–they can build a prosthesis that it so closely matches the patient's skin coloring and texture that it's almost impossible to tell from the real thing."

"FTM?"

"Transgender female to male. You can either have a full flaccid penis and testicles or an erect one. And from what I've been told, they are working on one that will go from one state to the other." The man nodded. "We are beginning to do some amazing things."

Jim glanced around to see if anyone was eavesdropping on the conversation. Fortunately there wasn't. Already Tristin had told him way more than he ever needed to know.

"The same goes for nose, ear, and ocular prosthesis," he said. "I've seen a whole lower facial and jaw with movement and agility that I would have sworn was the man's natural face."

"Really?"

"I specialize in designing limbs. Our socket designs of today are made out of new alloys and materials so strong and light that—and this is what pleases me—we can have people running in marathons and leading normal lives that wouldn't have been possible twenty years ago. Maybe five years ago."

Jim drained his cup.

He had opened the man's floodgates and everything was pouring out. The trouble was how to close them again.

He made a show of looking at his watch. "Oh, wow," he said, realizing he sounded like Billy Riley. "I'd better bring Dodee her coffee or I might end up needing your services. Interesting talking to you, Tristin."

He went back inside, refilled his mug, got a cup for Dodee, and ran into Joppa Harp as he left the Great Room.

She was dressed in a great expanse of bathrobe with flip flops on wide feet slapping against the floor. "Top of the morning, Jim. Finally over your out-of-raft experience?"

"All over the one from yesterday. Let's hope we don't have one tomorrow."

"I know I won't. I'm leaving tomorrow."

"You're not going rafting? You're breaking up the team?"

She smiled. "You're probably better off without me. Some business has come up that I have to take care of." She pointed to his cups. "More coffee in there?"

"At least one more."

He went downstairs, set his mug on the floor, and opened the door.

The bed had been made and there was noise from the

bathroom. He knocked. "I have coffee out here."

He couldn't have done better if he was Ali Baba shouting "open sesame."

She came out dressed in a short-sleeved tan shirt, cargo shorts, white socks and hiking boots. She had on a fresh face and a fresh smile and a fresh perfume and she gave him a fresh kiss, tasting of peppermint toothpaste.

"Good morning, sweetheart," she said, relieving him of the Styrofoam cup. "Thank you."

"You'll never guess who I've been talking to upstairs?"

"Tristin Fontaine."

His jaw dropped.

"Really?" The big blues opened wide and she smiled. "I just made a wild guess at the least likely person I could think of."

"Okay, smart ass broad. What does he do for a living?"

She stuck out her free hand and let it wander about. "He makes cigars in Cuba?"

"Close. He works for the CIA."

Her eyes popped open again. "Really?"

"No, not really. He's a prosthetist."

"Really?"

"Really." He shook his head. "You don't have any idea what I'm talking about."

"He's a prostate doctor?"

"He makes prosthetic devices; artificial limbs and things like that."

"Really?"

"Yes, really."

She gave him another kiss. "I have a more important question to ask you." And gave him one more kiss. "Are you going barefoot to breakfast, or are you going to put on shoes?"

"Boots."

He slipped on socks and hiking boots, and they headed for the chow hall.

She slipped her arm under his. "How did this come

about, that he's... a prosthetist? I never heard him say five words."

"I asked him what he did for a living and then I couldn't shut him up."

"Maybe he's making it up as a cover."

"A cover for what?"

"For killing Howard."

"If he was going to make something up, I can think of a million things easier than a prosthetist."

"But don't you see?" She pointed at him with her thumb and forefinger together. "It's so unusual no one would know enough to question him about it."

"Except a semi-retired physical therapist. We work with these guys all the time, and believe me, Tristin told me more about prostheses than I ever wanted to know. He couldn't have done that without knowing the field."

He held the door for her and they entered the dining room. He glanced around for Tristin, not wanting to get back in that conversation, but he wasn't there.

He followed Dodee to the buffet table and scooped out scrambled eggs, a few pieces of bacon, and a couple of sausages and headed toward a table occupied by Duke and Babs Penny.

"Morning, guys."

"Hi, Jim. Ready for the hike?" Duke asked, holding a forkful of eggs.

"I think so."

Dodee sat beside him. "High cholesterol breakfast there, sweetheart."

He studied her tray—cut pears and a bowl of bran flakes—and shrugged. "I'll burn it up on the hike."

"We're starting from two ends of the same trail," Babs said. "Leave a van at each end so we don't have to backtrack. Which one are you going on?"

"The one with the steep climb first and then the long descent. Get the climb out of the way then relax on the way back down."

"That's the one I'll be sweeping for," Babs said. "Old bad Penny here will be sweeping for the other."

"Bad Penny? I'm the good Penny." Duke flicked his eyebrows. "The bright and shiny original Penny. I just let you have my name because I felt sorry for you."

"You gave me your name because you wanted to sleep with me, dear."

He shrugged. "That, too."

Jim scooped up a forkful of scrambled eggs.

The two wore the teasing well, as though the act had been on the road for some years. Harmless little things couples did, sometimes without realizing it. Like before Penny had died. She had always introduced them as Jim and Penny Dandy. That had given just enough separation from Jim and Dandy to stave off the Jim Dandy jokes. Now, with Penny gone, he had to use the formal James P. Dandy name.

"Funny about names." He picked up a piece of bacon and took a bite, enjoying its distinctive taste. "A lot can be used for either a first or last name. Like your last name is Penny while my wife's first name was Penny."

"Like Howard," Dodee said. "And Leslie, and Martin—remember on the Santa Fe Trail we met Martin J. Martin?"

"You're kidding," Duke said.

"No." Dodee jerked her thumb at Jim. "The two of them had a routine. When they met in the hall, Jim would say, 'How you doing Martin Martin?' And Martin Martin would answer, 'Just Jim Dandy.'"

Babs's deep blue eyes brightened. "Well, Duke's real name is Benny. How cheesy does that sound, Benny Penny?"

Her husband leaned his hairy arms on the table. "It's not Benny, it's Benjamin."

"Which also could be a first or last name," Dodee said. "Like Jack Benny."

Babs nodded. "The actor Richard Benjamin. And Duke, for that matter, could be a first or last name, or a title."

Jim raised his hands and let them clunk on the table. "I'm sorry I brought the subject up."

Dodee smiled. "I think it's a Jim Dandy subject."

He glared into her big blues. "That's not funny."

But speaking of separating Jim and Dandy, how did Jim and Dodee Dandy sound?

TWENTY-TWO

They loaded up their backpacks with lunches and water and her camera, then met the others outside the chow hall where they loaded into two vans and headed out to pick up a southern section of the Appalachian Trail. They wound down the mountain to the crossroads at Dillard and turned north on Highway 23.

A few miles up the road Jim nudged Dodee. "There's a Dairy Queen."

"I'm surprised you didn't ask to stop."

"Probably too early for it to be open, but maybe I will after the hike. We passed it on our trip down."

"And you didn't stop?"

"You were asleep and I didn't want to wake you."

"You're sweet."

"I am."

Somewhere along the way they parted company with the other van. They pulled into a small, tree-shaded parking lot at Wayah Crest, a trailhead that led between outhouses and up the hill into the woods. The smell of mold hung in the chill air, and night dew still clung to the graveled ground and grass and leaves, waiting for the June sun to climb higher in the sky and burn it off.

Jim slipped on a light jacket, did some leg stretches to ease the stiffness from sitting cramped in his seat, and glanced around at his hiking companions.

They came in all sizes and shapes, age and gender—well, only two genders. Carmel was the leader again with Babs as the sweep. Valerie, Kelli, and Paul were holdovers from Monday's hike, but Sam Moskowitz and his mustache were along this time. Also three others he'd had seen in the chow hall and on the rafts, but hardly knew: Louis Field, a man with an eagle's beak nose; Iona Schmidt, a woman in her late fifties with auburn hair pulled into a severe bun and a stern face; and Rabin Hetch, a perky blond who looked to be in her thirties, but had to be at least fifty-five to be on the Elderhostel, unless she had an older roommate.

"Notice the outhouses up there?" Carmel Graves asked, pointing with her walking stick. "I think the boys are on the right and the girls are on the left, but it probably makes no difference. May I be so indelicate as to suggest you use them before we start off through the woods to grandmother's house?"

When everyone had taken her advice, Carmel led the way up the trail. Kelli and Valerie and Paul followed. Then the mustachioed Sam Moskowitz, the guy who had taken Howard's Jaguar out for a spin.

So what was that about?

Jim motioned Dodee to go ahead of him.

Was there some connection between Sam and the explosives? Like maybe Howard had really picked up the Jag in Washington, ferried explosives down here, and the loan to Sam was actually a clandestine handoff?

He adjusted the straps on his backpack and fell in behind Dodee.

But if that was the case, why kill Howard?

"Remember," Carmel called from the head of the line, "if you need a rest let me know, or ask about a bit of flora or fauna and I'll stop for that."

Unless Howard had already come under the suspicion of the FBI because of the car blowing up in Washington. Then once Sam had the explosives, why keep Howard around?

"I gotta say my hiker's prayer," Paul said, turning to give them a crooked smile. "Lord, you pick 'em up and I'll put 'em down."

Of course, that kind of thinking could get him conjuring up conspiracies everywhere. But if, on the off chance, it were true, then the question became not why Howard was killed, but how Sam had accomplished it?

Carmel stopped beside a rotten log alongside the path.

"We're on part of the Appalachian Trail now and different volunteer groups maintain sections of it. I'm captain of a group that takes care of a five mile section forty miles north of here." She tapped her walking stick on the log. "I don't know if this tree blocked the path at one time or not, but if it had, volunteers would have moved it off."

"How much work does that entail?" asked the perky Rabin Hetch.

"Moving the tree?"

"No, maintaining the trail."

"Oh, a few weekends a year."

"And they have volunteers to take care of the whole trail?" the stern-faced Iona Schmidt asked.

"I think so."

"Kelli and I belong to a group that takes care of a section in West Virginia," Valerie said. "Near where we grew up."

"How long is the trail?" Rabin asked.

"Twenty-one hundred and sixty miles, from Georgia to Maine. We'll be covering five miles of it today."

Sam turned to Carmel. "Have you hiked it?"

"I'm still working on it. I'm about half done." She tapped her walking stick on the fallen tree again. Lichen, moss and small plants grew out of it. "We call this a nurse log. When one falls and rots on the ground, it supplies nutrients for the next generation to renew the forest. And I was thinking this little spot here ..." She dug her hiking stick into the log, pulled away some bark where it met the ground, and exposed some scrambling bugs. "Ah yes. Know what these are?"

"Wood roaches?" Jim asked.

"Right, we have a family of wood roaches. They eat decaying wood, but I don't believe any living thing can digest wood. These guys get around that by having bacteria and protozoa in their stomachs that digest the wood for them. But the young are not born that way. So if you are a wood roach baby, how do you get the bacteria and protozoa you need to survive?"

"Find some wood that has the bacteria?" Valerie asked. "You eat the feces of the adults to introduce it into your system. That's why they have a nuclear family. Both males and the females share parental duty. In order to grow they have to shed their exoskeletons along with their stomachs. Every time they do, guess what happens? They have to introduce the bacteria all over again."

Paul's face spread in a crooked grin. "Is that where that famous expression comes from, eat shit or die?"

They started off, again, up the winding trail.

The waxing sun defeated the last of the lingering nighttime chill and, combined with the exertion of the climb, brought on the heat of the day. The next time Carmel stopped them, Jim took off his jacket and stuffed it in his backpack.

"This is a flame azalea," she said. "I pointed them out to those of you who were with me on Monday. But see this little animal here?" She touched a glossy growth on the leaves. "This is a fungus gall. It's sort of a hijacker that forces the azalea to contribute to its growth."

"Does it kill the plant?" perky Rabin asked.

"No, it doesn't seem to. But if you're thirsty and the gall is fresh, you can eat it." She pointed to a tree fifteen feet down the slope with sawtooth leaves. "There's another American Chestnut."

They continued up the trail and a half hour later broke out onto a meadow with a steep grassy slope leading up to a hilltop framed against the blue sky.

"This is Siler Bald Meadow," Carmel said, "and you'll be happy to know it's lunch time. We can either eat here, which is the highest point on our hike, or we can eat at the top of Silar Bald Mountain"–she pointed her walking stick up the steep, grassy slope–"which then becomes the highest point on the hike and where we'll have a great view. Or some can stay with Babs and some can go."

Jim nodded. "I'm going." He turned to Dodee. "You coming?"

"Wherever you go, sweetheart."

"Charge."

He took off, leading the way up the steep, grassy slope. The conqueror storming the castle.

"Why are you in such a hurry?" Dodee asked.

"I want to be king of the hill."

Two hundred yards later, storming the castle was more like crawling to the keep. And after a thousand feet of tough going, chest heaving, feet turning to lead, he was having a tough time keeping the mountain goats–Valerie, Kelli and Carmel–at bay.

He finally topped the crest and stood with his hands on his hips, too weak to raise them over his head, too busy sucking in air to shout "king of the hill." He looked down to see a granite plaque cemented into a rock outcropping.

Siler Bald, El. 5216 Ft.

Sonofabitch.

No wonder he was huffing and puffing.

At this elevation he was back in Denver.

TWENTY-THREE

He lumbered across to a rock outcropping sticking further out of the ground, sat down in a controlled collapse, still gasping, and stared down at foothills spread out before him like a sun-ripened green carpet splotched with moving cloud shadows. The skeletal trunk of a lone tree stood on the grassy knob as a testament to the storms of winter and the droughts of summer, and a lone bird perched among the leaves of its one living branch and sang a song of life. A cool breeze picked it up and broadcast it to an amphitheater of higher mountains surrounding him on the remaining three quadrants of the compass.

He closed his eyes and said a little prayer of thanks for making it to the highest spot on—

He snapped them open to see Carmel taking a picture of Valerie and Kelli posed beside the skeletal tree.

"You did say this was the highest spot on the hike?"

"From here on it's all down hill."

Dodee rounded the crest and sat down beside him. "That was more of a climb than I thought."

"You're telling me. We're back in Denver." Her big blues turned to him. "Elevation-wise. We're back up to fifty-two hundred feet. No wonder we're out of breath."

She smiled. "Thank God. I thought it might have something to do with our ages."

Then the bald head of Sam Moskowitz came into view, nose flaring above his black mustache as he struggled the last few steps, his breathing hard, his skin pale.

"You okay?" Jim said.

The man plopped down next to him, held one hand over his chest, and waved the other in front of his mouth as he tried to catch his breath.

"Came up too fast. I have a slight heart condition." He

reached into his pants pocket and came out with a small plastic container. "Always carry some nitroglycerine tablets with me." He pried the top off, stared into the distance for a few moments as his breathing eased and the color returned to his face, then shrugged, recapped the case, and put it back in his pocket. "Think I'm okay." He smiled at Jim. "But if I suddenly keel over, stick one in my mouth."

Paul came over the rise and stood round-shouldered, hands on hips, jaw hanging open as he puffed away. "I kept telling the Lord that if he'd pick 'em up, I'd put them down, but darned if I didn't feel like I was picking up mine and His too."

Jim turned back to Sam.

"You sure you're all right?" The last thing he wanted to do was fish pills out of the man's pocket and stick them in his mouth. "Maybe you ought to take a nitroglycerine now."

"Nope. I'm okay," Sam said, pulling his brown bag out of his backpack.

"Now that's the best idea since we started," Dodee said, digging out her own lunch.

"I'll agree with that," Carmel said, grabbing a seat beside Kelli and Valerie on the rock outcropping that stretched in a straight line across the hill, like they were all spectators in the first row of a theater watching cloud shadows play on the foothills below.

Jim bit into his ham and cheese sandwich and chewed it slowly to let the flavor swirl around his taste buds. "It was worth it."

"What's that?" Paul asked.

"The climb up here, just to sit and have lunch on top of the world."

"Well, look who's here," Dodee said.

Joppa Harp plodded into view, waddling from side to side on wide-spaced legs. "I should have stayed down with the people in the meadow."

"I thought you did."

"I got half way up and it seemed just as hard to go back

down as it did to go on. So I decided to make it if it killed me, and it damn near did."

Jim looked up at her. "Sorry you didn't go home this morning rather than tomorrow morning?"

"You're leaving tomorrow?" Carmel asked from the other end of the line. "Not going rafting?"

Dodee snuggled next to Jim to make room and Joppa sank on the rock next to her.

"I've got things that need doing. Have to leave in the morning."

Jim looked down the line to Carmel. "So how many stayed down in the meadow?"

"Three or four. Babs is with them."

"Seems like we have different plants up here than back on The Mountain," Valerie said. "Difference in elevation?"

"About a thousand feet difference," Carmel said. "For each thousand feet it's like shifting the climate two hundred and fifty miles north. The Mountain is on the border of North Carolina and Georgia, so the extra elevation here puts us up around Virginia. But we're way north of that if we compare it to the weather on the coast. It's really noticeable in the fall. The leaves will be green at the lower elevation, be in full fall colors at halfway up, and already fallen up here."

Kelli stood up, raised her arms, and took a deep breath. "The air smells so clean and fresh up here compared to Washington, D. C."

"That's because it is so clean and fresh up here," Valerie said. "We haven't mucked it up at this elevation yet. Give us time."

"You know, Dodee and I had an environmentalist on one of our Elderhostels, Santee Cooper in South Carolina." He finished his sandwich and opened a small bag of chips. "One of the things she said really got to me. Suppose, she said, there is a point of no return in our environment. Suppose there is a point at which the hothouse gases and car exhausts and smokestack toxins change our climate for all time? Like a snowball hurtling down a mountain, building up momentum and mass until it can no longer be stopped. It might not affect us, but what about our children and grandchildren?"

"So what did she think?" Carmel asked.

"She said she didn't know if there was a point of no return, but that if there were, wouldn't it be better to quit studying the thing to death and start doing something to stop the snowball before we reached it?"

Out on the skeletal tree the lone bird hopped around on the one live branch and sang out in the pure joy of freedom.

Paul balled up his brown bag and stuffed it into his pack. "Anyone hear what kind of weather we're supposed to have for our rafting trip tomorrow?"

"According to our local station, WHLC, it's supposed to be fair," Carmel said. "Oh, and we made the news."

"We?"

"The Mountain campus. A local reporter was talking about Howard Leslie's death and speculating that it might have been murder."

Paul stood up and stared down the line at her. "How could it be murder? It was out in the middle of the woods."

"I don't know. I'm just telling you what he said."

"What else did he say?"

"That fake FBI agents showed up and when they found out the sheriff was already there, they beat a hasty retreat."

"What about the real FBI?" Jim asked, standing up as well. "Did they say anything about that?"

Carmel nodded. "The newscaster said they showed up yesterday, but he couldn't find out if they were here to investigate Howard or the fake FBI agents."

Paul palmed up his hands. "I don't see how they could call it murder. You see anything that made you believe it was murder?"

She shrugged. "I'll leave that to the sheriff. He and his people searched the area and if there's something to find, I'm sure he'll come up with it."

"Did he say anything about a laptop on the radio?" Jim asked.

"Just that the sheriff found some CDs in Howard's things, but they contained only music."

Jim stared out at the distant mountains.

So much for the CD theory.

"I found some CDs." Sam Moskowitz nodded. "In the Jaguar. I found them in the glove compartment under the rental agreement and assumed they had been left by the previous renter. I was going to ask Howard about them, but"–he turned down his lips and shrugged.

"Did you tell the FBI about them?" Dodee asked.

"I didn't tell anybody."

"Were they still in the Jaguar when the FBI took it?" Jim asked.

Sam combed his mustache with his fingernails and wrinkled his brow. "To tell you the truth, I forgot about 'em. Someone had written on them with a felt tip pen and I assumed they were music. You know, like maybe they copied them from Napster or something."

"Did you check them out?"

"I don't have a CD player."

"Where are they now?" Joppa asked.

"In my cabin. Think I should have turned them over to the sheriff or the FBI?"

"Jim has a CD player in his car," Dodee said.

"Maybe we could check them out when we get back?" Jim asked.

"Sure," Sam said.

Paul folded his arms, emphasizing his round shoulders. "I still don't see how anyone can call it murder."

"Look." Joppa pointed down to the meadow as the other group of Elderhostelers trailed out of the woods, those who had started from the other end, and joined those who stayed with Babs. "They going to come up here?"

"If we watch," Carmel said, "maybe we'll see."

"Can I go back with them?" Joppa asked, struggling to her feet. "It's shorter, isn't it? I'm all tuckered out from climbing up here."

"No problem, just as long as we let Josie and Duke know. And Babs so she's not looking for you when she's sweeping the end of the line."

They packed up their trash and Dodee got Jim to pose next to the lone tree and against various scenic backgrounds.

"I need to get a sense of the place. Maybe I'll turn something into a painting when I get back to my studio."

"Why do you need me in the photos?"

"Maybe it's you I want to paint."

"Then maybe you want me to strip down to the buff."

"Nobody would buy your buff." She snapped the case on the camera. "I need you to give perspective to the landscape."

"Oh, well, glad to be of use. I might just as well be a park bench."

She wrapped both her arms around one of his and gazed down at the foothills. "What a beautiful day. Look at the clouds, all swirls and whirls, and puppy dog twirls."

He glanced at the sky and down into her big blues. "Swirls, whirls, and puppy dog twirls? What are puppy dogs twirls?"

She shrugged. "I needed something to make it rhyme."

He gazed back up at the swirls, whirls, and puppy dog twirls painted against the blue sky as the straight white line of a jet's contrail bisected it.

He pointed to it. "You know, lady, all the Wright brothers anniversary hoopla last year brought back a memory of when I was a little boy. I remember my older sister pointing out a plane to me, going through a lot of effort to make sure I saw it. I was so young I just accepted it, but now I realize a plane was still a rare thing in those days. Today you can hardly look up in the sky without seeing some evidence of their passing, if not the actual animal itself."

"Know what this tells me, dearie?"

"Dearie?"

"That, dearie, you're much older than I," she sang, barely keeping the tune.

He patted her on the rear end and glanced over the countryside once more. "Anything pique your interest up here enough to want to paint it?"

She turned and stared up at him. "I'm looking at it."

"Very funny." But he bent and kissed her, lips soft against his, the taste of her warming him all over. Then he took her hand, holding tight, and they started off the mountain.

They met Josie Blue two hundred feet down the grassy slope, leading the other hikers on the way up. Quentin puffed along fifty feet behind, sweat on his brow, and Hallis fifty feet behind him.

"Is it worth it?" she asked.

Jim nodded. "Worth every step."

"Thank God. I don't want to die for nothing."

Behind her came Elcee.

"Where's Aunt Debra?" Jim asked.

"That traitor." She put her hands on her hips and gazed down toward the meadow. "The only reason I started up this damn hill was because she was adamant about coming up here. Now I find out she stayed behind." The clear brown eyes turned to him, freckles sprinkled about her nose. "Well, I made it this far and I'm not turning back."

"It's worth the climb," Dodee said. "The view is forever."

"Thanks." She ran a hand through her soft yellowish-brown curls. "I needed that little bit of encouragement."

They continued down to the meadow where the hikers who had stayed behind with Babs sat talking with those who had come up from the other end. Duke sat next to Babs, Aunt Debra next to her.

"Your niece is calling you a traitor for not climbing the hill," Jim said.

"I changed my mind," she said, opening her brown bag. "A woman my age has that privilege."

Tristin Fontaine wandered out of the woods and sat down next to her, his pale face flushed and sweaty, as if exhausted from the long climb. And in spite of, or maybe because of, his new hiking boots and trail clothes, not nearly so new, he seemed out of place, this seventy-something man who signed up late for the Elderhostel.

So why was he here?

TWENTY-FOUR

The hike down ended at a sign posted on the side of the highway announcing it to be a crossing point of the Appalachian Trail. Naturally everyone had to pose next to it. Jim stood with Dodee while Sam took the picture with her camera. Then they piled into the van and started the long haul back.

He fell asleep five minutes into it and woke as they turned off Highway 23 and started up the winding road toward camp.

"I guess I conked out," he whispered to Dodee

"No guess, sweetheart. You were gone."

"And you didn't wake me up when we passed the Dairy Queen?"

"I had other things on my mind," she said.

"You okay?"

She leaned close and whispered in his ear. "I have to go to the bathroom like crazy."

He smiled at her. "Thank you for sharing that with me."

"But I want to know about the CDs."

Right, he had forgotten about them.

He looked around the van for Sam's bushy mustache and bald head, and found him in the seat behind.

"You want to check out those CDs sometime?"

"Walk me to my cabin and we can check them out now."

"Sounds good."

Dodee gave him a little gig in the side. "I said I want to check them out with you, sweetheart."

"We have to listen to them in the car, lady, right outside the back door of the lodge. You can meet us there."

"Oh, right." She caressed his side where she'd gigged him and smiled. "Sorry."

They turned off the road at *The Mountain Retreat and Learning Center* sign and he caught a glimpse of a green SUV parked beside it, and an even shorter glimpse of two men in the front seat.

He had seen a green SUV the night the phony FBI guys took Howard's laptop. A coincidence? Or were they back?

They passed the dining hall, pulled up the hill to the upper parking lot, and everyone piled out. Dodee strode straight for the second floor entrance while Jim and Sam headed down the hill.

Jim stopped at his Avalon and pulled off his backpack. "Might as well leave this here," he said, setting it on the trunk. "You told Howard you always wanted to buy a Jaguar. What do you think of it now that you've driven one?"

"Impressive." They continued down the hill. "When I get home I might count up all my nickels and pennies and see if it's prudent to buy one." He shrugged. "Well, forget prudence. The Jaguar is sex for the senior citizen. The question is, how much is sex selling for these days?"

They veered off the road at a wooden cabin, a duplex with a common balcony, painted gray on the outside like the other buildings in the compound.

"You have a roommate?" he asked.

"Paul Fetgatter. Two old bachelors."

"You're not married?"

"I'm a widower, Paul's divorced."

Sam opened the door for him and Jim entered a room with knotty wood walls and ceilings. A rug covered the floor around twin beds, clothes stacked on top of blue bedspreads.

Sam followed him in and staggered a step, throwing up his arms. "What the heck happened here? Why are our clothes piled on top of the beds?"

"You didn't leave them this way?"

"Gosh, no. Paul's finicky as hell. And what is my suitcase doing open?" He picked it up from beside the bed and dangled it in his hand.

Jim glanced out the windows toward the road and to the woods, then back to the room. "Looks like someone's already searched the place and beaten us to the CDs."

Sam combed his mustache again, then pointed a finger at him. "Maybe not." He rushed to the head of the bed, bent down between it and a night table, and came up beaming with four CDs in his hand. "Knocked them off the table this morning when I was reaching for my alarm. Meant to pick them up, but I went to the bathroom and forgot."

The CDs were packed in individual clear plastic cases. Each had been labeled with a felt tip pen: *John Denver*; *Beatle Classics*; *Johnny Cash*; and *Chicago*.

He turned back to the windows.

If the guys who searched the place were the same ones who killed Howard for a laptop, what would they do for the CDs?

"What do you think?" Sam asked.

"I think we ought to call the sheriff." He stared at the CD cases again, then gripped them by their edges. "Of course, if there had been any fingerprints we've probably already destroyed them"

Sam's brow wrinkled. "Hadn't thought about that."

"You have a plastic bag we can carry them in, just in case we haven't completely contaminated them?"

Sam dumped a pair of shoes out of a plastic grocery bag and Jim wrapped the CDs in it and looped the handles around his wrist. He snapped back to the window at the sound of a car's engine and saw a green SUV pull up outside.

"Oh shit."

"What's the matter?"

"The phony FBI guys are back. C'mon, we gotta get the hell out of here."

He rushed out with Sam at his side and ran for the woods in back of the cabin.

"Stop," someone yelled as a car door slammed.

"Stop," called a second voice, "FBI."

"What do we do?" Sam asked.

"Keep running."

He swung around a mountain laurel as a shot rang out and shifted into high gear, swinging south, paralleling the road towards the lodge and the office.

Another shot, this time emphasized by a slug slamming into a tree near his head.

Great, just great.

He dodged around bushes and trees, trying to put obstacles between him and the phonies with Sam gasping along behind him.

"Oh man, oh man. I can't take much more of this."

"Stop, FBI," the voice shouted again, punctuated by another gunshot. "All we want are the CDs."

Yeah, right.

Another shot rang out and he heard a soft thud, like it connected with soft flesh, and swung around to Sam. "You all right?"

"Oh man, this isn't doing my heart any good."

Behind them came the sound of elephants stomping through the bush.

"C'mon." He spun around and got slapped in the face by a witch hazel.

Great, just absolutely great.

He took off running again with Sam chugging after him.

"Oh man, oh man."

He charged through a mountain laurel, glanced back, and the ground suddenly fell out from under him. He snatched at bushes and branches, but it all slipped between his fingers as he plunged down a rocky bank and slammed—crotch, chest, and face—onto a horizontal log.

He had the breath knocked out of him and gasped for air as the lights dimmed and threatened to go out, and became dimly aware of Sam crashing about above him and smashing onto the same log, rocking it like a hobby horse.

When he finally sucked air back into his lungs, and the pain in his crotch subsided, he opened his eyes to see that he lay spread-eagle on a tree growing out of a cliff. Down below, with only fifty or sixty feet of air in between, jagged boulders grinned up at him.

He heard a groan and saw Sam further out on the limb, legs on one side, arms on the other, eyes bulging out of a pasty face, the added weight hobby horsing the tree up and down. Beyond him the trunk curved upward, its branches reaching for the sun. But back the other way, the roots tying them to the cliff threatened to weigh anchor at any time and cast them onto the rocky shoals below.

And Josie Blue's warning came back to him in a rush.

"Do not go wondering around behind the lodge or the cabins where the trees and underbrush might hide a step off into the great beyond."

Absofuckinglutely great.

TWENTY-FIVE

Somewhere up above elephants stomped around in the bushes while somewhere a few feet from his ear someone whispered.

"Nitroglycerine."

"What?" he whispered back.

"Need my nitroglycerine. My heart's acting up."

"Where is it?"

"In my pants pocket. Can you reach it for me?"

Jim lifted his head and stared at Sam, draped across the tree trunk with his legs on one side, head and arms on the other, bulging eyes staring back up at him from a bleached-white face. He shifted his gaze to his own hands clinging to the bark in a death grip, the plastic bag of CDs still dangling from his wrist.

He was supposed to let go of the one thing that separated him from a sixty-foot drop to a rocky death, scramble further out on a limb that ain't anchored too well in the first place, while guys with guns were ready to blast his ass at the first opportunity, and reach into another man's pants pocket?

Oh yeah.

Had to be one of the high points of his life.

He released his death grip, shinnied three feet further out on the swaying limb, shifted the plastic bag from one wrist to the other–sonofabitch if he'd lose it now–and gingerly reached into Sam's pocket.

"The other one."

"What?"

"On the other side."

That's it. Tell him right now.

Sam, you is going to die.

He shinnied a little further out, the tree really swaying now as it sloped downward toward the valley of death, and reached across Sam's rear end–if the sonofabitch broke gas he was dead–and slipped his hand into the pocket.

"It's in a plastic bottle. Hurry."

Hurry?

He was doing Sam the favor of his life and now he was supposed to hurry? On the other hand, if he didn't hurry there might not be a life to favor.

He groped in the pocket, wondering which side Sam hung his guys on, then felt the container and yanked it out before he got snake bit. He had trouble twisting the top off–-a childproof cap, of course–but finally got it open and shook out a pill. He reached down and for one horrible moment thought he'd have to stick the thing in the man's mouth, but Sam took it in his hand.

"Thanks," he whispered in a rasping voice.

"Don't mention it."

Jim stuck the plastic bottle into his own pocket and looked down at the rocks below–jagged rocks below–way down below–and shook his head.

Sonofabitch. If he had just minded his own business–advice he so readily handed out to Dodee–he wouldn't be in this mess.

He craned his neck and studied the cliff face. Not a sheer drop-off like a rock face on Mount Everest; more like a sixty or seventy degree angle with bushes and handholds. Going up wouldn't be bad. He could see where to put his hands and feet. But if he reached a dead end and had to come back down, it could be with one long step to eternity.

A crack rent the silence and the tree's slope got a little more slopey.

On the other hand, staying put wasn't a great option either.

"I'm going to shinny back to the base of the tree," he whispered. "Wait until I get there, then follow me."

"Then what?"

"Then we climb the cliff."

Sam's wild eyes stared him. "Screw that. I'm staying here until help comes."

"Two things. The help that's up there is carrying a gun. And I think this tree is ready to let go."

The eyes blinked at him. "Okay. I'm right behind you."

Jim inched backwards along the trunk, the shinnying complicated by broken branches and stubby ends, and by the tree swaying and groaning with each movement, but it dampened as he neared the cliff. When he reached it, he sat up, swung around, grabbed a small pine and a rock-hold for support, and gingerly climbed to his feet. He glanced down at the roots tenuously anchoring the tree, and immediately climbed off onto the rock face.

"Okay," he called in a stage whisper. "Swing around and straddle the trunk."

Sam swung around and straddled the trunk, the black mustache vivid against his ashen face, and shinnied toward Jim, inch by inch, with shaking hands. When he made it, Jim reached down and helped him struggle to his feet.

"What do we do now?"

"We climb out."

"I can't climb all the way up there."

"It's only about ten feet. Follow in my footsteps."

"And suppose you fall?"

"Find another footstep."

"I could wait until you get help."

"It might be a long wait. Suppose the phonies get me? You could spend the night down here before anyone knew you were missing."

"Okay, okay. I'll follow in your footsteps. Just don't get too far ahead."

Jim gazed up at the top of the cliff.

Ten feet?

It looked like a hundred.

He found a handhold and a place to put his foot and moved up. He found another, but was on the wrong foot and had to do a little hop to shift feet, then moved up again. He found more handholds and kept on moving. He paused to watch Sam's trembling hands snatch onto a rockhold two paces behind, then looked at his own hands to see they weren't all that steady either. He started up again, but froze when he heard rustling in the bushes above.

"Why are you stopping?" came a voice from down below.

Muffled voices from above.

"Why are you—"

"Someone's up here," he whispered.

"Mr. Dandy," a male voice called out.

Screw, they knew his name.

Then a woman's voice. "Sweetheart."

He let out a long sigh of relief and clamped down on his sphincter muscle to keep from embarrassing himself.

"We're down here," Sam called.

The branches of a mountain laurel parted and Jim saw the flame-red hair and freckled face of Billy Riley. Some more branches parted and Dodee's cornflower eyes and wheaten hair came into view.

"What are you doing down there?"

"Just hanging around."

"That's not funny."

"What the hell do you think we're doing down here? We were running from the phonies and fell in a hole."

"Are you hurt?"

"I don't think so."

"What phonies?" Billy asked.

"Hey, how about letting me climb onto solid ground before you begin the interrogation."

"Sorry. Need a hand?"

"In a minute."

He climbed up a few more feet then took Billy's hand, clambered over the side, and sat on the ground. A few seconds later Sam plopped down next to him.

"You got my nitroglycerine?"

Jim found it in his pocket and handed it over.

"What phonies are you were talking about?" Billy asked. He was dressed in a shirt and tie again, his short stature and slight build giving him the appearance of a cub reporter.

"The phony FBI guys."

"Oh, wow, that's great."

"Why were you running from them?" Dodee asked.

Sam cocked a forefinger and thumb in the form of a gun. "Because they were shooting at us."

"Oh, wow, that's great."

Jim raised his hand to Dodee. She took it and he got to his feet, surprised to find he was a little unsteady.

"A slug slammed into a tree not three feet from my head."

"Wow, that's great."

"No, it wasn't great." Jim glared at him. "We damn near got killed."

"Oh, right. Sorry."

Dodee put her hands on his shoulders and stared up at him. "You okay, sweetheart?"

"Yeah, I think I'll live."

"Then we slipped into a hole," Sam said. "If we hadn't landed on a tree growing out of the cliff, we'd have fallen three hundred feet to our deaths."

Jim nodded. "Damn near did that anyway."

She combed his hair with her hand. "Didn't you remember Josie telling us not to wander behind the cabins—"

"Don't start, lady. When you got killers after you, you don't have a lot of choice." He shook his head. "Didn't you see those guys?"

"We heard some shooting, then a car came racing up the hill. That's when we came searching for you. What I don't understand is why were they after you?"

Jim held up the plastic bag still wrapped around his wrist. "The CDs. Somehow they found out about them."

"Right." Sam nodded. "They drove up to the cabin and

started shooting at us."

"Wow, that's great."

Jim spun around and glared at Billy again and the redheaded man slapped a hand over his mouth. He turned back to Dodee.

"They knew Sam had the CDs, and they knew we were at the cabin. In fact, they had already searched the place and come up empty."

"That's because I had knocked them off the night table this morning, and they were on the floor under my bed."

"So they waited for us down the hill and when we got back from our hike, they came after us. You know what that means?"

He scanned their faces.

"Someone on the hike had to have tipped them off."

TWENTY-SIX

Dodee's big blues stared back at Jim. "You know what you're saying?"

"Yes, I do."

Billy stuck out a hand and leaned against a tree. "I don't. Like what are you saying?"

Jim shrugged and shook his head.

Without hard facts he didn't want Billy broadcasting his suspicions to the world.

But that didn't stop Dodee. "It means that someone on the Elderhostel has to be working with the phony agents."

Jim glared at her. "We don't know that."

"Then who else would have tipped them off about the CDs?"

"How do you figure?" Billy asked.

"We don't know that."

"Sam only told us about the CDs this morning."

"That's right, up on the mountain." Sam got to his feet. "Jim said something about the sheriff finding CDs in Howard's room, and that's when I remembered I had taken them from the Jaguar. I never mentioned it before. Then when we got back here, the bad guys were waiting for us."

Dodee pointed with her thumb and forefinger together. "Someone had to have tipped them off."

"We don't know that."

"So it had to be someone on the hike, ergo"—Sam's eyes widened—"it must be an Elderhosteler." And he beamed as if proud of his own deduction.

Jim shook his head. "We... don't... know... that. These are all assumptions and there could be a more rational explanation. C'mon." He started trudging through the underbrush towards the road. "Before we jump to any more conclusions, let's see if there's anything on the CDs besides music."

"Cool." Billy followed along. "And if there is?"

"We call the sheriff."

"And if there isn't?"

"We call the sheriff. Those guys tried to kill us."

They started up the road toward the lodge and Billy fell into step with him, his red tie flopping over one shoulder.

"Who do you think it could be?"

Jim glanced at him. "You, too?"

"You know who I think?" Sam asked.

"I don't want to know."

"I do," Dodee said.

"Who switched groups so she wouldn't have to walk so far? Joppa Harp."

Jim turned to him as they reached his Avalon. "Don't go spreading rumors. If an Elderhosteler did contact the phonies, it could have been anyone up on that hill."

"Maybe," Sam said, "but would the bad guys have had time to search the cabin?"

Jim opened the car door. "She could have told everybody. Do we place them all under suspicion then?"

"Hey"—a smile lit up Bill's freckled face—"works for me."

Dodee shook her head. "Besides, if it had been Joppa, she would have used her satellite phone to tip off the phonies from up on the hill."

"Like phone the phonies?" Sam asked with a grin.

"And if she did that, she would have tagged along with us to avoid suspicion."

"Oooo-kay," Billy said, "so who do you figure—"

"Hello?" Jim held up the plastic bag. "We going to keep fooling around or do you want to listen to what's on these CDs?"

That shut them up.

He climbed into the car and shook out the CDs on the seat beside him. He opened the first CD, handling the case by the edges to keep from messing up any fingerprints, and fed it into the player.

The overture from *Chicago* came though the speakers followed by Catherine Zeta Jones singing about *All That Jazz*.

"Okay, sweetheart, we don't have to listen to the whole song."

"I like it. I bought the CD after seeing the movie."

"To quote somebody I know, 'Are we going to keep fooling around or do you want to see what's on these CDs?'"

"Okay, okay." He changed the tracks, going through all eighteen of them to make sure there was nothing out there but music before popping it out. The next CD had John Denver written on it, and that's who they heard. He followed with Johnny Cash and then the Beatles.

He shrugged. "So much for finding secret stuff."

"Then why were the bad guys shooting at you?" Billy asked.

He shrugged again and put the CDs back into the plastic bag.

"Yeah, why?" Sam asked, combing his bushy mustache.

Dodee pointed her thumb and forefinger again. "Because they didn't know what was on the CDs any more than we did, and they couldn't take the chance they might contain something incriminating."

"What do we do now?" Billy asked.

"We call the sheriff." Jim climbed out of the car and locked the door. "Tell him what happened and turn the CDs over to him. You got a cellphone?"

He shook his red head. "I've got one, but it doesn't pick up anything from here."

"There's an emergency phone in the office," Dodee said.

"Is it open?"

Billy jerked his thumb toward his Hyundai Tiburon in the upper parking lot. "I'm on my way to cover a dog-feud story in Highlands. Want me to call the sheriff and fill him in?"

"That would be good."

"Cool."

"What were you doing here anyway?"

"Oh wow, this is my big story. Since I was coming up here anyway, I thought I'd check on any new developments, but I didn't think I'd be in on a shooting. That's great. I mean, that's—Billy shrugged—"you know."

Jim turned to Sam. "You want to hold onto the CDs?" He palmed his hands to Jim. "Not me. I've been shot at one time too many this afternoon," he said, and headed down the hill toward his cabin.

Jim turned to Dodee. "They fit into your purse?"

"You mean so I can get shot?" she asked, but stuffed them in her purse all the same.

"Well," Billy said, "I gotta go." They walked to the upper parking lot and he climbed into his car. "Can I give you a ride somewhere?"

"We can walk," Jim said.

They watched Billy charge off for his dog feud in Highlands.

"We going down to the social hour?" Dodee asked.

He nodded. "I want to see who's there."

"Like Joppa Harp?"

"Like Joppa Harp."

They strolled hand in hand to the Heritage Room. He poured two glasses of wine while Dodee got two cups of popcorn. They made the exchange of a wine for a popcorn and went back outside to the rocking chair deck.

He glanced around for Joppa Harp and found her sitting at the end between two Elderhostelers whose faces he recognized, but whose names he didn't know. There were a lot of vacant seats, but none side by side, so Dodee sat near the door next to Elcee and Jim took a chair across the deck from her next to Quentin.

"See you made it back from the hike okay," the man said, a smile splitting his chocolate face.

"It was nip and tuck for a while." He looked up as Duke appeared in the doorway with a beer in his hand. "We seem to be light this evening. Are we missing people?"

Duke flicked his eyebrows and nodded. "A few got back early from the hike and went into Highlands. Maybe the others are worn out and decided to skip the social."

Hallis leaned forward to gaze at Jim. "You were right about the hike up Siler Bald. The view was worth every step."

"And some of us missed it," Elcee said from across the deck, rubbing a finger under her freckled nose so it pointed at her aunt.

"It's the privilege of a lady my age to change her mind," Aunt Debra said.

"Not after insisting her dutiful niece make the climb, thinking her aunt was following along."

Dodee smiled. "In a moment of exuberance, Jim charged up the hill like he was a trail blazer."

"I wanted to be the king of the hill. I was too, but it damn near killed me."

Hallis nodded. "So did Quentin. Tried to run up there in one fell swoop. Must be a testosterone thing."

"Not a testosterone thing," Quentin said, running his hand over his curly head. "Thought I could make it in one burst of energy then rest on the top. I just misjudged the distance and height."

One of the people sitting next to Joppa went inside and Jim moved down to the empty seat.

"How was the trip back?" he asked her.

"Okay, but I'm glad I didn't go the long way with you. That climb up to the top of the hill did me in. I came home and took a nap. How about you?"

"Like you said, it was a long hike, but it was mostly down hill so it wasn't too bad." He took a sip of wine and studied her. "When we got back we checked out the CDs Sam found."

Her eyebrows raised. "CDs?"

"Sam told us he found some CDs in Howard's Jaguar."

"Oh, right." She half turned in the chair. "What did you find?"

"Just music, the sound track from *Chicago*, John

Denver, Johnny Cash, and the Beatles."

"Nothing special then?"

He shook his head. "Did you happen to tell anyone about the CDs?"

"No, I had forgotten all about them." She bit her lip. "No, wait." Her large brown eyes stared at him a moment, then she nodded, jiggling her double chin. "I did, now that you mention it." She scanned the people on the deck. "Who was it? I can't remem—yes." She pointed toward three men coming down the steps, the round shouldered Paul Fetgatter, the short and mustached Sam Moskowitz, and the lanky Tristin Fontaine. "It was Tristin. Why? Wasn't I supposed to?"

"No reason not to, I guess." He watched the three men disappear into the Heritage Room. "Just that we have to turn the CDs over to the sheriff, and he'll ask who knew about them."

So did that narrow the field to Tristin?

Joppa half turned to him again. "But then you'd have to include everybody, I think, because I told him while we were riding back in the van."

He nodded.

So much for narrowing the field.

TWENTY-SEVEN

He and Dodee headed back up the hill to the lodge's Great Room after dinner. Birds were bedding down in the trees as the long June evening stretched out toward twilight. A small breeze carried a woodsy perfume. His stomach was full and Dodee's hand felt smooth and warm in his.

Only one thing nagged at him.

"I'm surprised the sheriff hasn't shown up."

"Maybe he was out when Billy called."

"And maybe Billy forgot."

She glanced over her shoulder, then wrapped both her arms around one of his and lowered her voice. "I noticed you talking to Joppa out on the porch. I didn't want to bring it up with everyone around at dinner, but what about—"

"Sam's theory that she tipped off the phonies? He's getting to be as bad as you."

"What do you mean?"

"Sticking his nose into police business."

"Oh. And who was it who wanted to find out what was on the CDs? And who was it who jumped at the first chance to sit down next to Joppa Harp? And who was it—"

"Okay, okay. I surrender."

"Are you going to tell me what she said or not?"

"Not." Than grunted as she gigged him in the side. "Okay, okay. I asked her if she mentioned the CDs to anyone. She said she told Tristin about them."

She twisted around to bring her big blues to bear on his face. "Right, Tristin, that figures because—"

"No, it doesn't figures because. I thought it did until she said she told him in the van on the way back. They could have all heard it."

They strolled on, side by side in each other's warmth, and he wondered how to refer to her in their relationship.

Girlfriend didn't quite fit the bill.

Lovers is what they were, but that didn't sound right. This is my lover?

Might as well call her his mistress, which would probably get him a gig in the side and a fist in the gut.

Significant other?

Too sterile.

The big blues turned up to him again. "You okay?"

"Yeah, why?"

"After falling halfway down the mountain?"

He smiled. "A lot better than falling all the way down the mountain. But I'm a bit drained physically from the climb back up and emotionally from hanging in the tree when I thought Sam was having a heart attack."

"What happened?"

He glanced around to make sure no one was within earshot, and told her about retrieving the bottle of nitroglycerine from Sam's pocket. "Don't tell anyone about that."

She grinned. "What's it worth?"

"I'll spank you if you do."

"You sure know how to turn a girl on."

They climbed the steps to the lodge entrance and stopped in the hall at the top of the stairs.

"You know," she said, "if you're tired, sweetheart, go back to the room. I'll stay and find out what's happening tomorrow."

He shook his head. "I'm not that tired."

The chairs in the Great Room had been arranged in a circle. A few people had already gathered, and Dodee sat down next to Babs and Duke Penny.

"Got another name for you," Duke said as Jim sat next to Dodee. "You know, first and last names. Like Jack Benny. How about Trader Jack."

"That's Trader Vic," Babs said, "and it's not a real person."

"No," he turned to her, "I knew someone named Trader Jack. Real first and last names. And to top it off, I was in the service with someone named Jack Trader." He turned to Dodee. "What do you think of that?"

"I think it's just Jim Dandy."

That brought smiles to Babs and Duke, but Jim only shook his head. "Don't encourage her. She's going to end up with a spanking."

"Promises, promises, sweetheart."

The room filled as Elderhostelers came in bunches.

Jim turned to the Pennys again. "What about this rafting trip tomorrow?"

"Ah," Duke said, flicking his eyebrows, "with the water as high as it is, it's going to be exciting."

"Not enough to worry about," Babs said.

"You guys keep saying that. It scares the hell out of me."

Josie Blue strode into the room. "Everybody here? All those who aren't here, raise your hand."

Valerie and Kelli immediately raised their hands; Paul, Aunt Debra, and Elcee joined them.

Josie hung his head. "Why do I keep walking into these things?" He used his index finger to start counting heads around the circle.

"Six, eighteen, twelve," Valerie said with a wink.

"Three, seven, twenty-two," Aunt Debra said.

Josie shook his head as he continued counting. "You're not helping."

"We're all here," Babs said, as he got halfway around the circle.

He kept his finger pointing as a marker and glanced at her. "Not kidding?"

She palmed up her hands. "We're all here."

"All right." He rubbed his hands together. "Tomorrow we raft down the Chattooga River. It's one of the most famous whitewater rivers in the country. It goes from wild to mild. We'll be on the less wild side, but with some challenging rapids and falls. Nothing is over class three, which you experienced on the Nantahala on Monday, with one exception. That's called the Bull Sluice. There is a place to portage around it, so when we get there we'll pull to shore and everybody can climb up on the rocks and look it over. Then it becomes your choice. You can either continue the portage to the downriver side or take the ride."

Elcee licked her lower lip and raised her hand. "What class is the Bull Sluice?"

"I believe it's a four. But you don't have to go over it."

"I'm goin'," Aunt Debra said, the seventy-something nodding her head as her niece rolled her eyes and everyone laughed.

Josie clapped his hands for attention. "Because the Chattooga is more challenging than the Nantahala, we'll be wearing helmets along with our PFDs. Safety is our primary objective. Any questions?"

"Yeah," Sam said with a smile. "How do I get out of this?"

"Well, that's a good question. No one has to go—"

"No, I'm just kidding. I'm going. I figure if it's set up for—have Elderhostelers done this before?"

"Many times."

"Well, if it's set up for Elderhostelers, how dangerous can it be?"

Jim nodded.

What Sam said was a nice thought, except they weren't putting on helmets for a stroll in the park.

Yeah, buddy.

"We won't have to pack a brown bag this trip," Josie said. "The outfitters will supply us with lunch along the way. And at the end of the trip, since we'll pull out late, we'll have a fried chicken picnic waiting for you. Also, we won't leave until mid-morning, ten-thirty. This will give you some free time to wander around or relax. The town of Highlands is just down the road with a lot of quaint shops if you're interested in that sort of thing."

"How far is it?" Elcee asked.

"Fifteen minutes," Louis Field said. "We went in this afternoon."

"One more bit of housekeeping," Josie Blue said. "On Friday morning after breakfast, we'll have what we call a no-sweat hike. We realize you'll be leaving right after lunch, which is included by the way, so we'll have a gentle hike to point out some more of the flora and fauna of the Appalachians. If you can't make it—we're aware some of you have long drives ahead and want to get on the road—we'll understand. But please, let us know so that we can account for you. Any questions?" He looked around the room, then nodded. "All right then, I'll turn this over to Babs and Duke who have some fun things to do."

"Yes," Babs said, standing up in the circle. "Remember how we kept pulling chairs out from under you the other day ? Well, we're not going to do that tonight."

"Instead," Duke said, standing up next to his wife, "we'd like to hear an anecdote from your life that you feel comfortable sharing. For instance, we had a man here once who told us that he let his beard grow when he went off on an extended fishing trip to Alaska. When he came back his fianceé gave him an ultimatum. Either he got rid of his beard or he got rid of her." Duke flicked his eyebrows. "He never saw the woman again."

A little ripple of laughter floated around the room.

"I'll start off," Babs said, "and then I'll pick someone to follow me. When I was a junior in college I started dating a man who I thought was refined and intelligent—"

"And handsome," Duke threw in, folding his hairy arms across his barrel chest and turning his head to give them a profile. "Don't forget about handsome."

"And ... not too terrible looking. So I invited this refined gentleman home to Sunday supper to meet my folks. Anyway, I was standing out on the lawn when this biker rolls up on a motorcycle, all dressed in leather with a Luftwaffe jacket and a German helmet. So I'm wondering who this lowlife is when he takes off the helmet, and it's this guy." She jerked her thumb at her husband. "It was like a Dr. Jekyll meet Mr. Hyde thing; like a different person altogether. So I wondered if I really wanted this guy to meet my folks." She took his hand. "But then he smiled and I knew I was lost."

Duke Penny flicked his eyebrows gave them all a big phony grin.

Jim shook his head. "With a smile like that, you should have introduced him to the guy who grew the beard."

"No, now that I've housebroken him, I think I'll keep him around," Babs said. "Okay, we need someone to start off and since you opened your mouth, Jim, why don't you go next."

"Me?" He glanced at Dodee.

She shook her head. "Don't look at me. She asked you."

He held out his hands. "I don't have anything."

"Well," Dodee said, imitating Duke's phony grin, "why don't you tell us about your swell name?"

"That's not funny."

"Go ahead," Babs said, "tell us about your name."

"There's nothing to tell. My mother named me James after her father, the only thing I ever faulted her for. No one in grade school seemed to make the connection with my last name, but ever since high school people have been making lame Jim Dandy jokes. I've heard them all. So I want to commend this group for not stooping so low as to make a game of someone's name."

Duke grinned. "Sounds like a Jim Dandy story to me."

"Right on," Paul said, his crooked smile twisting his face. "A Jim Dandy story on a Jim Dandy night."

"To a Jim Dandy group of people," Quentin said.

Jim held up his hands. "All right, all right."

"I have a name story," Elcee said, standing up, her posture finishing-school straight.

Babs nodded to her. "We'd love to hear it."

"My maiden name was Caron, and my real name is Leslie—

"She was named after her aunt," Aunt Debra said. "Her other aunt, not as good looking as me. We were all living together after the war, and to keep their names straight we called the baby, Leslie Catherine, and then by her initials, LC. The name stuck and became Elcee."

"Thank you so much, Aunt Debra."

"Well, I had to explain it, dear."

"Anyway, my maiden name was Caron, and in school and at work I used Leslie, so I had the same name as the dancer and movie star, Leslie Caron."

Jim felt a hand on his shoulder and turned to see the sheriff who motioned toward the door.

"Then when I got married, darned if my husband didn't give me the name of another movie star."

Jim tapped Dodee on the arm and headed after the sheriff.

"Now my name is same as an old time movie star, Leslie Howard."

Jim stopped at the door and stared back at the woman.

TWENTY-EIGHT

Jim turned to Dodee. "Her last name is Howard?"

She nodded as she followed the sheriff out the front door.

"You knew that? Why didn't you tell me?"

"It's on her nametag."

Gordon Grigory, one of the real FBI agents from the day before, waited outside, along with Jonesy, the sheriff's deputy, who was holding a three cell flashlight

"Mr. Dandy and Ms. Swisher, right?" the Sheriff asked, turning to them. "Billy Riley tells me you have some CDs for us?"

Jim turned to Dodee who took the plastic bag out of her purse and handed it to the sheriff who in turn passed it to the FBI agent.

"We put them in the bag," Jim said, "in case there were any fingerprints."

"Mind telling me how you came by them?" Gordon Grigory asked.

"We were on a hike up Siler Bald when Sam Moskowitz mentioned that he had found them in the glove compartment of the red Jaguar."

"He *found* them?"

Jim went through the story of Sam trying out the Jaguar and coming across the CDs in the glove compartment.

Grigory turned to the Sheriff. "Let's get him out here."

"I'll go," Jonesy said, heading for the Great Room.

"They only contain music," Jim said. "We checked them out on my car's CD player."

"I understand someone shot at you?" Sheriff Graham asked.

The door opened and Sam came out.

"You took these CDs out of the Jaguar?" Grigory asked.

"How come you didn't tell us that when we picked up the keys?"

Sam's lips and bushy mustache turned down. "It didn't cross my mind. I thought they were just music CDs."

"And someone shot at you this afternoon?"

Jim nodded. "The two men from Monday night who claimed they were FBI agents."

"They were after the CDs," Sam said. "Searched my room and everything."

Jonesy crossed his arms. "How can you be sure they were after the CDs?"

"Why else would they shoot at us?" Jim asked. "A slug slammed into a tree six inches from my head."

"Think you can find the tree?" Sheriff Graham asked.

"Maybe, but not in the dark. Where were you earlier? They shot at us this afternoon."

"This afternoon?" The sheriff's brow wrinkled. "Billy Riley only called it in an hour ago."

"Billy Riley, that's the radio newsman?" Agent Grigory asked.

"Yep. Probably trying to protect a story scoop."

The agent turned to Jim. "How come you didn't call it in yourself."

"Cellphones won't reach out of here and there's only one phone for emergency use in the Center's office."

"And you didn't think this was an emergency?"

"I didn't know if the office was open. Billy was on his way to Highlands and offered to call. I assumed he'd do it when he got there."

Sheriff Graham glanced up as the door opened. He waited while Quentin and Hallis came out and headed down the hill toward their cabin. "Riley mentioned running into some of your group in Highlands. Anything there?"

Jim shrugged.

Grigory chewed on the side of his thumb for a moment. "What about the false agents? Can you give us a description?"

"They were the same ones who were here Monday night.

One was pasty white with a shock of brown hair–"

"That was agent Smith," Dodee said.

"–and the other had Hispanic coloring, black hair and eyes, overweight–"

"His name was Brown."

Grigory's gaze shifted to the sheriff.

The man nodded. "That's what we got. Anything else we can do here tonight?"

Grigory turned as the door opened again and the rest of the Elderhostelers poured out, the meeting in the Great Room apparently over. "I guess we can wrap it up." He turned Jim. "You be here tomorrow?"

"In the morning."

"We leave at ten-thirty for whitewater rafting," Dodee said.

Jim nodded and forced himself to keep a straight face. "Of course, I could always skip it if that would be of help."

Grigory shook his head. "Might want you to show us that tree with the slug in it, but we can get out here before ten."

Jim nodded again.

So much for that great idea of skipping the rafting trip.

"That's it, then?" Jonesy asked.

"Appreciate you folks keeping quiet about this," the sheriff said. "Thanks for your help."

The three men descended the steps and veered off toward the parking lot.

Sam turned to Jim. "What do you think?"

"I think I'm glad they didn't want us to go looking for that tree in the middle of the night. I've had enough hiking for one day."

Dodee nodded. "Me, too. I'm ready for bed."

"Me three." Sam clumped down the steps. "I'm going back to my cabin. See you all in the morning."

Jim watched him head down the hill then held the door for Dodee as they went inside.

"Wait a minute," he said, hearing voices in the Great

Room. "I want to see if Elcee's still here."

"You go ahead," she said with a yawn. "I've had enough for one day. I'll meet you in the room."

He followed the voices and peeked into the small kitchen.

"Hi, Jim," Babs said, drying the coffee pot. "We'll have everything ready for you to switch on in the morning."

He nodded. "I thought maybe Elcee might be here."

"I think she already left," Duke said.

Jim checked the balcony, but no one was out there either.

Any questions about her name would have to wait until morning.

"What did the sheriff want?" Duke asked.

Jim held out a hand and let it fall. "Just had some more questions about the other night. See you tomorrow."

He went down to the room.

"Are you as worn out as I am?" Dodee asked, emerging from the bathroom in a pink nightgown.

"Even more so, but I've got to take a shower. After falling through those trees and crawling around in the brush, I feel like I've got creeping things on me."

"Should I wait up, sweetheart?"

He stuffed his shirt in his laundry bag. "Not for me."

"What was that business about Elcee?"

"Think about it." He pulled off his pants and stuffed them in the laundry bag as well. "Her real name is Leslie. Leslie Howard, Howard Leslie."

"Her name is the reverse of Howard's?"

"You really are sleepy."

"I don't see—"

He grabbed his shaving kit and faced her. "We've been assuming all this time that someone wanted to kill Howard."

"They did a pretty good job of it."

"But suppose they got it all wrong? Suppose instead of Howard carrying explosives around, suppose someone planted a bomb in his car to kill him. Only someone stole the car and had the unfortunate experience of it blowing up in his face."

A small smile spread on her face. "A very unfortunate experience."

"Disastrous. So imagine the killer's surprise when they discovered Howard Leslie was still around."

She yawned again. "As you said, they were inept."

"But suppose they were even less epted than inept. Or more inept than we thought. Suppose instead of wanting to kill Howard Leslie, they were supposed to kill Howard comma Leslie."

It took a couple of ticks before the big blues popped open. "You're saying they were out to kill Elcee–Leslie Howard–and killed Howard Leslie instead?"

He palmed up his free hand. "It's a possibility."

"But why would they want to kill Elcee?

"That's the question I wanted to ask her."

"That means all our brilliant deductions are out the door."

"All your brilliant deductions, and don't go jumping to any more conclusions." He opened the door to the bathroom. "These are only supposes. They might not have anything to do with reality."

He took a shower, brushed his teeth, and came out into the darkened room lit only by pale moonlight. He climbed into bed and Dodee snuggled up to him, more asleep than aware.

Outside the owls resumed their hooting again, and the cool night air wafting through the open window brought with it a woodsy odor to mingle with the smell of soap and Dodee's perfume.

He studied the dim ceiling.

What did he know about Elcee?

She was a programmer for the government, same as Howard.

Another reason why the killers could have gotten the two mixed up.

And they worked on opposite sides of the mall.
Did that tell him anything?
And she was worried about her job.
What was that about?
He ran through the questions again, then put them aside.
Whatever it was about, it would have to wait.

He closed his eyes and, with the warmth of Dodee's body next to him, slipped down into a deep slumber.

TWENTY-NINE

He crept out of sleep rather than popping up fully awake. Like tunneling through cobwebs. And he ached in odd places, from muscles that had been stretched and wrenched in the fall off the mountain and the crash into the tree. He yawned and looked over Dodee's prone form to the gray light giving shape to the shadows of the room.

Should he try to snuggle back down and forget the day?

It would be one antidote to the dawn breeze slipping through the open window to raise chillblains on his skin. But any hope of actually creeping back to sleep was doomed by the damn birds squabbling in the trees outside and by the resurrection of last night's unsolved problem that ran on a treadmill in his mind.

Howard Leslie, Leslie Howard.

A question or a coincidence?

A coincidence and who cared?

But if it was a question, it was one of mis-identity; not Howard Leslie, but Howard comma Leslie.

And if one of the Elderhostelers was tipping off the phony FBI guys, last night's revelation by Elcee, Leslie Howard, could be a wake-up call for those who had killed Howard Leslie.

He crawled out of bed and, in an attempt to work out the kinks, went through the stretching routine he did at home as part of his daily workout. It helped. Some. But little twinges twanged on his pain meter as he struggled into the bathroom. He washed up, shaved, and slapped on some PS For Men aftershave. He climbed into his comfortable old pair of faded jeans and a sweat shirt, grabbed his mug, and barefooted it up to the Great Room kitchen to turn on the coffee Babs had set up the night before.

Someone had beaten him to it. A fresh pot, three quarters full, sat on the coffee-maker's hot plate.

Had he missed Elcee?

Or had she not come up yet?

He filled his mug, added a dollop of half and half, and carried it out onto the balcony, the deck cold against his bare feet—eventually he'd remember to wear shoes.

Once again he stood on the high mountain and surveyed the land below, like he could see all the kingdoms of the world, murky this morning as clouds hung heavy in the sky. He cradled the hot mug in his hands, gathering its warmth against the cool air, breathed in the aroma of the surrounding woods, and waited.

Let the clouds gather, let them burst with rain, let them delay the day with mists that obscure the way, still they can not hold back the light that disperses the shadows of night.

Then the sun rose from the land to burn through the gloom and command the sky.

What manner of Being is this who even the heavens obey?

He heard the door open and swung around, hoping for Elcee, but instead saw Kelli Kee dressed in a housecoat and holding a jug of orange juice. "Morning, Jim. What kind of a day are we having?"

"Gloomy right now, but it looks like the sun is burning through." He motioned to the jug. "I know, hydrate first, then caffeinate."

She nodded and poured some in a Styrofoam cup. "It's a fact that a large majority of seniors are dehydrated which leads to a host of health problems. So"—she held up the cup in a toast—"hydrate first, caffeinate second." And she took a drink.

"I'll remember that." He took a sip of coffee and leaned on the railing. "Ready for today's rolling river?"

"Looking forward to it." A smile spread on the oval face with the heavy jaw. "It should be exciting."

"Bet you like roller coasters as well."

She nodded again and took another pull from her cup. "You staying for the no-sweat hike tomorrow?"

"Probably not. I have a long trip home."

"We do too, but we're going to break it up. Stop off and do some antiquing."

"Where do you and your sister live?"

"Northern Virginia. Val lives about ten miles from me."

"You're both married. Your husbands didn't want to come?"

She glanced skyward and shook her head. "They're stick-in-the-muds, both of them. Val and I had the leave and it sounded exciting, so here we are."

"You said you had the leave. Work for the government?"

"At Langley. Both of us. Our husbands work on Capitol Hill." She took another sip of juice. "I better go get dressed."

He turned to the windows as she went back into the kitchen.

At Langley?

She placed the jug in the fridge.

She worked at Langley?

She drained her cup, filled it with coffee, and carried it out of the Great Room.

Langley was the CIA.

He turned back to the railing.

Just great.

Murder, bombs, the FBI—both real and phony—and now the CIA.

Who the hell had been after Howard?

And was there anyone on this Elderhostel he could rule out? Aside from Dodee, that is, and maybe he wasn't too sure about her.

Oh yeah.

And after Elcee's revelation last night, was it even Howard they'd been after?

But Dodee had the right question about that.

Why would they want to kill Elcee?

He went back inside, poured coffee for Dodee, and topped off his mug. He heard flip flops padding across the

Great Room floor and turned to see Joppa Harp come around the corner dressed in her expansive bathrobe.

"Top of the morning, Jim. Any coffee left?"

"Hi, Joppa. Still a few cups. You packing up?"

Her eyes widened as her brows wrinkled.

"Didn't you say you were going home today?"

"Oh, yes I did." She nodded, jiggling her double chin. "But the problem at home resolved itself, and I'm excited about the rafting trip today."

He carried the coffee down to his room and, with his hands full, rapped a knuckle on the door. It opened a crack and Dodee's big blues peered out.

"Brought you coffee."

"Thank you, sweetheart." She let him in and took the coffee. She was dressed in shorts and a bra with a blouse laid out on the bed. "See anyone upstairs?" she asked.

"Yeah, Kelli. Guess who she works for? Both she and her sister."

She sipped from her cup and shrugged.

"The CIA. Shit, we have everyone here. Is this a coincidence or are all these guys implicated in Howard's murder?"

She sipped and shrugged again.

"Which might not have even been a murder to begin with. But if it was, did they mean to kill him or was it a case of mistaken identity?"

She sipped and shrugged a third time.

"And I saw Joppa, too. She decided not to leave, but to stick around for the rafting trip. You know who should be getting the hell out of here? You and me. Too much crap going on."

The big blues fixed on him over the rim of her cup. "You want to leave?"

He stared back at her.

She shrugged once more. "You don't seem crazy about going on this rafting trip. We could leave if you like."

"We could. Go down to the coast to Sea Island and spread out in the sun." He chewed on his lip. "Agh, you want to go on the rafting trip. Let's do it."

He exchanged his jeans for a pair of cargo shorts. "Besides, I want to see if there's anything Elcee's involved in that might get her killed. Thought maybe she'd come up for coffee, but no. Have to catch her at breakfast."

They left the lodge and started down to the dining hall, running into Babs and Duke Penny coming out of the host couple's cabin.

"Ah, two more chow hounds," Duke said. "Gotta get a good breakfast to fortify ourselves for the long day ahead."

"We have to wear helmets this trip?" Jim asked.

Babs nodded. "That's because it's rockier and has more twists and turns than the Nantahala. And it's a lot longer with a lot more falls. But nothing we'll face today will be any harder than on Monday."

"Except for the Bull Sluice," Duke said as they headed down the steps to the rocking chair porch.

"Except for the Bull Sluice. But you'll be able look it over before you decide to go around or ride it down."

"Sounds like fun," Dodee said.

"Oh, it is," Babs said.

"Doesn't it, sweetheart?"

He passed on answering as he held the dining room door and entered after them. He scanned the room already full of Elderhostelers, but Elcee and Aunt Debra were not among them.

Neither was Tristin Fontaine.

He followed Dodee to the buffet table. Thick pieces of french toast rested in a stainless steel pan. He took three, added a scoop of butter between each, doused it all with syrup, and, remembering Duke's admonition to fortify himself for the long day, took a piece of coffeecake for good measure.

Maybe he could fortify himself so much he'd have to stay home.

They joined Duke and Babs at a table with Sam Moskowitz. The small man smoothed his mustache and leaned in close. "Heard anything new about the CDs?"

He shook his head. "You going on the raft trip?"

"You bet. Want to try it all. I've already made up my mind." He turned to Duke and Babs. "I'm riding the Bull Sluice. You done it before?"

Duke flicked his eyebrows. "Only about five times. Whenever we've come as a host couple. But it's always different depending on the level of the Chattooga. We've had a lot of rain this spring."

Jim buttered his coffeecake. "Is that good or bad?"

"Well"—Duke scratched his cheek—"if the river is down, we go bumping along the bottom and sometimes even have to get out and drag the raft through some spots. Today should be a breeze."

Joppa plopped down at the table with them. "Top of the morning, everyone." The plump woman had a full tray: cereal, banana, juice, coffee, and a stack of four french toasts floating in a sea of syrup.

Duke turned to her. "Hear you're going to stay and go whitewater rafting with us."

She spooned in some cereal and nodded. "Hearing you talk about it last night made me want to do it."

Jim stared at her.

Was he the only one in the whole place that was apprehensive?

Or the only one who admitted it to himself?

He scanned the room again. Still no Elcee, no Aunt Debra, but at the buffet table was the lanky figure and long face of Tristin Fontaine.

THIRTY

He watched Tristin collect his breakfast from the buffet table and waited for him to sit, but the man came straight up to their table and took the place across from him, setting down a tray containing a bowl of cereal, an orange, a steaming cup with a tea bag tag hanging over its side, and an empty saucer.

"Morning," he said, glancing around the table, as though it were a necessary all-purpose greeting.

"Hi," Dodee said. "Jim tells me you're a prosthetist."

His pale lips thinned in what could be interpreted as a smile as he nodded and sat down.

Duke turned to him. "What's a prosthetist?"

"I design, make, and fit prostheses."

"Artificial limbs," Jim said.

"You design them?" Babs asked. "I thought, you know, well"—her brow wrinkled—"I guess I don't know. Never stopped to think about them to tell you the truth. What's to design?"

Tristin squeezed his tea bag over the cup then set it on the empty saucer. "We're always trying to make them more functional as new materials become available. For instance, we now make artificial feet out of carbon graphite. It's light and strong, providing a store and energy return, like a spring, that gives the wearer a natural gait." He ate a spoonful of cereal. "We use titanium in connectors now, again to give us light weight, but also strength. We now use computers to scan limbs which allows the carver to design a better fit for the prosthesis. We do everything we can to make the patient comfortable and functional."

Sam shook his head. "Wow. I never thought about artificial body parts before. You like it?"

"It's the reason I'm still working at my age."

"And you can make a living at this?"

Another of what could pass for a smile crossed Tristin's

long face. "A very good living, especially when you're at the cutting edge where I am. I can't tell you everything I'm doing because of patent rights that are still in the mill, but I'm working with things like myoelectronics. They pick up impulses from arm muscles and transfer them to microprocessors in prosthetic hands which, in turn, gives function to the fingers nearly as good as flesh and blood. The same with other body parts. I'm also designing brain implants that will send electronic impulses to muscles that are no longer functioning. My hope is that someday we will be able to empower those suffering from spinal cord injuries with some functionality. I serve a small segment of the population, but I expect great things over the next ten years."

Jim scanned the room again as he tried to think of some way to change the subject before Tristin got into yesterday's conversation about transgender, female to male sex prostheses, far more than anyone at the table needed to know.

"I haven't seen Elcee and Aunt Debra this morning," he said.

"They're not here."

He turned back to Tristin.

"They went into Highlands." He ate another spoonful of cereal. "They were going to have breakfast, do some shopping, and be back in time for the rafting trip."

Jim stared at him.

Tristin shrugged. "Told me last night. I was going to go with them, but I didn't wake up in time. I wanted to get some heavy socks for my hiking boots."

"I noticed your boots," Babs said. "They look brand new."

"I purchased them last week."

Jim forked up the last of his french toast. "Nothing like waiting until the last minute. When did you decide to come?"

"Last week. Since I didn't have any roughing-it clothes, I went to REI Outfitters and told them I was coming on this trip and they"—he shrugged—"outfitted me. Boots and shorts and everything."

"How come you didn't have any outdoor clothes?" Duke asked, leaning his hairy arms on the table. "I mean, if you didn't have any outdoor clothes, does that mean you didn't do any outdoor stuff? Then why did you decide all of a sudden to come on this trip?"

Jim nodded.

That was the question he wanted to get around to.

Tristin finished his cereal, moved his bowl aside, and took a swallow of tea. He glanced around the table and blinked, as if suddenly realizing that everyone was looking at him.

"Oh, I didn't have any outdoor clothes because my wife was a recluse. For the last twenty years of her life she never went out and didn't want me to go out either." He set his cup down and gripped the food tray along the ends. "So, aside from going to work and attending church, I stayed home. I even arranged for a lawn maintenance service so I wouldn't have to be wandering about outside. When she died a few years ago, I guess I just continued what had become a habit." His eyes moved from person to person at the table. "I wasn't even sure I had the social graces to carry it off anymore." He stood and picked up his tray. "But when I heard about this trip at my church, I was determined, dagnabbit, to come on it if I could. I had to make a lot of phone calls, but, dagnabbit, I'm glad I'm here."

"We're glad you are, too," Babs said.

Dodee nodded. "It was nice hiking with you on Monday."

Tristin again gave them what passed for a smile, nodded, and headed for the kitchen cleanup window.

Dodee let out a long breath. "What a touching story."

"Yes, it is," Babs said, the lips turning down on her broad East European face. "I'm glad he made the effort to come."

Jim looked at the two women, then turned to Duke. "But you know, he didn't really answer your question. Why did he decide to come at the least minute?"

"I think he did, sweetheart. He said he heard about it at church and decided to come."

He watched Tristin head out the side door carrying his orange. "But doesn't that sound phony?"

Babs drained her coffee cup. "He told me the other day that a friend mentioned it to him." She turned to Duke. "We'd better get going, honey, if you want to go into Highlands this morning. How about you two." She turned back to Dodee. "Want to come with us?"

Sam stood up. "I'll go with you."

"Sure, we have a van."

And Dodee's big blues came around to Jim.

He shook his head. "Better not wait for us. The sheriff said he might want to come by this morning and talk to me. If we decide to go, we'll drive in ourselves. But thanks for the offer." He watched them go as he finished his coffee. "Tristin's story still sounds phony to me."

"Why? If a friend told him about it and it sounded good—"

"But why the all-fire rush to come on this trip? Elderhostel has a zillion other trips. Why would he have to drop everything, get outfitted with clothes, and make all those last minute phone calls just to come on this trip? What drew him to this specific trip?"

"So he could kill Howard?"

"I don't know." He glanced around to see they had the place to themselves. "Maybe he killed Howard and now he's stalking Elcee, if the reversed names mean anything."

"Then why didn't he go into town with them?"

"I don't know."

Her brow wrinkled. "Thinking back on it, it seems that Tristin was everywhere Elcee was."

"No, he was with us on Monday while Elcee took the short hike."

"Oh, right." Then she turned and pointed at him with her thumb and forefinger. "But you know, that wasn't the original plan. Remember Elcee told us she changed hikes at the last minute because she didn't think Aunt Debra was up to it?"

"He wasn't with them on the rafting trip."

"That was because he was sick."

"Or maybe because we didn't know Elcee's real name was Leslie Howard then."

"You didn't know, sweetheart. That doesn't mean others didn't. You're not the greatest with names."

He nodded.

She was right there.

But if someone else hadn't known her real name before last night, they certainly did now.

"If Elcee doesn't show by the time we load up for the rafting trip, I'm calling the sheriff. Maybe Tristin doesn't have an ulterior motive, but if Howard was killed by mistake, somebody does. And if they haven't already taken her out—"

"Taken her out?" She turned to him. "Taken her out, sweetheart? You're starting to sound like a cheap detective story."

"No, I'm getting to sound like you, which is really frightening."

"Go ahead. If they haven't taken her out—"

"Maybe they'll still try. Maybe just to cover all the bases."

The side door opened and a head with flaming red hair and a freckled face poked in, looked around, and broke into a smile.

"Billy Riley, cub reporter, has arrived."

The boy-faced man hurried up to the table. "Been looking all over for you."

"All over?" Jim asked.

"Well, like up at the lodge. I was hoping I'd catch you here." He turned and glanced toward the buffet table. "Think they'll mind if I sneak a cup of coffee?"

"In fact, I'll join you." He looked at Dodee. "You want another?"

She shook her head. "It's a long trip down the river."

They filled their cups from the coffee urn and Jim started back only to find he had lost Billy. The cub reporter had paused to place three pieces of coffeecake on a paper plate.

"Think they'll mind if I have a piece of cake?"

"I suppose not."

"Cool. I haven't had any breakfast." He stuffed a bite into his mouth. "What have you got for me?"

"Got for you? What have you got for us?"

"Oh, wow, you don't have anything new? We've got to solve this thing by tomorrow."

"What do you mean, 'we'?"

Dodee rested her arms on the table. "What happens tomorrow?"

"Tomorrow you all go home. Hey, if we don't solve it by then, it probably won't get solved. At least not with the lightning I need to take me to bigger and better radio stations."

"You keep saying 'we'," Jim said. "As far as I know this business belongs to the FBI and the sheriff."

Billy stuffed another piece of cake in his mouth. "They were here last night, right? They picked up the CDs?"

"That's another thing. How come you waited so long to call them? I thought they'd be here in the afternoon."

Billy held up his hand as he swallowed his cake and washed it down with coffee. "I was covering a story about a dog feud. Neighbors ready to go to war over a dog, okay. First I talked to those who owned the dog, a gnarly pit bull who kept barking at me through the chain on the door. Very uncool. These guys want to keep it. Then I went to talk to their neighbors who are demanding they get rid of it. Then I went back to the owners again, but by that time they had left, went grocery shopping as it turned out."

"Is this going to be a long, drawn out shaggy dog story?"

"Let him tell it, sweetheart."

"I'm coming to the end. The owners were gone, okay. But I wanted to get a look at the dog again so I opened the gate to the back yard, to get a peek through a picture window. But the gnarly beast was in the back yard. It backed me into a corner, and I couldn't get out for two hours until the people came home and called the dog in."

"Even more reason for you to call the police, so they could rescue you."

"My cellphone was in the car."

"Is this a true story?"

He stuffed the last of the cake in his mouth, raised his right hand as if taking an oath, and nodded.

Dodee turned to Jim. "Shall we tell him about Elcee?"

"About Elcee?" The eyes popped wide in the freckled face. "Who's she?"

Jim took a breath and let it out. "This might be nothing, but last night we found out that one of the women on the trip is named Leslie Howard."

The cub reporter nodded a few times, then palmed up his hands.

"It's possible the killer got the reverse names screwed up and killed the wrong person."

"Oooo-kay." Billy pulled out his notebook and scribbled in it. "So what else?"

"What else? We keep feeding you. What do you know?"

"Okay. We're in this thing together. But remember, we've got to come up with something before you leave otherwise I'm stuck here at WHLC for, like, eternity." He took a sip of coffee and looked back at the buffet line. "Wait a minute."

He carried his paper plate back to the coffeecake, took two more pieces, leaving one behind, held a wavering hand over it for a moment, then took that one as well, shoving it into his mouth.

"If they're going to hang me, might as well give them a reason to do it." He sat down and took another swallow of coffee. "Oooo-kay. I learned that Howard, Howard Leslie, the murdered man–"

"There's still a slim possibility it was an accident."

"No, it's murder. It's no good to me unless it's murder. Anyway, do you know he worked for the Department of Agriculture? He'd been working on a computer program to calculate the predictability of genetically altered crops. Not only that, he'd invested heavily in a genetic engineering company that has some new products coming down the pipeline."

"What new products?" Dodee asked.

Billy shook his head. "Don't know."

"How did you find out?"

"The sheriff got it from the FBI and told me on the promise I wouldn't tell anyone. But hey, you're, like, already in it anyway."

Jim placed an open hand on the table. "Is that enough to get him killed?"

The freckled face grimaced. "There's a group in Seattle—Extreme Environment or something—that has been hounding Howard, saying he was trying to foist genetically altered plants on an unsuspecting world."

"Seems hardly a reason to kill him."

"Seems like it." He grimaced again. "But you know, sometimes if you get enough big money involved, so much you don't know what to do with it, and someone comes along with a harebrained scheme you figure"—he shrugged—"why not give it a shot." He blinked, then smiled. "Or a push off a cliff." He stood up, pulled out another business card, and slid it across to Dodee.

"We already have two," Jim said.

"Cool. Take another. Keep it on you in case you come up with something. Oooo-kay?"

Dodee smiled, like the motherly instinct kicking in, and nodded. "We'll keep it with us."

"Thanks. I really need this story. Please let me know if you hear anything. And, hey, I'll do the same for you. I promise. Later."

And, since there was no more cake left in the pan, the

cub reporter left the building.

THIRTY-ONE

Jim held the dining room door for Dodee and they ambled up the hill.

"We could take a quick trip into Highlands," she said.

"We could. Want to go shopping?" He watched her shrug. "How about tomorrow instead of the no-sweat hike? Or if we decide to go down to the coast, we'll probably run into plenty of shops."

"You're serious about going then?"

"We could. Go down to Sea Island and soak up some sun."

She turned to him. "You told Billy that Howard's death could have been an accident. You believe that?"

He shook his head. "Not with people blasting guns at us. I was just pulling Billy's chain."

"Apparently they don't think it's an accident either," she said, motioning to the top of the hill where the sheriff's car was parked.

Then the sheriff himself came out of the lodge followed by Jonesy. He stood on the stoop a moment, hands on his hips, then spotted them and waved. "How are you folks this morning?" he said, coming down to meet them. "You remember those CDs you gave us? You said they were music CDs?"

Jim nodded.

"You're sure? You listened to all of them?"

He stared at the sheriff's ruddy face. "I went from track to track on each one, but I didn't listen to the whole thing."

"Could there have been something else in the middle of the tracks or at the end or something like that?"

"I don't know. Didn't you listen to them?"

"That's just it." He played with his nose a moment. "The darn FBI confiscated them."

"We were hoping you could shed some light on it," Jonesy said.

"Me? I know only what I told you. Why would the FBI confiscate them?"

Sheriff Graham shook his head. "Said they'd become government property."

"I thought you were working together," Dodee said. "This is the agent from last night?"

"One and the same."

"Can you ask him to make you copies?"

"I would, ma'am, if he hadn't hightailed it back to Washington, D. C." Graham stuck his hands on his hips again and set his jaw. "See, they think I'm just a small town sheriff so they can push me around. Think I won't be able to solve this case without them. Well, I ain't being pushed around and I will solve this case if it's the last thing I do."

"Someone higher up called them off," Jonesy said. "Sounds like a cover up."

"Damn right." The sheriff's jaw set again. "And not only did Grigory leave, he took the other agent with him, the one who's stationed in Asheville. What does that tell you?"

Jim shrugged.

The sheriff took a deep breath, let it out, and glanced down the road past the lodge. "Guess it won't hurt to search around the cabin, Jonesy." He looked at Jim. "You said last night a slug hit a tree. Think you could help us find it?"

"We could give it a try."

They started down the road toward Sam's cabin.

"How many shots you say were fired?"

Jim shrugged again. "There could have been a hundred. After the second I had more important things on my mind than counting."

It took them half an hour of examining woodpecker holes, all the while being damned careful not to step off into the great beyond, before they found the right tree and the right hole and Jonesy dug out the slug.

"All right, this is a start," the sheriff said, putting it into a plastic bag and buttoning it in his shirt pocket. "Nothing else you can think of that might help us?"

"I do have one thing," Jim said, "but it's not much. Howard Leslie was the name of the man who was murdered–"

"Do you know he was really murdered?" Dodee asked.

"Yes, ma'am. Plenty of evidence for that."

"As I was saying"–he glanced at Dodee–"his name was Howard Leslie, but last night we found out there's a woman on this Elderhostel named Leslie Howard."

The sheriff nodded a couple of times, then held out a palmed up hand.

"I'm wondering if maybe the killer got the names screwed up and went after the wrong person."

The lips turned down on the man's ruddy face as he stared off into the distance, then finally shook his head. "I don't think so. There's a preponderance of evidence that says Mr. Leslie was the target. You heard he was involved in a car bombing?"

Jim nodded. "And about working on genetically altered crops."

Graham's jaw dropped. "How did you hear–Billy Riley, right?" He turned to Dodee. "Right? For the Department of Agriculture? He told you about that?"

She lifted one shoulder and let it drop.

"And he told you about Mr. Leslie being heavily invested in a genetic engineering company? And the Extreme Environmental group out of Seattle?"

Jim repeated Dodee's gesture while trying to keep a smile off his face.

Sheriff Graham turned to Jonesy. "I am going to kill Billy Riley." He turned back to Jim. "I'll keep in mind what you said about Howard Leslie and Leslie Howard, but someone had to have a lot of political clout to pull the FBI agents back to Washington. Some high-powered people want this thing swept under the rug, which means there has to be a ton of money involved. But they haven't figured on one thing." He poked himself in the chest. "One way or the other, this small town sheriff is getting to the bottom of this, even if it means shining a reeeaaal bright light on the rats in the shadows. C'mon, Jonesy, let's see what else we can find around here."

Jonesy hung back as the sheriff stomped through the woods toward Sam's cabin. "The way the FBI handled this thing has hurt his pride. I wouldn't want to be in his sights when he finds the evidence he needs. Thanks for your help, folks," he said, nodded, and hurried after his boss.

"What do you think of that?" Dodee asked as they hoofed it back to the lodge.

"So much for the Howard Leslie, Leslie Howard thing."

"Maybe the FBI just finished their investigation. They came down here because of a car bombing, found Howard, concluded he was the source of the bombs, and went home."

He held the hall door of the lodge for her.

"You're forgetting about the two phonies. The FBI wouldn't leave without trying to get those guys, not unless someone ordered them to."

"Then who were the phonies?" she asked. "Guys from the Extreme Environmental group?"

He turned her around, lifted her chin, and stared into her big blues. "Listen, lady, I am finished with it." He kissed her. "As long as nobody is shooting at us, I don't care. I don't know and I don't care."

"I suppose you're right."

"Damn right I'm right."

"Be nice to help Billy though."

"Screw Billy."

"Well"–she smiled and batted her eyes at him–"if you insist."

THIRTY-TWO

Elcee and Debra were back by the time everyone gathered outside the chow hall–dressed in the same assortment of shorts, ankle length Spandex, light jackets, and backpacks as they had been on Tuesday–and loaded up for the van trip to the Chattooga River for their rendezvous with the class four Bull Sluice.

Screw that.

No way, not unless Dodee insisted on going over and testosterone forced him to follow.

Sonofabitch.

He sat scrunched up behind the driver's seat again, Dodee piling in after him, and Elcee sitting next to her.

"How was Highlands?" Dodee asked her.

"Very nice." She smiled, crinkling her brown eyes. "We had a big breakfast and wandered about the shops. I bought some earrings and Aunt Debra bought a pair of men's socks."

"Top of the morning." Joppa climbed in the van, tilting it slightly. "We keeping our same rafting team? The one from Tuesday?"

Elcee shrugged and turned to Jim. "I guess. We're experienced now."

"Think I could join you?" Tristin asked from the seat behind him. "If you can fit me in."

"Sure you can," Aunt Debra said, sitting next to him.

"What about Paul?" Jim asked. "He was with us the last time."

"He's in the other van."

"We'll trade him," Joppa said, smiling as she moved toward the back. "Like the Yankees and Giants. We'll trade Paul for Tristin and give them three draft choices for next year."

Jim turned to the window as the van pulled out.

Yeah, right. And who was going to have the awkward job

of telling Paul he was heading down to the minor leagues?

They moved down the sharp curves of The Mountain Center's drive.

Or maybe he was heading up to the majors.

Instead of having the sixty-something outdoorsie Paul, they now had the seventy-something indoorsie Tristin. Just what they needed to go along with the seventy-something Aunt Debra. Were these the guys he wanted to pop over the Bull Sluice with? On the other hand, was there anybody he wanted to pop over the Bull Sluice with?

He glanced past Dodee to Elcee.

He still had that tingle about the Leslie Howard, Howard Leslie thing. Only now Tristin was part of their raft crew. Maybe the sheriff was absolutely right about Howard's death, but he'd still feel better if Tristin wasn't tagging along wherever Elcee went.

Dodee fingers curled around his. "Okay, sweetheart?"

"Just absolutely great."

They pulled up to the Nantahala River Outfitters. Unlike the six or eight buildings at Tuesday's site, this one had only two rustic buildings set in the trees. The main one housed combination restrooms and dressing stations, a store selling mementos, and an outfitting room where they gathered for helmets, paddles, and PFDs.

They had to watch another video and listen to another lecture on whitewater safety, and Jim paid attention to every word.

He had heard all about the out-of-raft experience before, but after falling into the drink in the first ten minutes on the Nantahala, he wanted to make damn sure he heard it all again before tackling the Chattooga.

Then the guides helped him find a PFD, checked when he had it on to make sure it was tight enough, and fitted him with a helmet. He collected a paddle and walked outside to find his team standing in a group, Elcee wearing a lone yellow PFD in a sea of reds.

"Okay, everybody," the lead guide called out. He also wore a yellow PFD, as did the rest of the guides, but theirs were abbreviated jackets to allow for mobility in steering the raft. "Before we get on the bus, the Chattooga is a national river. The land on either side is national forest so we'll have to disembark on the roadside. We depend on everyone to help donkey the rafts to our launch site. The quicker we can get down there, the quicker we can get on the water. Okay, let's load 'em up."

They piled onto an old, gray school bus with yellow rafts loaded onto a rack welded to the top. Jim sat next to Dodee midway back, across the aisle from Elcee and Debra, with Tristin in the seat behind them. And they roared down the road, not so much in speed as in engine noise.

Dodee put her hand on his. "You okay?"

"Sure. I'm looking forward to some of it."

Her eyebrows raised at that. "You are?"

"Yep, two things. Lunchtime and dinnertime when it's all over."

"It will be fun."

"No doubt it will."

But he'd be damned if he was going over the Bull Sluice.

Elcee leaned across the aisle. "I saw you with the sheriff last night. Anything new on Howard?"

He told her about the genetic engineering and the FBI being pulled off the case. "The sheriff thinks someone put pressure on them to drop the investigation."

"They really think he was murdered then?"

"They seem pretty sure. At least the sheriff does. Says he's going to solve the case if it's the last thing he does." He looked at her. "When I heard your full name last night in the Great Room, I realized it was the reverse of Howard's."

She nodded. "We had talked about that."

"You and Howard? When I heard it I got to thinking that maybe the killers might have picked the wrong target."

Now she turned to face him squarely, brown eyes wide.

He raised one shoulder and let it drop. "I got to thinking

that instead of them being after Howard Leslie, maybe they were really after Howard comma Leslie." He lowered his voice and leaned close. "And then there's Tristin who showed up late for the Elderhostel and seems to be shadowing you."

She gave him a small smile. "I have my own ideas on that." She looked towards the front of the bus. "Did you mention this to the sheriff?"

"Tristin?"

"No, about my name?"

"Yeah, I did. He's sure they were after Howard. With the car bombing and everything."

The brown eyes turned to him again. "But if they got the wrong name, maybe they were really trying to bomb my car."

"Yeah, but Howard was involved in the genetic altering of crops and had an environmental group after him. Or so they think. The sheriff said there was a lot of money involved." He stared back into the brown eyes. "You doing anything that can match that?"

She stared at him a moment, then shook her head, but when she turned toward the front of the bus, she licked her lower lip.

THIRTY-THREE

They pulled to a stop at a cleared spot barely off the highway and barely big enough for the bus. A shaded lane with a slight grade led down through the woods for a hundred feet before disappearing around a bend.

"This is a Forest Service road," the lead guide said. "It's not for public transportation so we have to carry our own stuff down to the water."

"Didn't he already tell us that?" Hallis asked in a low voice.

Quentin leaned on his paddle. "Young people think that when you've passed a certain age you have to be told loudly and often."

"And some of us do, honey."

"Is that how you treat your patients?" Jim asked.

"Well," Quentin scratched his cheek, "yeah. But those people are sick."

"So are you, honey," Hallis said.

Quentin held out his hands, tilted his head back, and gazed towards the heavens.

Jim glanced around and was relieved to see that Paul had joined another group.

Two guides began throwing the yellow inner-tube rafts off the top of the bus to those below.

"They look so young," Dodee whispered in Jim's ear.

"That's because we are so old," he whispered back. "Actually, they're college students on summer vacation."

"How do you know?"

"I asked."

"They certainly look strong and ready for the rough and tumble."

"I hate 'em. All that energy is wasted on the young. It should be given to those who really know how to use it, like us who are mellowing into fine wine."

"You will never mellow into anything, sweetheart. But the whine part might fit. "

Plastic plates, plastic cutlery, and plastic bags containing lunch were divvied up among the groups and placed on the floor of the rafts. Then everybody grabbed hold and away they went, through woods that smelled of moss and mold, the twists and turns of the shaded lane giving no hint of their destination until they broke out into a clearing at the water's edge.

"Looks nice and smooth here," Paul said.

"Yeah, here," Kelli said.

"Don't worry," Duke said, "there'll be plenty of white water to make it exciting."

Jim shook his head.

Exciting shit. Terrifying.

A blond ponytailed guide placed half the raft in the water, his foot on an inner-tube side to steady it. "Okay, whoever is going on this raft, let's load up."

Jim climbed in, moved forward and sat on the inner-tube side, then realized he was right up front.

Hmm, is that where he really wanted to be?

Looking into the teeth of death as they rolled over a falls?

He turned to swap places, but after looking over the candidates, Dodee and Joppa behind him on the right, Elcee, Tristin and Aunt Debra on the left, he realized there was no one to swap with.

Sonofabitch, he should have kept Paul Fetgatter.

Ponytail shoved off and suddenly there was no turning back.

Great, just great.

"Okay," the guide said, "my name is Roland. I'll be your pilot today, and we'll be flying at minus three inches." He gave them a big smile. "Let's go over some of the commands we'll be using and then we'll be ready to head downriver. All forward, means everyone paddles. All forward."

They moved out into the sunshine, still in smooth water,

but with some boiling spots here and there indicating the current was heaving up from rumbling over rocks below. Roland led them through the commands they had learned on the Nantahala, then they swung upriver and all-forwarded enough for their ungainly, overblown inner-tube to keep pace against the flow. When all the rafts were ready, they swung around, got into the line, and headed downriver.

They were on their way.

"Okay," Roland said, "we can rest and let the river take us for awhile."

"Sweetheart."

He turned and Dodee took his picture.

"Want me to take everyone's picture?" Roland asked.

So everyone turned while Roland lined them up and Jim gave him a big smile. This was the shot that was going to be seen on the television documentaries.

The last known photograph of the crew of the Rubber Duck, taken by a waterproof throwaway camera, the only thing that survived the dunk in the drink.

He turned forward again and held the paddle across his knees, one hand at the end to keep from shlocking anyone in the head.

Rock outcroppings sprinkled with wild flowers and yellow dandelions lined the banks, topped by tall conifers and deciduous trees that made it seem like they were traveling down a deep canyon. The smell of the deep woods had given way to clear, fresh air filled with the sound of songbirds. And high over head, against a backdrop of blue sky cluttered with Dodee's clouds of swirls and whirls, and puppy dog twirls, a lone eagle's freedom cry sang out to the faint accompaniment of water rushing over rocks.

It would have been a nice day except that the rushing water accompaniment grew steadily in volume until it threatened to drown out the world.

He braced his right foot under the front of the raft and his left against the thwart as up ahead the first raft wobbled and dipped as it hit the rapids, followed a moment later by the second in line, and third, then—sonofabitch—they were there, right in front—

"All ahead hard," Roland called above the din.

He dug in his paddle and put his back into it.

They charged into the rapids, slammed down into a trough, and bounced up the other side like they were airborne.

"Left forward, right back."

He froze in a moment of panic until he figured out he was right, then back-paddled as a boulder rose up directly in front of him.

Not good.

They smashed into the rock on the left side, bumper-balled around it, fell off a falls, and pounded down into roiling water as flying spray filled the raft. They bounded up the other side, rumbled over some smaller rocks, and glided into smooth water.

"Good job," Roland said.

Everyone started laughing, as if they had just zoomed down a roller coaster drop-off and realized they were still alive.

And he had to smile himself, turning to see Dodee's face alive with excitement.

So what had he been so anxious about?

Hundreds of people had ridden this before and come out okay. Would they take Elderhostelers if there was a danger of losing—

"Right forward, left back."

He swung around to see a massive rock dead ahead.

Oh shit.

He dug in his paddle as they raced sideways toward it, pulling for all he was worth. They made some ground, not enough, and the river slammed them into the damn thing and held them against it while water flowed over the inner-tube sides and filled the raft.

"All forward, all forward."

He was willing, but the current had a mind of its own. It

spun them around and shoved them backwards into another trough, bouncing and rolling from side to side, all the more scary because he couldn't see where the hell he was going.

"Right forward, left back."

He dug in again, and again, and again. The raft swung around until—holy shit—the river dropped off into an abyss, and he was no longer sure he wanted to see where he was going.

"Hold up."

They rumbled over the falls, plunged to the bottom, smashed into something hard, then shot up again, water splashing and sloshing—

"All forward."

He bowed his head and dug in again, concentrating only on his oar and the circle of water around it.

"Hold up."

He raised his head.

Bad move.

They rushed toward a narrow channel between two protruding boulders where the river raged and roiled. They smashed into the rock on the right, ricocheted off onto the one on the left, and rumbled down a washboard-road times four that set his teeth chattering in spite of the dampening effect of the inner-tube sides.

Then everything flattened into calm water on the other side.

"Okay," Roland said as he bailed out water, using a Clorox bottle with the bottom cut off to form a scoop. "You can relax for awhile."

Relax?

Don't tell that to his bladder.

"All right," Elcee said, face bright with excitement. "That was a good one."

Jim turned to see Aunt Debra's face mirroring Elcee's, and Dodee's and Joppa's as well.

Only Tristin looked like he was giving the situation the serious attention men knew it deserved. But even he—the traitor—had that slight stretch of the lips that passed for mirth on his face.

"Good job," Roland said, scooping out the last of the water.

Over the guide's shoulder the next raft in line came rumbling down the slide, and from this side, the plunge into the abyss didn't appear to be more than three feet.

So how come it looked like Niagara Falls from the top?

"I haven't seen any bridges overhead," Joppa said.

"I don't think there are any on this stretch of the river," Roland said. "Well, yeah, there is an old abandoned railroad bridge we'll pass under after lunch."

Jim gazed downriver as they trundled over a series of smaller rapids, a piece of cake compared to what they had already been through. Then the lead raft pulled over to a sandy shore beside some large flat rocks and the others followed.

"What's going on?" he asked.

"Lunch," Roland said.

"All right." Joppa rubbed her pudgy hands together. "I'm ready."

Jim climbed out when the raft nudged the beach and pulled them up so that they were high and dry. He helped Dodee and Joppa out and turned to see Elcee already on shore. Tristin gave his hand to Aunt Debra and when she alighted, they moved up the beach together still holding hands.

He felt Dodee's arm on his shoulder. "What are you looking at, sweetheart?"

He motioned to Tristin and Aunt Debra. For the first time there was a smile on Tristin's face, not one of his half-hearted attempts, but a full-on smile as he responded to something she said.

Dodee looked up at him. "Think we just found the reason Tristin has been shadowing Elcee and her aunt?"

He gave a half shake of his head. "Maybe. And maybe Aunt Debra was the friend from church that mentioned this trip. And maybe that was the reason Tristin was determined to come on this particular Elderhostel at the last possible moment."

Still, could it be that simple?

He looked around as the others landed. Two of the guides had turned over one of the rafts, washed the bottom, spread a white plastic cloth on it, and were busy laying out plates of cold cuts—baloney, ham, beef—and three or four kinds of cheese. At one end they placed jars of pickles and mustard and catsup. At the other, plastic knives, forks, and plates along with loaves of rye, white,and wheat bread.

"Remember, folks," called out the lead guide, "this is a national forest so we want to leave everything as we found it. We have a large plastic bag to collect all our trash, so I ask you to make sure we leave nothing behind."

Jim slipped off his PFD and helmet, helped Dodee out of hers, and placed them on some pine needles at the edge of the small clearing. When he turned back, the chow line had already formed. He saw Elcee halfway down the line staring toward him, but her eyes were focused on eternity as a pink tongue patrolled her lower lip.

In the background, at the far end of the clearing, Joppa stood alone, resting her weight on one hip, and looked out over the water as she talked on her satellite phone.

THIRTY-FOUR

He sat on the sand beach with Dodee and ate a sandwich of ham, boloney, two different kinds of cheese, mayonnaise, mustard, and two sliced pickles, all packed in between two pieces of rye bread. He chewed slowly, masticating it to a pulp, savoring each bite before taking the next. He breathed in the clean smell of the surrounding pines and heard again, far overhead, the lone cry of the eagle, ruler of the sky.

A smooth hand caressed his forearm and he turned to see Dodee's big blues fixed upon him. "What are you thinking in there?"

He raised his eyebrows.

"You enjoy food more than anyone I know."

"And that's what I'm thinking. Umm umm, this is living. The only thing that could make it better is if we were making love at the same time."

"Out here on the gritty sand? With everyone watching?"

"*Carpe diem.*"

"You'd have to seize more than the day to pull that off." She leaned over and gave him a kiss on the cheek. "I'm getting some cookies. Want one?"

"No, I want five or six."

He took another bite of sandwich, savoring both it and the sight of Dodee's figure as she walked across to the upside down raft-table, where–sonofabitch–she became embroiled in conversation with Paul.

What the hell was that?

Where were his cookies?

Elcee came to squat beside him, sitting on her haunches, clear serious brown eyes staring at him.

"You know that comment you made about my name being the reverse of Howard's? You wondered if maybe they killed the wrong person?"

He shook his head. "Elcee, I'm sorry. I didn't mean to worry you. It was just something that crossed my mind."

"No, no. When you mentioned that someone had pressured the FBI to drop the case and go back to Washington, it got me to thinking that maybe I am doing something as controversial as Howard was."

He stopped chewing his sandwich.

She took a small breath and let it out. "I've been under a lot of pressure the last four weeks to drop something I've been working on. It's come from my supervisor, but I think that's only because someone is putting pressure on him. I'm even wondering if I'll go back to find I've been transferred."

Dodee sat back down beside him, holding out a handful of cookies.

He took one and turned back to Elcee. "What have you been working on?"

"I'm a computer programmer. One of the things I did last year was set up a program to monitor proposed government regulations. Did I tell you that? It's an Internet connection where the public can check on new regulations that are being promulgated and register their comments. The comment and the sender's email addresses go into a large database which in turn is accessed by various agencies. Hopefully, someone then scans the statements and takes them into consideration before finalizing a regulation."

Dodee held the cookies out to Elcee. "They've been ignoring the comments?"

"No, that's not it. Or if it is I don't know it." She took a cookie, but ignored it as her eyes shifted back to Jim. "When I put the programs on line, I continued to spend a lot of time making sure the logic worked. I took long lists of regulations and registered positive comments. Then I took the same list and registered negative comments. For and against the same regulations."

"And they registered?" Dodee asked.

Her eyebrows rose and she nodded. "Oh, yes. Perfectly.

To make sure I used two different address, one for the pro comments and one for the cons. Replying to either will get back to me, but one will go to my home and the other to my office."

"So it all worked—"

Jim laid a hand on Dodee's arm. "I have a feeling there is a *but* in here somewhere."

Elcee licked her lower lip, the clear brown eyes shifting between them as if deciding what to say. "Everything worked fine as far as the programming went. It has been up and running for over a year without a glitch. But, as you said, there is a *but*. A few weeks ago I got a political email urging me to vote for the reelection of the president and it listed those issues the president was concerned with. And guess what? They were generally the same as all those positive comments I registered using my home email address."

"And your office address got the opposite?"

She nodded. "I got another political email urging me to vote for the reelection of the president, but this time all the issues the president was concerned about were the exact opposite of the first."

"That doesn't make sense," Dodee said.

"Oh yes it does," Jim said. "If you want to reelect the president it does."   He turned back to Elcee. "So what happened next?"

"Next is what's getting me into trouble. I tracked down the organization that sent the emails to me and threatened to turn them in to the FBI."

"You think the President was involved?" Dodee asked.

She shook her head, then nodded. "I don't know. I haven't found anything to link the organization to the president. From what I can determine this is a rogue group like the Dirty Tricks Committee under Nixon. I'm hoping they hacked into the database, created profiles depending on the responses, and are sending out promotional emails based on those profiles."

"What do you mean, you're hoping they hacked into the data base?" Jim asked.

"Because if they didn't hack into it, that means they have official access, which makes it worse. And the pressure on me has to be coming from somewhere. Either way, it's a federal offense."

"There's a problem." He chewed on his lip for a moment. "What's to prevent two normal people from discussing their responses and seeing the discrepancy you saw right off?"

Dodee turned to him. "Didn't you say those guys were inept?"

"Yeah, but somewhere among all this ineptness you'd think someone would be epted." He chewed his lip again. "Unless they were just testing the system."

Elcee nodded again. "That would make sense. I entered all those responses while I was setting up the program so my addresses would be the first ones that registered and the first ones they'd try."

He stared at the guides who were gathering the remains of lunch and packing it into bags.

The whole thing was crazy.

Even if it was true, would somebody kill to keep it quiet? What's the worst that could happen? Negative headlines across the country? On the other hand, suppose that was the only thing between them and a federal prison?

He turned back to her. "You said your boss is pressuring you to drop it? What did you tell him?"

"I told him I'd take it to the Inspector General and the FBI."

Holy shit.

Would someone kill to prevent that?

Like someone so inept they blew up a car in the middle of Washington that killed the wrong person who was a different wrong person from the one they were really trying to kill? And then killed that wrong person? And now were so deep in the muck they had to kill the right person to cover up killing both wrong persons as well as to cover up the thing they were trying to cover up in the first place?

"You have any proof of this?"

"I made a CD at work."

He grimaced. "They've probably got that and have covered their tracks by now."

"Well." She smiled. "I also made two more. I left one at home and I have the third in the glove compartment of my car."

He smiled back at her. "Good thinking. Okay. Here's what we do. First we borrow Joppa's satellite phone. Then we get hold of Billy Riley"–he glanced at Dodee–"you got his number?"

She patted the pocket of her shorts.

"Okay, this is the story Billy Riley's been praying for. We call him, tell him where the CD is, and you give him permission to break into the car and get it. He broadcasts it over the radio, then he contacts the sheriff, and it's all over. Even if it had nothing to do with Howard's death, it's over. Once the story is out in the open, those guys and everybody connected with them will be more worried about scurrying out of the spotlight than with trying to keep you quiet." He looked from one to the other. "How does that sound?"

They both nodded.

He nodded himself.

Sounded damn good.

They crossed the clearing, weaving through Elderhostelers climbing back into the PFDs and helmets, to where Joppa stood munching on a bag of potato chips.

"We ready to go?"

"I wonder if we could borrow your satellite phone before we go. There is a chance that someone might be after Elcee and I'd like to call the sheriff."

"Can't do it." She shook her head. "Be glad to let you borrow it, but I just tried it. The battery is dead."

THIRTY-FIVE

"Well, so much for that idea." He turned to Elcee who looked like someone had let the air out of her balloon. "No big deal. We'll just have to wait until the end of the trip."

"We'd better get going," Dodee said.

"What's it all about?" Joppa asked as they started back across the clearing.

He gave her the two-minute version.

"You can't be serious. No one would kill somebody over that."

Jim shrugged. "Maybe not, but it wouldn't hurt to let the sheriff know."

They pulled on their PFDs and strapped on their helmets. Dodee got Paul to take a picture of their rafting crew, lining up three to a side with Tristin next to Aunt Debra and Roland the guide in the middle.

Jim gave the camera another big smile.

It could be used to identify the body if he decided to go over the Bull Sluice.

They piled in, but at the last minute, as the other rafts shoved off, Joppa had to trudge into the woods to go to the bathroom. By the time the plump woman waddled back, the other rafts had started downriver.

"Sorry," she said.

"No problem," Roland said. He waited until she took her place. "All right, all back."

They moved off the beach and out into the main stream, swung around, and started downriver, the last in line with the nearest raft a couple of hundred feet ahead.

"All forward, all forward."

They dove into the thick of it again, the current along the bottom slamming into unseen rocks and ricocheting to the surface in a swirling, frothing cauldron that rang out in a discordant bubble-concert.

"Left forward, right back"

Jim looked up as he back-paddled.

The river whirled on either side of a three-foot boulder, a small rumble ride on one side, a fall off the end of the earth on the other.

"All forward, all forward."

They steered for the rumble ride as the current swept them toward the falls, so that they met in the middle, smashing into the boulder and spinning around. The water grabbed them again and shoved them backwards down the falls.

Sonofabitch.

The unstoppable raft plunged into a hole and jolted against the immoveable bottom, then they shot skyward as the current picked them up again.

"Hold on, hold on."

Hold on?

What kind of a command—

Roland's yellow PFD slipped alongside the raft with Roland inside.

Jim dropped his paddle, grabbed the arm-straps of the PFD, and fell backwards into the raft, pulling the guide back on board as they rumbled into herky jerky rapids that shook them from side to side like a dog with a rag.

"Hold on." Roland crawled over him on his way to the back of the raft. "Hold on."

Hold on?

To what?

Head, heart, or testicles?

"Right forward, left back."

He grabbed the paddle and dug in again. The raft came around to point at another falls dead ahead.

"All forward, all forward."

Sonofabitch, this time he got to watch as they slipped off the edge and plunged into a trough, water splashing over him, then they bounced up again, rumbled over a few more rocks, and settled down into flat water.

"Good job. You can relax a while."

Relax, hell, he needed a bathroom.

And a towel or two.

"Was that anything like the Bull Sluice?" Tristin asked.

"No," Roland answered, scooping out water with the cutoff Clorox bailer. "But that series was not a whole lot worse. It's just that here it was spread out while the Bull Sluice comes all at once."

"How long have you been doing this?" Dodee asked.

"Two weeks."

Jim stared downstream as the abandoned railroad bridge came into view.

Two weeks?

"All ahead, four strokes."

Two weeks is exactly what he didn't want to hear.

They moved over to the left side of the river.

Here he was trusting his life to someone with–

"You're doing very well for only two weeks," Aunt Debra said.

"Oh, that's two weeks this year, on summer break from college. I've actually been a guide for the last three years."

Jim closed his eyes, opened his arms to the sky, and raised his face to the sun, basking both in the warmth of the June day and Roland's revelation that he had three years experience versus two weeks.

Actually, the trip hadn't been all that bad.

He opened his eyes and watched the line of rafts ahead of him, those in the front disappearing around a bend in the river, the one at the end passing under the abandoned railroad bridge three hundred feet downstream.

In spite of the excitement, or perhaps because of it, he was having fun.

Two men started across the railroad bridge and stopped a quarter of the way out.

Maybe he'd live through this rafting trip after all.

Then the men pulled something out of their pockets and snapped into a two-handed shooter stance.

Oh shit, maybe not.

Two cracks rang out and the raft jerked to the left.

"Oh, god," Roland shouted, "I been shot, I been shot."

Two more explosions and something thumped against the front inner-tube, and two more thumped in the same spot.

Jim glanced at the raft and then back up.

Sonofabitch, they were shooting at him.

"I been shot, oh, god, I've been shot."

Jim swung around to see Roland holding his hands across the front of his PFD, his yellow PFD, then Jim jerked back to Elcee in her yellow PFD.

"All forward, all forward," Jim yelled, grabbing Elcee and yanking her onto the floor of the raft. "Stay there." Then he dug his paddle into the water. "All forward. Head for shore."

More gunshots rang out, echoing off the river's tree-lined canyon walls.

"Row for your lives."

He ducked his head and put his whole strength into it, but with the hiss of leaking air and the raft wallowing, it was like paddling through a sea of molasses.

"I've been shot, I've been shot."

Thank God those guys didn't have rifles or the whole damn raft would be gone, but the closer they got to the bridge, the better the aim would be.

He looked for the other rafts, but they had all disappeared around a bend in the river, then glanced toward shore where the current was driving downstream toward two boxcar-sized rocks that jutted out into the river. If they could make it to the first one they'd have some cover.

"All forward, all forward."

Then as suddenly as it started, the shooting echoing around the tree-lined canyon faded away.

He looked up to see the men were reloading.

And—sonofabitch—running across the bridge to their side

of the river.

Great, just great.

He turned and dug in again, trying to reach the first boxcar boulder before the current swept them past it.

"All forward, all forward."

They crept closer and closer, but then drifted past it in the stream. A gap opened up between the boulders and a new race was on to make it before they were swept away again.

"All forward, all forward."

"We're trying, sweetheart."

They slipped past the first rock and banged into the second at the edge of the gap.

He jumped off before the raft could slip away and grabbed the line, held on, knee deep in water, feet braced on the bottom, muscles straining as he tugged with all his strength. But the current fought him and the current was winning.

Then Tristin popped up beside him, and Dodee too, and as gunshots rang out again, ricocheting off the boxcars, they yanked the raft between the boulders and slipped out of the line of sight from the bridge.

He plopped down in the water, Dodee beside him, the sound of gunshots replaced by heavy breathing all around him.

Elcee's wide eyes peeked over the raft's side. "Everybody okay?"

"No, I'm shot," Roland said, "I'm shot."

Jim went to him as the others clambered out of what was left of the raft and helped him remove the PFD. Blood drained from his left shoulder.

"See, I told you I was shot," Roland said as his eyes started to roll up.

"Stay with us. We're not out of this yet."

The eyes refocused, but fright and shock stood sentry in them.

Jim yanked off his own PFD, ripped his T-shirt, and wrapped it over Roland's shoulder, stemming some of the blood flow. Not good. Some antiseptic to slap on would be better. An ambulance ready to rush him to a hospital would be even better. But for now it was better than nothing.

He looked around for a way out.

The gap opened to a bank leading up onto a wooded hillside. They could climb out of here, but what would they find at the top of the hill? A road or more wooded hills?

A shot rang out, ricocheted off the upriver rock, and zinged across the gap where they were standing. Wide eyes all around. Then another shot followed the same path.

"Shit. Everybody down."

"We've got to get out of here," Tristin said. "We've got to get out of here now."

"Keep down and crawl," Jim said. "Dodee, get moving. Up the hill and into the trees."

He helped Roland out of the flaccid raft as Dodee led the way with Elcee next helping Aunt Debra. Tristin gave Jim a hand with Roland and between the two of them they clawed their way up the bank with him to where Dodee and the others waited.

"Where to now?" she asked in a stage whisper.

"Keep under the cover of the trees," he whispered back.

"They'll find us, sweetheart. All they have to do is cross the bridge."

They had already crossed the bridge.

He stared uphill.

Even if they could slip by the men, what would they find up there? A railroad track through thirty miles of forest? Roland wouldn't make three miles much less thirty.

He glanced along the bank, upriver and downriver, and pointed down.

"Parallel the river under the bridge," he whispered. "They probably won't expect us to be coming toward them. And keep quiet."

He led the way for fifty feet of tough going, until another boulder forced them higher up the hill. A shot rang out and splattered against a tree twenty feet below them and another struck the ground above.

"Down, down," Tristin whispered

Jim scanned the white faces staring back at him.

How the hell had they found them so fast?

He stared at Elcee's yellow PFD?

"Get that damn thing off. Where the hell did you get it?"

"From Joppa." She popped the clamps and shrugged it off. "She asked me to trade because it didn't fit her."

He glanced around again.

And where the hell was Joppa?

He grabbed the yellow PFD and tossed it down the hill. A gunshot rang out and hit something close to where the PFD had landed.

Was it just the yellow PFD or did those guys on the bridge know where they were going?

"Everyone stay here," he whispered. "Don't move and keep quiet. I'm going back to find Joppa."

He hurried through the woods toward the gap between the boulders, moving up hill and circling back to sneak up on the blind side, hoping he was quiet enough for the sounds of the rapids and the birds in the trees to cover him. He stopped behind a large red oak and peeked over the edge of the boxcar boulder into the gap below, but the plump lady wasn't there.

Sonofabitch.

Then he heard the loud ringing of a phone, almost on top of him, and eased around the red oak.

Joppa stood not more than five feet away, downhill, staring in Dodee's direction, as she talked into her satellite phone, the one with the supposedly dead battery.

THIRTY-SIX

He heard Joppa mumble something into the phone and moved around the tree to get closer to her.

"I'll get back to you," she said and punched a button that apparently broke the connection.

She tried to take a step up the steep bank, but slid back down. She shifted the phone to her left hand, grabbed hold of a witch hazel branch with her right, and pulled herself up a step, cutting the distance between them to two feet. She took a firmer grip on the witch hazel and pulled herself up another step, which brought her right next to him.

He reached out and snatched the phone before she could blink.

Her head snapped around and her brown eyes fixed on him. "You."

"I might say the same thing."

"I didn't want to do it." She shook her head and palmed up her free hand. "I had no choice." She shook her head again, then she lunged for the phone. "Give it back."

He jerked it out of her reach and she lost her balance. Her feet slipped out from under her. She landed on her stomach and slid all the way down into the gap between the rocks.

"Give me back my phone," she yelled.

"Yeah, right."

He climbed the slope and hurried downriver again.

Okay, he had the phone and the damn thing worked, but he wasn't out of the woods ... he stopped, glanced up at the surrounding trees, and shook his head.

Yeah, buddy, he wasn't out of the woods, literally and figuratively. Wouldn't be as long as the men on the bridge had a bead on them.

He looked back toward the gap in the rocks where he had

left Joppa, up to the railroad bridge, and downstream to where he had left Dodee and the others.

"Come on back," he shouted. "They know where we're going. We have to head upstream. Come on. This way."

Then he took off running through the woods.

It wasn't much of a misdirection, but it was the best he could do.

He met Dodee and the others heading his way and held up his hand.

"Stop," he whispered and showed them the phone. "Joppa's been telling them where we are."

"Do we head upstream or not?" Dodee asked.

He glanced up at the railroad bridge again and shook his head. "We take a chance no matter what we do, but I think we're better off heading downstream. He scanned the faces of Elcee, Dodee, Aunt Debra, and Tristin who supported Roland's good shoulder. "Make as little noise as possible and maybe we can scoot under the bridge without them knowing it." He turned to Dodee. "You got Billy Riley's cellphone number?"

She fished the soggy card out of her pocket and handed it to him.

He turned to Elcee. "I'm telling him to break the window of your car and get the CD."

"I left the keys on my night table. Upper floor, last door on the right, room twenty-one. The car is a green Ford Taurus parked in upper lot in front of the lodge. The CD is in the glove compartment."

He gave her a nod and a smile. "Good." He turned to Dodee and Tristin then back to Elcee. "You all go on."

"I'll stay," Dodee said.

"No, I'd rather you go. Tristin might need some help with Roland and Elcee has to help her aunt."

"I don't need help," Aunt Debra said.

Jim took a deep breath and let it out through clenched teeth. "We can stay here and argue until they shoot us." That seemed to chasten them. "I'll call the sheriff and catch up. You all move out and be quiet. No talking."

He dialed Billy's number, pressed the send button, and held the phone to his ear. It rang, and rang, and rang.

Sonofabitch, Billy–

"Billy Riley here."

It sounded like an answering machine, but when he waited for it to go on, nothing happened. He put his mouth right up against the phone. "Hello?"

"Hello?"

"Billy? Can you hear me?"

"Who is this?"

"Jim Dandy from up on The Mountain. I can't talk any louder because people are shooting at us."

"Hey, cool–"

"No, dammit, it ain't cool. We could get out heads blown off. Call the sheriff and tell him we're down here by an abandoned railroad bridge going over the Chattooga River, on the east side. Got that?"

"East side of the Chattooga River near an abandoned railroad bridge. Coo–right."

"Someone's shooting at us, and we need help as soon as he can get here."

"Right, I'm on my way–"

"No. Don't come down. Hello, you there?"

"Hey, yeah, but–"

"I'm going to give you the biggest story of your life. First you call the sheriff, then go up to The Mountain." He told him about the keys and the CD and outlined Elcee's tale of using government data for presidential campaign profiling. "Get the CD, get the story on the air, then no one will be able to stop it."

"Oooo-kay, I'll take a laptop and do a remote broadcast from right up there."

"Call the sheriff first."

"I'll call the sheriff first."

"No fucking around about this. Call him right away."

"I'll call him right away. You have a number?"

Jim blinked. "A number?"

"Of your cell phone. I'll give it to the sheriff."

He looked over the phone and found a number written with a felt tip pen and gave it to him. "I don't know if it's for this phone, but it's the only one I see."

"I'll call you back."

"No, I don't need the phone ringing to pinpoint where I am."

He punched the end button and hurried through the brush. He heard some shouting from behind, too far to make it out, but it was Joppa's voice from higher up the hill. Apparently she had made it out of the gap.

But the voices were behind them.

So far, so good.

He caught up with the others, and Dodee turned to him with a finger to her lips.

"What's up?" he whispered.

"There must be a road on top of the hill. We heard a car stop and a door slam. Then it went on."

He scanned the woods, saw no one, and turned back to them. "The sheriff's on his way. All we have to do is hide out until he gets here."

"Do we stay here?" Elcee asked.

She was propping up Roland who had one arm over her shoulder and he didn't look too spiffy.

Jim checked up the hill again.

If they just sat down and kept quiet, maybe they could get by. But if that car had dropped someone off, and he came lumbering down the hill and got within fifty feet, they'd be dead.

He turned back, scanned their faces, and did it again.

"Where're Tristin and Aunt Debra?"

"He wanted to go ahead," Dodee said. "Circle up the hill and see if he could find help."

"Aunt Debra insisted on going with him," Elcee said.

Get help, shit. Get them all killed was more like it.

He turned to Roland. "Think you can go on?"

The young guide's eyes rose to his, not fully focused. "I don't know."

Jim checked the makeshift bandage and shook his head. "Not important."

The important thing was that Roland was still losing blood, was obviously in pain, and was threatening to go into shock. In fact, it was a miracle that he hadn't already. They needed to get him to a hospital, like in the next five minutes, and in the meantime they weren't going anywhere.

Where was Quentin Quaries, MD, when you needed him?

And some blankets would be nice.

And then the satellite phone rang.

He punched the receive button and stared up the hill.

"Hello?" he said when he didn't see any movement above. If it was Billy—but nobody answered. "Hello?"

He shrugged and clicked off.

"Who was it?" Dodee asked.

"No—"

And it rang again.

And again he punched the receive button.

If it was Billy he was dead meat, that simple.

"Hello?" But again no one answered.

"Maybe you're not getting through to them," Elcee said. "It's a satellite phone. They should be able to get—"

The damn thing rang again.

He stared at it.

"Why would someone keep calling—"

Sonofabitch.

He swung around and rared back to throw the phone, but a gunshot split the air and a bullet splintered tree bark above their heads.

"That's enough," called a voice from up the slope. Phony FBI agent Smith marched towards them through the trees, a white face with a shock of brown hair on the balding head. "I don't want to lose that phone at this stage." He stopped ten feet away. "Toss it here. Underhanded and easy or it might be the last thing you do."

Jim did as he was told.

Smith caught it in his free hand, keyed in a speed dial number, and listened. "You were right. They circled back downstream. Thought they might have left the phone behind, but I tracked it right to them."

He listened for a moment as the sound of more cars raced by somewhere up the slope.

"Yeah," Smith said, his eyes shifting to Elcee, "she's with them. Just come on down the road until you get to the railroad track. We're not far down the hill from that. Call on the phone and listen for the ring. It worked for me."

Smith clicked off and shook his head. "This has turned into a major mess."

"You know it's all over," Jim said.

"For you all it is."

"Hey." Roland staggered a little then regained his footing. "I'm just a guide. I don't know anything about anything."

"I know, and I feel bad about that. For all of you. But you"—he motioned to Elcee—"you wouldn't let go of that bone. See what a mess you created. Now everyone has seen us—"

"That's not what I meant when I said it was over. I called a radio newscaster and any minute now the whole business will be on the air."

"And the sheriff is on his way," Dodee said.

A smile spread across Smith's pasty face.

"I'm not kidding," Jim said.

"Nice try."

"Elcee has a CD in the glove compartment of her car with everything on it. Billy Riley is on his way to get it right now. He's a newscaster with WHLC. It will be all over the country in half an hour."

"I admire your tenacity, I do. But to use a football analogy, you're on your own two yard line and the clock only has two seconds left."

"The sheriff *is* on his way," Dodee said again.

Jim nodded. "If I were you, I'd be more worried about getting a head start than with trying to figure out what to do with us."

"That's it? That's your Hail Mary pass?"

"They'll be able to trace you, you know. They have Joppa's name and address up at The Mountain."

"Well, I'd be worried if Joppa was her name. The real Joppa met with an accident and landed in the hospital. How else could we get someone in here at the last minute without raising suspicions?" Smith shrugged. "Besides, we've screwed up by the numbers so much it doesn't make any difference anymore. The bombing—who the hell figured someone would steal his car? We thought we caught a break with the satellite phone and finding the big guy all alone. Instead of shooting him, a bop on the head and it's an accident. Who'd figure we'd be that lucky? But, of course, we weren't. It's not the big guy at all. The names were reversed. Who'd figure that when we looked it up in a government directory that we had the names reversed? And that it's a woman? Who the hell would figure that? Bad luck on this thing from beginning to end." He shrugged again. "So you see, at this stage another three or four more accidents are not going to make any difference."

They heard a car pull to a stop somewhere up the hill, and the slamming of doors. Then the satellite phone rang and Smith held it up in the air to provide a clear signal.

"Your Hail Mary pass just landed incomplete." He shrugged one more time. "Game's over."

"The sheriff is still on the way," Jim said.

Only, would they still be around when he got here?

But over Smith's shoulder he saw Tristin's lanky frame move across the slope. He tried not to look and give him away.

The phone rang again as Tristin slipped behind a tree.

If he was going to do something, now would be–

"Don't turn around." The voice was strong and

commanding. "Try and my deputy and I will drop you where you stand."

Smith eyes popped open for a moment, then a small smile spread across his face.

Jim mentally shook his head.

This wasn't going to work.

"Jonesy, you hear? Drop him if he flinches."

Now the smile faded a bit.

"I've got a bead on him, Sheriff," a second voice called off to the right, sounding like Aunt Debra in a disguised voice.

This wasn't going to—

"You understand what I'm saying down there, mister? Nod if you do, but be careful. Anymore than that and you can kiss your ass goodbye."

Smith gave a little nod, but his lips tightened, his jaw set, and he spaced his feet apart, as if in preparation for spinning around and snapping off a shot.

This wasn't going to work—

"Now toss your gun on the ground."

And there was nothing he could do—

"By the way," Tristin said in his deep, commanding voice. "Since you're in such a talking mood, you have the right to remain silent—"

Smith's jaw dropped.

"—you have the right to an attorney—

The eyebrows raised.

"—but if you choose to speak, anything you say may be used against you in a court of law."

He let out a long breath and his shoulders sagged.

"Now put the-gun on the-ground."

Smith stared at the gun in his hand for a moment, then tossed it.

"Take two paces away. Mr. Dandy, be so kind as to pick up the gun and bring it to me."

He didn't have to be told twice. He scrabbled over and grabbed the gun before Smith could react, then trained it on the man. "Great job, Sheriff."

"Oh, Lord." Tristin sagged against the tree with his hand over his heart. "Oh my God."

Aunt Debra rushed to him. "Are you all right?"

"I didn't think I could pull it off." He put an arm around her. "I'm too old to be playing these games."

Smith spun around, stared at Tristin a moment, then swung back to Jim.

"Uh uh." Jim raised the gun a little higher and shook his head. "I just caught that Hail Mary pass." He pointed to the phone that was still ringing in the man's hand. "I'll take that as well. Dodee."

She took it from Smith and handed it to Jim. He pressed the receive button. "This is Sheriff Graham," he said, "and we just got your boy down here."

"Who is this?" asked the voice on the other end.

"Sheriff Graham."

"Well, Mr. Dandy, then who am I? And what am I doing with all these deputies up here on top of the hill?"

THIRTY-SEVEN

By morning Billy Riley had scooped the country and was appearing on television stations all over the world.

Sheriff Graham, grinning broadly, told the *Today* show how a small town sheriff solved a crime that even the FBI had given up on.

And phony FBI agents Smith—"I'm just a political consultant"—and Brown—"I was only driving the car"—were booked for murder one, and the plump Joppa Harp—not her real name—was booked as an accessory.

In the meantime, the official Committee for the RE-Election of the President, CREEP, denied any foreknowledge of, and foreswore any connection to, the rogue group that had illegally hacked into the Commerce Department's computers with the intent to illegally obtain the comments of private citizens, with the intent to illegally profile said private citizens for the purpose of illegally soliciting votes.

The Committee did not categorically deny that some funds may have been diverted to the rogue group from its campaign fund of two to three hundred million dollars. Two to three hundred million. How were they supposed to keep track of two or three hundred million dollars? But they were not acknowledging that the funds had been diverted either. Furthermore, unnamed sources within the Committee speculated that private business groups who raised large sums might be to blame, because with so much money floating around, how was it possible to know where it all came from, much less where it all went.

Jim sat in his car listening to it all play out on the radio as he sipped from his mug of coffee.

Not bad.

And it was also not bad that he had gotten out of riding down the Bull Sluice, although that was not all good since the rest of the Elderhostelers had taken the plunge and were still high-fiving each other over it. Made him feel left out.

Someone tapped on the window and he jerked around to see Elcee.

"There you are. Been looking all over for you."

He lowered the window. "Wazzup?"

"First I wanted to thank you for saving my life—our lives—yesterday."

"Hey, don't thank me. I was trying to save my own skin."

"Second, that Billy Riley had an interview with Roland in the hospital. He's doing fine and credited you with being the hero."

"Not me. Tristin is the real hero."

"Finally I'm relaying a message from Billy Riley. He's on his way up here with a television crew to interview you."

"Oh, shit. I'm out of here."

He hopped out of the car, gave Elcee a hug, and rushed to his room.

"I'm out of here, lady. You goin' with me?"

"What about breakfast?"

"Billy Riley's on his way up here with a television crew to interview us."

"I'm goin' with you."

They packed stuff helter-skelter, threw the bags in the trunk and stuff on the back seat. They wadded their bedclothes into a pillow case, dropped it outside the door, and were ready to go.

Except...

"We have to put the beds back the way we found them."

"Screw it, they can put them back."

Her jaw set. "Then everyone will know."

"They already know."

"Are you helping me put them back?"

He manhandled the twin beds back into place.

"Tonight," he said, grunting the night table in between them, "we're getting a place with a king-sized bed."

"Yes, sweetheart."

"We're out of here."

They rushed out to the Avalon, climbed in, and buckled up. He goosed all six cylinders to life, rumbled down the curving switchback driveway to the main road, and took a left just as a string of television trucks slowed for the turn in. He sped past them and glanced over to give Dodee a big phony grin.

She gave him big phony grin back. "That was cutting it close, sweetheart."

"Thanks to those twin beds—"

"Would you like to have twin beds tonight?"

"As I was saying, a miss is as good as a mile."

"Mind telling me where we're going?"

"Told you. Down to the coast. Get a place with a king-size bed on Sea Island and rest up."

"Okay with me."

They came down off the mountain road into what was supposed to be Dillard, except that there was nothing there, and turned north onto highway 23.

Fifteen minutes later he slapped the steering wheel. "Sonofabitch."

"What's the matter?"

He pointed out the windshield. "We're too damn early for the Dairy Queen."

The corners of her lips turned down and she shook her head. "Don't worry, sweetheart. I'm sure we'll see a lot of them on our way to—where?"

"Sea Island. Gonna go down there, get a place with a king-sized bed, make love all afternoon and all night."

She broke out into a full-toothed smile. "Sea Island? Sounds more like Fantasy Island?"

"What do you mean?"

"Like we really *can* make love all afternoon and all night."

He shrugged.

　　　"I figured you'd want to save the mornings for stretching out on the beach and studying the swirls, whirls, and puppy dog twirls."

The End